THE TROUBLE WITH DEMONS

DEMON GUARDIANS
BOOK 1

TERRY SPEAR

PUBLISHED BY:

Wilde Ink Publishing

The Trouble with Demons

Copyright © 2010 by Terry Spear

Cover Copyright by Terry Spear

Discover more about Terry Spear at:

http://www.terryspear.com/

Print ISBN: 978-1-63311-034-2

Ebook ISBN: 9781458176639

SYNOPSIS

Demons, witches, warlocks, and ghosts are real and deadly, as these teens discover.

Witches and warlocks hide their true identities from the rest of the human population, while three teens with demon heritage living with human families become unlikely companions in a race against time to deal with a demon threat to humankind in their quirky way.

Alana Fainot, a witch and half-Kubiteron demon, witnesses a Matusa murder his summoner, and she knows he'll target her next. Raised by her mother, she has no idea who her demon father is. But when she's pulled to a demon portal, she meets Hunter Ross, half Matusa, half human, who returns demons to their world, but who's been poisoned by a Matusa and is more dead than alive. His human mother gave him up for adoption, and he doesn't know who either of his birth parents are. His friend Jared Kensington, a full-blooded Elantus demon, less powerful than the Kubiteron, is a whiz at electronics and helps Hunter track demons in the city but was abandoned by his parents on Earth world for reasons unknown. He's determined to find help to save Hunter. Alana knows aiding any Matusa is a mistake, but when she learns Hunter is half-human, she makes a deal—he protects her against the Matusa who will come for her, and she helps find his dad in the demon world to save Hunter's life.

Often at odds, the three teens work together to stop the plans of a group of Matusa to take over the human race before it's too late.

Jump in and have some fun with the demon guardians who are out to save our world in The Trouble with Demons!

Thanks to Jack London and his White Fang and Call of the Wild that made me see wild creatures in a different way.

1

Alana Fainot felt eerily unsettled while she celebrated the end of her junior year of high school with her mother at a Spanish restaurant in Baltimore, Maryland. Alana suddenly envisioned three women in a darkened alleyway, the women's voices whispering in her head. She feared they were attempting to summon a demon.

"Why did we have to do it here in this stinking, filthy place?" a woman whispered. "Why not on the outskirts of Baltimore, somewhere in a field or something?"

"For the atmosphere. How can we summon a demon without having the essential mood?" another responded with derision.

Using white chalk, the two women drew a pentagram inside a circle against the black asphalt, over grease spots and globs of old gray chewing gum. Per the summoning ritual, the third woman lit the remaining fifty candles in the darkened alleyway between two brick buildings. A slight, humid breeze fussed over the flames, threatening to blow them out.

"Smells like rotting garbage. The heat and humidity have made my hair spaz. This long gown is making me sweat, and I'll have underarm stains for sure. *Real ambiance*. Let's hurry and get this done. I've got half an hour before I watch *The Shining* with Denni-son," the first said.

The second snorted. "Kim, after the demon does what we tell it to, you won't want to go back to mind-numbing Dennison."

"Having the demon kill Clint at Saveway Grocers is the only reason we're doing this, agreed? We get a new manager, end of story. Then we send the demon back."

"Until we need him for another gig, Lillian," the third one said, raising her brows to emphasize her wish.

Lillian cast them a wicked smile. "Yeah, that two-timing louse, Johnny Cantos, is next on *my* list."

Kim didn't look like she approved but then changed her mind when the other two seemed adamant. "Sure, whatever."

They pulled black hoods over their heads, then with their voices raised high, and the candlelight's flames reflecting in their eyes, the women chanted, "*Stirrus, Demononus, Seplichus, Protinalium, Horrita.*"

The portal opened, filling the alley with shimmering blue-green light, and a brisk wind snuffed out the candles. Their gleaming teeth showed in giddy grins, and they began the rest of the chant. "*Demon of Seplichus, we command you...*"

ALANA GRITTED HER TEETH, fighting the pull from the restaurant. The portal opening somewhere down the street from where she sat sent a surge of energy rushing through her, and the roar of the wind filled her ears.

Everything faded—the Spanish music playing overhead, the aroma of Mediterranean dishes, steaming spicy paella and garlic chicken, making her mouth water. Conversation and laughter disappeared. The sound of her mother's worried voice and the sensation of her hand patting Alana's vanished.

She struggled to center herself, to return to the safety of the restaurant, but it was like a part of her melted away from her physical being, floating in pitch blackness, shifted into something surreal. Like a magnet, the demon gateway's energy drew that disembodied part of her into the narrow alley.

Silence cloaked her like a deadly veil as her astral projection drew closer to the portal. An innate fear warned her if she got too close, the vortex could suck her into the demon world.

Transfixed in place several feet from the shimmering light, the three women she'd envisioned stared at the gateway. Wearing ankle-length, black dresses, their hair dyed the same color half hidden under matching hoods, and sable shadow covering their eyelids, the women appeared to be Goths in their mid-twenties. Not witches. Foolhardy Goths.

Their mouths coated in grim-reaper ebony lipstick curved up, giving them a demonic appearance. The portal's illumination danced off their eyes, completing the hideous look.

Rotting garbage overpowered the smell of burning candle wax. Something scurried in the dark close to one of the brick buildings —a cat, maybe, or a rat.

The women chanted, "*Demon of Seplichus, we command you, come unto us. We command you...*"

Ice spread through Alana's veins. In her astral state, what could she do? Nothing! She couldn't save the demon from these women if it was one of the lesser ones, and if it was not...

She shivered.

What if...if she pretended to be the demon they summoned...

She moved out of the shadows but stopped. They couldn't see her. She couldn't prevent them from calling a demon. What was she thinking?

Then a demon stepped through the portal, his look amused in a sinister way. Long hair the color of bittersweet chocolate whipped across his chiseled face, half-hidden in shadows with the portal's light at his back. His head held high, he commanded obedience.

Alana's chest tightened as if a wall was crushing the breath from her. A Matusa, one of the Dark Ones. Shrinking back into the shadows, Alana shivered.

The gateway shut with a whoosh, silencing the brisk wind. Streetlamps stretched measly tentacles of light between the century-old buildings, replacing the portal's light.

The women's apparent fear mixed with heady elation. They had called forth a demon. They would wield the power of a Dark Lord. But not this demon. Never a Matusa.

Alana expected bedlam, and her heart shriveled. She couldn't save the women, destroy the summoning book, or send the demon back. Why was she drawn to the portal if she could do nothing to help?

To witness the suffering? To show her how useless and insignificant she was? To prove once again she was some kind of freak?

The woman closest to the demon recited new words from the book, seeking him to do her bidding. The creature's eyes glowed red, and Alana's heart hitched.

He reached his hand out to the woman, tore through her dress, and dug through her flesh. Her high-pitched scream died on her lips.

"Oh God, oh God," Alana said under her breath, the blood pounding like thunder in her ears. *Go, go, go!* she screamed at herself. Paralyzed, she couldn't shake loose of her astral projection.

The woman's body slid down against a brick wall, but the demon continued his work. Crouching before her, he broke through the ribs with a crunching sound until he held her beating heart, still inside the chest cavity.

Sheer terror swept over Alana, the loss of control, the futility, the meaninglessness. Immersed in a horror flick—only it was way too real—she couldn't escape. A scream rose to her throat, and she clasped her hand over her mouth, tears filling her eyes, blurring her vision.

The Matusa ripped out the woman's heart, rose to his full height, and held it up for the other women to see. His prize. His proof they couldn't control him. With eyes blazing like fire, a smile curved his lips.

One of the women fainted. The other collapsed on her knees, begging for mercy.

Alana wanted to dissolve into the pavement.

The Matusa took a step toward the sobbing woman, tears running black rivulets down her colorless cheeks. The copper smell of blood now mixed with the candle wax and putrid rubbish wafting in the air. A light breeze stirred. The roar of a lion at the nearby zoo drifted overhead. But none of these took his attention from the woman.

None of these, except for Alana. He turned and stared straight at her as if he could see her standing there in the dismal place. As if something about her had called to him, distracting him from his mission.

Holding her breath, she prayed he couldn't see her, but his dark look bored straight into her, his fathomless eyes capturing hers, holding her hostage. Frigid fear stabbed her heart. Her astral form had morphed into something else.

Now, the danger knew her.

2

"Alana, Alana," her mom called to her in the noisy restaurant, the chatter, and Spanish music finally reaching her ears.

Alana opened her eyes, then blinked a couple of times, unable to clear the horrific vision from her head.

"Were...were you having another one?" Her mother wore her blond hair swirled in a bun, faded blue jeans, and a T-shirt, her usual look when she spent the day dealing with poltergeists.

"Yes, *Mother*." Alana gave her an annoyed look, but her heart was still beating so hard she could barely think straight.

Poking at the garlic chicken resting on a bed of rice, her mom anxiously watched Alana. "I think you should see someone about it."

"Who? I mean, come on, Mom! Get real." Rubbing her frigid fingers to warm them, Alana hoped the astral out-of-body experiences wouldn't worsen. She shook her head. A week ago, the summoners or summoned demons didn't see her. This time...

Her mom gave her one of her long-suffering looks. "I know you're still mad at me about this."

"Right. Why didn't you tell me before what was wrong with

me?" Alana scooped up a spoonful of rice and shrimp, determined to enjoy her dinner. At this rate, it could be her last. Her stomach rolled with nausea. She couldn't eat. She set her spoon down on the plate and made another sour face. "You wanted to wait until when to tell me? Next year, when I turned eighteen? Another couple of years when I'd already gone completely mad?"

"I didn't know any of this would happen. How would I have known? You were perfectly..." She stopped speaking and glanced up at Alana, her clear blue eyes worried.

"Normal. You can say it. I was perfectly normal until my seventeenth birthday."

"It's not like I would know what might happen. I haven't had anything to do with your...your father since...since, well, you know."

"Since you summoned him to do it with you."

Her mom's brow creased. "That sounds rather crude."

"You summoned a demon for what reason then?" Alana asked, keeping her voice low.

Demons, witches, ghosts, none existed except in writers' over-imaginative minds and a few misguided souls'. At least that's what most people thought. Though before she turned seventeen, Alana hadn't believed in demons either. Yet, she should have known demons existed just like witches did. After all, didn't every culture write about them from the earliest times? Sure. And like witches, maybe demons had been just as maligned. Or not.

Shaking loose from her gloomy thoughts, she frowned at her mom. "You summoned a demon to have a new friend? To kill someone that you didn't like? Come on, Mom! Why did you summon one, then do it with him?"

"Some of my girlfriends from college and I found an old text that was supposed to summon demons. Except the other girls got spooked and left the party." Her mom set the rest of the garlic bread back on her plate and licked her fingers. "You know me. I have to finish what I start."

Alana rolled her eyes. "And that's how I came to be. So what happened to Daddy Dearest?"

"I told you."

"You told me he left, but not why. I thought when someone summoned a demon, he or she controlled the demon. Except for the Dark Lords. Anybody unfortunate enough to summon one of *them* is worse than dead." The image of the demon holding the woman's bloody heart assaulted Alana and an internal shudder rippled up her spine.

"I summoned a demon who, well, thank God was not one of the bad kind."

"He left you pregnant."

Her mom's cheeks colored.

"You were drunk, right? What else? Don't tell me you had a boyfriend who had just dumped you for your best girlfriend."

"No. Andy Carver dumped me for the girl I hated most at the University of Baltimore."

"So you summoned a demon to fix Andy Carver and his new girlfriend." Alana didn't really think so, but she was tired of her mother hiding things from her.

Her mom's brows furrowed, and she stabbed another strip of chicken. "You know me better than that, honey. I was fooling around with my friends. Sure, I was down about Andy, and sure, I'd had too much wine. But we were bored during spring break and playing around with the book like it was a game. We never thought anything would happen."

"A game." Alana shook her head, wondering if the woman the Matusa had murdered had thought it was just a game, too. "How come Daddy Dearest left?"

"Your father was very handsome and charming, but after he made love to me, he forced me to recite something else in the book." Her mother focused on her meal, avoiding Alana's glower. "It sent him back to his world. I think. He vanished, and it was the last time I saw him."

"And you never wanted to call him back?"

Her gaze caught Alana's, then she looked away. "Sure, I wanted to. I knew I shouldn't have loved him, but I did. No man has ever measured up to him since."

"So why didn't you? Call him back, I mean."

Her mom poked at her half-finished meal. "I couldn't force a demon to stay with me if he didn't want to."

"Right. He does it with you when you're drunk, gets you pregnant, then disappears, and that makes him the perfect soul mate." Alana wiped her fingers off her napkin. "We've never lived around witches, and I can't have normal human relationships. I sure can't have demonic friends." She sighed, then drank the rest of her water, but nothing quenched her bone-dry throat. "I'm an abomination, Mom. Worse, I'm afraid a Dark One will soon come after me."

Her mom's attention shifted from her dinner to Alana. "Why?"

"I watched him murder a woman, and he knows it. I didn't hang around to see him kill the other two." Thank God, she'd finally yanked herself from the alley before he finished his work. She'd have nightmares about it forever.

Speechless, her mom stared at her.

In one way, Alana wished she didn't know what was wrong with her. How in the world was she supposed to deal with something like this? "So I guess you don't know what powers I might have."

"No, honey. I'm so sorry. If I could, I would make it up to you. I would take back what I had done. I was so stupid. We all were."

"I wouldn't be here." Alana toyed with her napkin.

"What?"

Lifting a shoulder, Alana repeated, "I wouldn't be here if you hadn't done it."

"Oh." Tears formed in her mother's eyes—which was *so* not like her! Not that she didn't have feelings, but she never let anyone know how hard things were for her when it got bad. Her mother quickly averted her eyes and leaned back on the chair, distancing herself from Alana, her whole-body language shouting, *I can keep it together if I have my space!* "I don't know how to tell you this without just coming out and saying it."

A million scenarios raced through Alana's mind, but when her mom spoke again, not one of them came close to her proposal.

"I want you to live with your Uncle Stephen for the summer."

Alana's mouth gaped before she gathered her wits and could think how to respond. "No. He's a neat freak!"

"Alana—"

"He can't stand kids, especially teens. And...and he's inflexible. Everything is by the book, no deviation."

Her mother frowned. "Alana, dear—"

"I thought I would go insane after spending two weeks with him last summer. All summer? No way." Alana crossed her arms in a huff.

"He believes you're capable of a higher-level magic than me. If you are, you need a master to train you. I would never be able to help you develop your potential—"

"Mom, no. I refuse to stay with him."

"It'll just be for the summer." Her mother wrung the napkin through her fingers.

Alana could see her normally persuasive powers over her mother were having no effect, and she wondered if her mom had some other agenda. "Why?"

"It's as I've said." She pursed her lips like she always did when she wasn't about to reveal the truth.

Alana hated to do it but considering the trouble she could be in... "All right," she begrudgingly said. "Uncle Stephen is more powerful. When the Matusa comes after me, maybe between the two of us, we can fight him."

"I'm so sorry, honey."

She wished her mom would quit saying that. "Yeah, well, you didn't bring *that* demon into the world, but I'm afraid your magic and mine won't be strong enough against him."

"I still don't understand how you know about the different kinds of demons."

Alana chewed on her bottom lip. "I think it's like an imprint. My dad's genes must have given me the knowledge. Anyway, what's frustrating is I don't know what kind I am. If I could see him, I could tell. I don't know why I can't tell from looking at myself in a mirror."

Her mother's brow furrowed. "This business with the portals—I don't understand how the demon saw you. You said when you went to them, nobody could see you."

"Yeah, well, like everything else in my life, my abilities are changing again. So when some idiot summons a gateway close by, I'm dragged to it. The Dark Ones kill the summoner. If a lesser demon is brought forth, the summoner controls them. Unless someone can release them, they're doomed to stay here as the human's slave. That's what I see."

Her mother sipped some of her water like she always did when she didn't know what else to say to smooth things over between them.

Alana let out her breath. "You always said we were given a purpose in this world. Yours is to free lost souls and send them on their way. What am I supposed to do? I see a horrible situation and I can't do anything about it."

"I want you to listen well to your uncle. Learn all you can from him. I packed your bags while you were at school. They're in the trunk of the car."

So much for giving Alana a choice. How long had Mom been

contemplating this? As much as she loved her, Alana could never understand why her mother kept things from her. Not when Alana could never keep a secret from her. Even when she wanted to.

"Can't you come with me this time?"

Her mom's face brightened, and she gave a short laugh. "That will be the day. I never could stand the way Stephen is so obsessive-compulsive about being neat and orderly."

"Good. I thought I was the only one he drove crazy." But she knew her mother's animosity for her brother went deeper than that.

Her mother's voice turned ultra-serious. "Besides, I can't leave my work right now. Listen, I can't impress upon you enough, Alana, I want you to learn all you can from your uncle."

"I know. Learning every bit of magic can mean the difference between life or death, freedom or enslavement—for someone like me." Alana couldn't shake the nagging in the back of her mind that her mother was up to something or knew more than she was letting on. "I'll do my best. But couldn't you come with me for a couple of days?"

"I have to exorcise a ghost at the Holloway Mansion and Trendy Donuts called about a poltergeist."

Alana tapped her fork on the table. "Do you think some demons summoned into our world are responsible for the plague of ghosts recently? I mean, most people don't believe in them, but the increased sightings even hit the local news channel."

When she didn't answer, Alana assumed her mother agreed with her that demons were stirring up the poltergeists. Anything to terrify the human population, as if they were playing some sort of demonic game.

Alana didn't know how she could manage, but every part of her screamed at her to fight the Matusa and free the lesser demons. Maybe her Uncle Stephen could teach her how.

All she had to do was convince him that demons were real. *That's all.*

"John, can you take out the trash?" his mother hollered to him from the living room.

"It's Hunter," he yelled back from his bedroom, determined to get his mother to accept his new name. Though he'd tried to train her since he'd turned fifteen, three years had passed without any success.

He read the newest email from Jared: *Demon sighted, Holiday Excursions Inn, room six. Be careful, Hunter. It's one of the Dark Ones. And there's another one, but I'll give you the location after you take care of this one. Jared.*

Two? What's going on? I'll call you as soon as the first job's done. Hunter.

He turned off the computer and then stalked out of the room. *Two Matusa's. Really not good.* The noise from his mother's vacuuming roared in his ears.

"Oh, John." His mother switched the vacuum cleaner off. "Remember that old box of junk in the garage. It goes out with the trash, too."

"Is Dad working late again?"

"Yeah, two more women arrived at the medical examiner's office. Hope they catch the bastard soon."

More of the Matusa's doing, he feared. "I'm meeting Jared at the library after I take out the trash. Do you need anything while I'm out?"

"Can you take Dara?"

"No."

"John."

"Hunter," he reminded her for the hundredth time. John had died when he took up the hunt.

With a hint of exasperation, she sighed. "I don't know why you want to change your name. I'll never remember it. Dara wants a couple of books, and I can't ever find the time to go to the library."

"She can give me a list of the titles, and I'll get them. Jared and I are discussing our next martial arts demonstration, and I don't want to drag my eleven-year-old sister around."

Eavesdropping as usual, Dara ran in from the den and gave him a list. He glanced at it and frowned. "Twelve books?"

She folded her arms. "Gifted class."

She only reminded him a million times a year.

"My teacher says I'm a voracious reader and I should keep it up."

He shook his head and strode toward the garage. "You'll never finish them before they're due back."

"Will, too." Dara returned to the den where cartoons played too loudly on the TV.

Hunter jerked open the door to the garage and strode inside. Grabbing the box destined for the trash, he paused when a stained and torn baseball glove caught his eye. His father's. Sports like that had never interested Hunter, unlike his father had always hoped. He picked up the glove and set it on a shelf with tennis rackets and beach balls. Maybe someday he and his father could spend some time tossing the ball.

Martial arts and kicking demon butt, now that was what Hunter lived for. But his father didn't appreciate his love of the former and wouldn't understand the latter.

Hunter dug around in the box, thinking he might find something worth keeping. Nothing but worn-out clothing, rusted tools beyond repair, and...

He pushed aside a pair of grease-stained jeans. A book. Really ancient looking, bound in ivory leather with gold print. *The Tome of*

Summonings. Hunter's skin chilled. Was this the book his mother had used to call forth the Matusa, the demon who was his birth father? Vowing to destroy it the first chance he got, he set it on the workbench and took out the trash.

Before he left the house, he secured the tome and slipped it between his martial arts books in his bedroom. Which brought to mind his new mission. Find the source of the summoning books and stop the demons from entering Earth world in the first place.

Slamming the door to the house, he headed for his truck. Concentrate on keeping a steady head, his training reminded him. Though his heart hammered with gusto.

Time to rid the world of another dark demon.

3

On the flight to Dallas, Alana had rehearsed how she would tell Uncle Stephen of her demon heritage. She didn't know any other way of convincing him she was half demon, except maybe to remove her contacts and show how her eyes glowed red when she grew angry.

She took a ragged breath. Maybe being only half demon meant she didn't have any other powers, which she was counting on if she had to face the Dark One.

But the minute she arrived at her uncle's house, he forced her to practice magic. Even before she unpacked her bags! Which was another reason she didn't want to stay with him. Who wanted to spend all summer studying?

Using her mind, Alana lifted the vase from the antique side table and held it five feet off the floor while her uncle supervised her every move. She thought Algebra II had been a pain. *Why levitate objects when I already know how to?* And Uncle Stephen knew she could do it!

The vase drifted lower.

"Concentrate," Uncle Stephen warned her. "Quit thinking of other things."

Other things.

How could she not think of other things? Any minute the Matusa summoned in Baltimore could come knocking at the door.

She raised the vase back to its original level. *"How long am I going to have to hold up this blasted vase?"* she asked telepathically. The zig-zag design and orange and navy colors blurred her vision.

Not replying, Uncle Stephen stood like a statue, his strawberry-blond beard trim and neat as usual, his hair shoulder length and shiny. His blue eyes were as clear as her mother's, staring at the vase, waiting for her to slip again.

She studied the pattern, getting lost in the maze, until her thoughts focused on the demon with the dark hair and fathomless black eyes in the Baltimore alley. He was beautiful in a cruel way. His lips had curved up, but the smile was an illusion, a hint of sinister amusement. The vision of him grew fuzzy, and she refocused on the hideous vase. It lowered again.

"Concentrate!" Uncle Stephen snapped.

"You know," she started to say, but the vase landed on the terra cotta tile floor, breaking into a million porcelain shards. She jumped back, looked up at her uncle's recriminating gaze, and made an irritated face.

"I *told* you to concentrate. That means you don't say anything to me either telepathically or verbally." His jaw clenching, he gave her a hard look.

"Why can't we use a pillow or something else that isn't breakable?" She figured that he should have known better.

"The incentive isn't there unless you have to protect something more fragile."

"Well, how about at least until I get the hang of this?" Then if she got distracted again—

"You already know how to do this."

She gave him a withering look.

"You have to get into the right frame of mind first. Then we go from there, like practicing your A, B, C's, then working into words, and from there, sentences. But your mind is somewhere else. What are you thinking of? Some cute warlock you left back at your high school?" He gave a disgusted snort.

"For your information, I don't have any friends, boys or otherwise."

His brows arched. "No witches or warlocks around?"

"No." Not when her mother made sure she attended a school where there were none. Why? Her mother had never confided in her until the demon issue came up. The fact Alana was a half-demon wasn't the problem, but that she wasn't a full witch. She scoffed at the thought. If she'd had a warlock for dad, things would have been different. Not that she cared anything about having a dad. She'd seen how controlling some could be. Best to live alone with her mother.

She straightened her shoulders. "Not only that, Uncle Stephen, but I'm—"

The phone rang and her uncle stalked off to the kitchen.

"I'm half demon which kind of puts a damper on relationships," she muttered under her breath. "Then there's this other problem with drop-dead gorgeous and dangerous who wants to rip out my heart."

She cast a collection spell and lifted all the vase fragments, then sent them into a wastepaper basket nearby with a tinkling crash. Her uncle peeked out of the kitchen, phone to his ear, a brow quizzically raised.

She pointed to the clean floor.

Taking a ragged sigh, he said, "Yeah, she got here safely, but now she's wrecking the place. Levitation. Broke a vase. Well, she might be all right at your place, but her mind is somewhere else. Do you want to talk to her? Okay."

He held the phone out to her.

Great. Alana crossed the floor and took the phone from her uncle. "Hi, Mom."

"What did you promise?"

She quashed the urge to roll her eyes. "To learn all I could."

"Are you having visions again?"

Alana looked in the kitchen where her uncle poured water into the teakettle.

"Alana?"

"For heaven's sake, Mom. I just got here. Why can't I have a week off from school at least?"

"You said one of the Dark Ones would try to locate you soon."

Her mother had her there.

"Did you tell your uncle?"

"What? He doesn't believe in demons!"

His gaze shifting to her, Uncle Stephen paused to set two coffee mugs on the counter.

"Alana, I told you I would leave it up to you to tell him when I sent you off, but he has to know if one is coming after you."

"He doesn't even believe..."

Uncle Stephen watched her, but when he caught her eye, he walked over to the cabinet and pulled out the decaf coffee.

Alana left the kitchen entryway and returned to the living room. "He doesn't even believe how you became pregnant. He's certain the guy you were going steady with who dumped you is my dad."

"Andy Carver. Yeah, I know. Our parents thought the same thing. How could they think otherwise? He was the only guy I'd been dating."

Alana flopped onto the couch, sinking into the squishy cushions, then leaned forward and ran her fingers over a crystal ball on her uncle's oak coffee table. "You could have summoned good old Dad back."

"I couldn't. He didn't want to live in our world, even if he felt something for me."

"Nothing permanent."

The teakettle whistled.

"Tell your uncle, Alana, before you go to bed. He has to know. He can teach you some important protection spells. Maybe he can figure out a way to help stop the visions you're having, too."

Uncle Stephen walked into the living room with two steaming cups of coffee.

"Okay, Mom. Love you. And be careful with those ghosts. They can be nasty. Especially," she said, then gave her uncle a pointed look, "if demons stirred them up in the first place."

"I'll be careful. Love you, honey. I'll call tomorrow."

Alana hung up the phone. She ran her hand over the soft velvet stripes of the brown and white couch cushions, preparing to speak again to her uncle about the other half of her family roots.

Her uncle sat on a wide-winged chair across from her and cleared his throat. "Demons? Don't tell me your mother's been filling your head with nonsense like that all these years."

No, just very recently. "We recognize another side of our world that most humans won't accept despite all of the legends about us. So why not demons? I thought witches and warlocks were supposed to have more open minds." She gave him one of her superior looks.

"Open-minded, certainly, but the next thing you'll be telling me that fairies exist in the flower gardens, and Santa Claus is real."

"Okay, Santa Claus is real. He was a 4th-century Christian bishop in Turkey who tossed gold coins in through a poor nobleman's window to provide dowries for his three daughters. I had to do a paper on myths and legends and how they are based on some truth. So see? If Santa Claus is based on a real person, and witches and warlocks are real, why can't demons be? I'm not sure about fairies. I would have to do some research on that. But let's pretend for a minute."

He shook his head.

She took a sip of her coffee and choked on the bitterness. "You forgot to put sugar in it."

"Sorry, I forgot your mother likes cream and no sugar. You like cream *with* sugar."

She rose. "Be right back. But I'm not letting you off the hook about being more open-minded."

When she returned, her uncle wasn't in the living room. She heard him in the guestroom where she always stayed and climbed the stairs to join him.

Leaning against the doorframe, she watched him lay one of her suitcases on the dresser, and the other on the bed. Even though she wasn't happy to be here, at least the room was decorated in all sky blue, her favorite color, and paintings of Texas fields of bluebonnets filled the walls. A television, stereo, and computer made it a teen's haven if she didn't have to study spells every waking hour of the day.

She took a deep breath. Time to tell her uncle the truth. "I'm half demon."

He swung around and gave her a look of contempt. "You might have a nasty temper at times, though I've never seen it, but you're not half demon. I can't believe your mother has filled you with that nonsense to protect that bastard, Andy Carver."

"A Matusa demon is after me, or at least I'm sure he will be." She walked into the room and ran her hand over the oak headboard, noting there was not a speck of dust anywhere. "Mom wants you to teach me some stronger personal defensive spells. And you need to apply more protection around your house."

His eyes hardened. "I won't play into this delusion your mother is feeding you."

"Fine, then I'll return home. No sense in me staying here if you're not going to help me. Mom's powers are too weak, but I'm sure that somehow together, we'll manage." Though she assumed being here might keep her far enough away from the Matusa, and he might not try to locate her. She whipped around and returned to the living room.

Uncle Stephen followed her. "I've been saying it all along, that your mother needed to see a specialist for her fantasies." He sat in the living room again and lifted his coffee cup. "I want to know what's going on. She wanted you to stay with me briefly last summer to learn more magic skills, but I can't understand why she wants you to stay all summer this year. Have the two of you been having problems?"

"No." Well, not that she wanted to discuss with her uncle. She still couldn't get over being mad that her mother had a fling with a demon, that she was the result of it, and hadn't told her.

"I wondered maybe if she has taken Dad's advice." Uncle Stephen's eyes were almost sympathetic.

Her mother hadn't taken her grandfather's advice since he kicked her out of the family when she became pregnant. Which meant Alana hadn't had anything to do with her grandparents either. She frowned. *I wonder what my demon grandparents would be like?* She'd never even considered she had another set. "What advice did Grandfather give her?"

"That she finds a warlock and settles down."

She snorted. "That would be the day." Yet a small niggling worry gnawed at her. What if her mother wanted to rejoin the secret magic users' circles?

She could, once Alana was no longer at home. Was that what her mother was up to? She wanted to find a life with her kind again? Clenching her teeth, Alana sat down and then took out her contacts. She had one more year left in high school. Couldn't her mother wait until she went to college at least? Whose fault was it that Mom had ruined her chances with a warlock?

Secrets, always secrets.

But…if her mother returned to the magic users' circles, where would that leave Alana? Out in the cold? Not able to be part of the demon world or fit into the human world…jeez, what had her mother done to her?

"What are those? Contacts? Why are you wearing them? None of us have vision problems."

"I have red eyes when I get angry." She tried to make her temper rise, but she couldn't. The feelings had to arise naturally and despite how annoyed she was with her uncle, she apparently couldn't make herself angry enough. And now she couldn't quit wondering about the way her mother shipped her off so suddenly.

He shook his head. "She has taken this thing too far. Why didn't you tell me about this last summer? I would have made sure you didn't return to live with her."

The way her blood boiled, Alana was certain her eyes glowed with fire, but her uncle didn't seem to notice anything different. Ignoring his question, Alana figured she'd better get to the point.

"I saw a Matusa demon summoned in Baltimore, then murder a woman. I'm sure the other two who had helped summon him were next on his agenda. He saw me watching him, but I wasn't physically there. I could sense everything in the darkened alley, the breeze, the odors, hear the words spoken, everything. It was an astral dream-walking experience."

"I'm worried about you." Uncle Stephen frowned at her.

"Listen, it's like being sleep-paralyzed. Hasn't that ever happened to you? Except I'm wide awake. So it's not exactly like the out-of-body experience, OBE, that scientists have studied. How could I be in two places at once if I wasn't part demon? No witches or warlocks you know can do that, can they?"

"A hallucination? You're not eating some of those mushrooms your grandmother was getting into last year, are you? She saw some of the most bizarre things until we realized what she was eating for a midnight snack."

"I *don't* do drugs, Uncle Stephen."

Her uncle's face turned stormy. "You haven't had a near-death experience, have you? If your mother didn't tell me…"

"No, Uncle Stephen. I've never been clinically dead, or nearly dead." Though if the Baltimore Matusa got hold of her…

He took a ragged breath. *"That's* good to hear. If you're done with your coffee, we'll return to work."

So that was it? No death experiences, no using drugs, dismiss the issue? She growled inwardly. "Defensive spells?"

"Levitation, until you get your mind centered where it needs to be."

Now, aren't my eyes glowing red?

A HALF-HOUR LATER, as the sun's fiery orange glow sank beneath the earth, Alana was levitating two coffee cups. Concentrating was proving to be more difficult by the second, but she knew focusing had a great deal to do with successfully casting any spell.

She squinted, trying to make out the title of the book Uncle Stephen was reading. *Barbecue recipes?* He looked up at her, making sure the cups hadn't moved.

Relaxing New Age music played overhead. The fragrance of the coffee lingered in the air. She licked her lips and could still taste the sweetened decaf. Outside, light rain pattered on the cement walk, and she smelled the shower-fresh air, totally attuned to her surroundings.

Closing her eyes, she concentrated on the cups. Before she knew what was happening, her eyes focused on a vision—a sign, Hayworth Motel, rusted, swinging loosely in the Texas breeze.

Then her gaze shifted. The yawning portal filled with light drew her forth.

The wind whipped at her hair and clothes, and the garbage odor from a nearby dumpster permeated the warm, humid air, a slight rain drizzling.

A man moved into her vision, not from the portal, but from a few feet away. A Matusa demon with long, dark hair, but not the same as the one in Baltimore. Her breath caught. He hadn't seen her yet, and she wanted to slip out before he did, but then she saw another. Much younger, maybe her age or a little older, he was tall like her Uncle Stephen, his brown hair long, his dark brown eyes sharp and wary.

He was like the other, but not. She couldn't pinpoint what made him different, besides being younger, but he was also a Matusa. She'd never seen two of them together. Was this something new? A gathering of the Dark Ones before they plotted to conquer the human race?

But where was the summoner?

The older man and the younger one turned to look at her, their eyes widening. *Ohmigod.* She took a step back. *Leave, leave, leave!*

The older one's lips turned up and his eyes reflected his sinister delight. "She's mine."

4

The golden-haired vision near the portal suddenly vanished into the dark. Hunter didn't need any distraction when it came to dispatching a Dark One, but the girl who appeared then disappeared, couldn't help but shake him. She wasn't just any girl, either.

Luckily, the older Matusa appeared astonished. More importantly, he didn't believe Hunter planned to return to his world. That was the only good reason for being one of the Matusa's kind. Well, that and the fact they were some of the strongest in existence.

"Did you get a fix on the girl?" the Dark One asked, his long jaw barely moving when he spoke.

Even though Hunter was six foot one, the Matusa towered over him. The guy played with a ruby-encrusted gold cross hanging around his neck. It looked ancient and Hunter wondered just how old he was and who he'd killed for the cross. It wasn't a symbol used in the demon world.

"Kubiteron, right?"

The demon's black eyes sparkled with humor and his lips curved up cruelly. "Yes. Easily enslaved. She's mine," he said again.

No Matusa was enslaving any lesser demon in Earth world. It

was time to make his move. Hunter gave a powerful side kick, slamming his size eleven sneakers into the demon's chest. He grunted and fell back. A look of surprise crossed his face, but before his eyes glowed red, Hunter swung his hand like a knife at the Matusa's throat.

Every move was meant to push the Dark One back through the portal before he could use his evil powers.

Choking and trying to catch his breath, the demon clutched his throat, and his head dropped forward. Hunter kneed him in the nose, breaking the cartilage with a crunch. Blood splattered the pavement. The Matusa howled.

Feeling invincible, Hunter followed up with another kick in the chest. One more shove and the bastard would be through the portal. Score another point for the good guys.

Hunter lunged for the final push. The demon smiled maliciously, the look in his dark eyes chillingly sinister. His trim fingernails extended into daggers. Before Hunter could dodge them, the demon swiped his claws at Hunter's arm. Like knives, the claws ripped through Hunter's sleeve and dug deep into the skin and muscle.

With the gouges burning like fire, Hunter did a jump kick and knocked the Matusa back a few more inches. But not far enough.

"You will die," the demon promised. He slashed at Hunter's belly.

Hunter fell back, his movements turning sluggish, his strength dwindling. His vision blurred and the Matusa's face wavered. He struck at Hunter again. Hunter feinted diving one way, then jumped the other and avoided the sharp claws aimed at striking his throat.

With a last kick, Hunter propelled the demon back to his world. Pain streaked up his bloodied arm, paralyzing it. Cradling his injured arm, Hunter said the spell to close the portal. He headed for his pickup, cursing himself for his ineptness. Never had he let one get the best of him. *Stupid. Just plain stupid.* He didn't even feel any elation over returning the demon to his world like he usually did.

Jumping into the cab of his pickup, he yanked his phone off his belt and called Jared.

"Hunter? How'd it go?" Jared asked, his voice strained.

It should have pleased him that Jared was concerned, but he didn't like being fussed over. His mother did enough of that. "I've sent the Matusa to his home world, but there's another demon I have to locate and send back. Not tonight though. I've had enough of a workout for one evening." Hunter drove toward the library, his skin overheating and sweating from the workout.

"Wow, Dallas is starting to have a real problem with this. But I didn't see a signature for another Matusa."

"She's a Kubiteron." Hunter gritted his teeth against a new wave of stabbing pain trailing down his arm to his fingertips. Even his fingernails hurt.

"She? Someone's love slave?"

"How do I know?"

"Her summoner must have been nearby."

"I didn't see anyone. Hey, have you got your first aid kit with you?" Hunter knew his wound would heal by morning, thanks to the demons' remarkably advanced healing powers. But he couldn't let his mother see the mess.

"How bad is it?"

Red streaks ran up his arm from the bloodied gouges in the skin —signs of an infection. "A few scratches, but Mom's going to have a conniption if she sees my torn shirt. It looks like I tangled with a mountain lion at the Dallas Zoo and lost."

"I'll be there in a minute. Kubiteron, eh? I don't see any signature for her."

"What are they capable of? Can you look it up for me? I'm not sure what to think. One minute she was there, then the next—"

Jared swore under his breath.

"What's the matter?"

"A truck nearly hit me. I have to concentrate on my driving. Be there in a few."

Hunter drove into the parking lot of the brightly lit library and cut his engine. It was open until ten, and luckily, they had another hour to spare. Glancing into the backseat of his truck, he realized the next time he would have to be better prepared: bring a change of clothes, a first aid kit, and anything else he might need after tangling with a Dark One.

Wiped out as if he'd had a rigorous ju-jitsu workout while suffering from a horrible bout with the flu, he slumped in his seat. Pain, like a hot poker, shot up the nerve endings closest to the wound and worked its way into his chest.

Trying to get his mind off the throbbing wound, he attempted to sort out how to locate the source of the demon summonings. Neither Jared nor he had come up with much of anything except for a summoning book in the possession of one of the summoners, which they had promptly destroyed.

A few minutes later, Jared's yellow Jeep roared into the parking space beside Hunter's pickup. Once Jared arrived, Hunter normally would be out of his truck and halfway up the steps to the library. But he couldn't call upon the strength to move a muscle.

Jared's mouth gaped as he bolted around to Hunter's door. "Got an extra sweatshirt you can wear." Looking at the damage to Hunter's arm, he cursed. "Man, you really did tangle with a wild cat."

"Yeah, but by morning it should be well healed."

Jared wrapped Hunter's arm with a bandage, then helped him into the sweatshirt. "You look like hell. Are you going to be all right?"

"Yeah." Though he'd never been clawed like that before, the burning sensation wasn't letting up.

"Did you want to go inside?"

"I have to get some books for Dara. Here, can you help me with this?"

Jared took the list and shook his head. "She won't ever be able to read all of these in time unless they're all picture books."

His head swimming, Hunter grabbed the hood of his truck, which sent more pain darting through his system.

"Hey, dude, are you going to be okay?"

"Yeah, yeah. Fine," he grouched. He was half Matusa and demons like him didn't show weakness, especially to a lesser demon like Jared. Not that he consciously thought of Jared as a lesser demon, but the pecking order seemed to be in their genes.

Somehow, Hunter made it to the library, though Jared grabbed his arm when he faltered like a drunken man. Again, Hunter felt the urge to scowl at Jared, hating that he looked too puny to do anything on his own.

When they walked inside the library, he couldn't smell the mold or dust like he normally could. His vision blurred slightly, and Jared helped him to a long wooden table. "Sit here. I'll get the books and be right back."

Hunter tried to ignore how bad he felt. As usual, after a fight, a broken movie reel replayed the confrontation with the demon in his mind. Hit, kick, chop. Everything was perfect until Hunter gave the demon enough time to extend his claws and get a swipe at him. *Faster.*

Every move had to flow into the next, fluidly with a deadly punch, no hesitation. Taking care of the other at the Holiday Excursions Inn, then this Matusa at the Hayworth Motel in one night, had probably been too much for him to handle. Yet, the sooner he sent the demons back, the less chance they had to harm anyone.

He still couldn't get over the fact that there were two Matusa in Dallas, which meant things were bound to go from bad to worse in a hurry.

The pounding in Hunter's head grew, and he shut his eyes.

The image of the Kubiteron demon appeared in his mind. She stood near the portal, the breeze sweeping her blond hair into her jade eyes, her lips parted. Her gaze had shifted from the Matusa demon to him, surprise reflecting in them. Petite, dressed in hot denim shorts that showed a lot of tanned leg and a tank shirt that revealed even more skin, stirred his blood. Why had she appeared before them and how? And where had she disappeared to?

An icy hand clapped over his forehead. Hunter jumped and cursed under his breath at Jared. "Don't sneak up on me!"

"Jeez," Jared said, "you're burning up. I checked out your sister's books, but I've got to get you home. Can you drive?"

His vision glazed over, Hunter stared at his friend.

"I didn't think so. Your parents are going to throw a fit. How are you going to explain this to them?"

Hunter shook his head and grabbed Jared's arm, then pulled himself up and reeled. "I'm driving home. I'll sneak in, leave the books for my sister, and go to bed. I'll be all right in the morning."

"If you die on me, your parents are going to be pissed. Are you sure you don't want me to drive?"

"No, I'll be fine, Jared," he growled, not liking that he had to waste what little strength he had arguing with him.

"I'll follow close behind." Jared helped Hunter to the truck. They both stood the same height, but Jared was a little stockier built. And right now, his strength came in handy. "I don't know, Hunter. Maybe you should go to the hospital."

"And what? Tell them a demon did this?" Hunter closed his eyes against the torment.

"You might need an antibiotic."

"I'm fine." Scowling, he climbed into his truck and leaned against the steering wheel, his mind drifting. All his senses seemed to be fading, except for the excruciating sense of touch, which was the only thing keeping him from passing out completely.

"Home, Hunter. I'll follow you."

Home. Hunter backed out of the parking area, felt a jolt to the truck that he'd never experienced before, and headed to his house. The center stripe along the route disappeared, and he didn't remember seeing any signals or stop signs on the way home.

Which was just as well, as wiped out as he felt. An angry car horn blasted somewhere in the distance a couple of times. The trip seemed to take hours instead of the usual fifteen minutes. When he parked the truck curbside at his home, the vehicle tilted to one side, and he struggled to open his door.

Jared pulled up behind him and hurried to the truck. "Hey, man, you parked your truck half on the curb. I'll repark it for you. Can you make it inside the house?"

When Jared pulled the door open, Hunter nearly fell out of the truck. Jared grabbed his uninjured arm and steadied him. "Jeez, this isn't good. Despite what you say, we've got to tell your parents."

"Dad's still at work."

"Well, your mom then."

Hunter couldn't even feel his feet taking the long journey to the front door, but no matter what, he didn't want to worry his mother over anything or do a lot of explaining. "What took us so long?"

"On the drive home?" Jared helped Hunter up the front step. "First, you drove over the curb at the library. You probably knocked your wheels out of alignment. Then you were weaving all over the place. You went through three red signals and two stop signs without pausing at any of them. We were lucky there wasn't much traffic and no cops." Jared twisted the doorknob and hollered into the house. "Mrs. Ross?"

Dara came running to the door, her pigtails flopping. "Did you get my...jeez, what's wrong with you, John?"

"Hunter," he croaked out, sweat pouring off his brow.

"Get your mother, will you? Hunter got scratched by a wild cat."

Jared handed Dara the bag of library books, while he held onto Hunter's good arm.

"Mom! Mom! John's hurt!" Dara screeched, not moving an inch from where Hunter leaned precariously against the wall.

A STRONG ANTISEPTIC filled Hunter's lungs with every ragged breath he took. Recognizing the smell, he assumed he was in the hospital as many times as he'd come here with his dad, hopeful he'd want to be a doctor, too. He wished sleep would take away the shooting pains in his arm and the ache from his head.

His mother's worried voice penetrated the fog. "John, I'm taking Dara home to bed. Dad is examining a patient who just died, but once he's through, he'll see you."

Opening his eyes, Hunter stared at his mother's anxious expression. She touched his cheek and flinched. "The nurse said the antibiotic should soon kick in. Animal control has been contacted. They need to know what the wild cat looked like, but it'll have to wait until tomorrow."

Wild cat?

"Get your sleep, honey. I'll be back first thing in the morning."

His mother left, and he closed his eyes. *Wild cat?* He couldn't understand what she was talking about. Then the room swirled like a whirlpool, around and around until everything turned gray. The last vestige of light disappeared, and a black hole sucked him in.

Hunter found the motel without any trouble and saw a flickering light in room 203. The demon was watching television? Probably enjoying all the world's troubles, natural and manmade. As soon as Hunter summoned the portal, the Matusa opened the door and smiled at him. A merciless smile. He tilted his head to the side when he saw the gateway. The demon couldn't figure out what was going on.

Did he think Hunter had been summoned? A demon couldn't open a portal. At least not a full demon. Thankfully, other demons could see only his demon half and not his human existence. It gave him the advantage when they thought he was one of them.

But the demon probably couldn't understand where the summoner was who brought Hunter here. No dead bodies, nothing.

Then the girl appeared like a breath of fresh air, quiet, innocent, one of the weaker demons, but not by much. As far as he could recall, the Kubiteron were only one notch down in strength from the Matusa. But they did not kill like the Matusa. Thankfully, Hunter's human side sought to control that dark part of himself.

Her eyes widened when he caught her attention, and then she vanished, like a puff of mist blown away on a windy Texas day.

Somehow, he had to find her and send her back to her world. Someone had to have summoned her and was keeping her hostage.

Had she come to him, seeking his help? He chided himself. All other demons were afraid of the Matusa. She would never have approached him willingly.

His mind hazy, Hunter chanted the words: "Stirrus, Demononus, Seplichus, Protinalium, Horrita."

The portal opened, a blue-green light filled the room, and a wind tugged at his stiff, white bed sheets.

The girl with the golden hair and jade eyes appeared again. He stared at her while she observed the portal. Turning her attention to him, her lips parted. He'd summoned her? He had to be hallucinating.

He looked back at the gateway. Was she drawn to the portal? Did she want to go home? He had to find out where she was being held prisoner, but his mouth felt like cotton, and he couldn't form the words.

Her gaze focused on his injured arm, but shifted to his face, still beaded in sweat.

"You're sick." Her words sounded surreal, airy, and sweet,

almost as if no words had been spoken. "Where's the other one?" she whispered, and he could hear the tremble in her voice.

Hoping to convince her he meant to help her return to her world, he opened his mouth to speak again, but the words failed him.

She tilted her head to the side. "Did *he* hurt you?"

Again, Hunter tried to speak but cursed his vocal cords for not working.

She stood taller and raised her chin. "You will join the other, Matusa." Her words were posed as a threat.

He would have smiled if he'd had the strength. Wondering why the portal was open, he quickly closed it. The girl vanished.

ALANA PACED across her guest bedroom, wishing the opening of a portal wouldn't draw her astral form. The injured Matusa had wanted to speak to her, but he didn't realize he was in a dreamlike state. He didn't seem to wish her any animosity, but then again, that's the way the Dark Ones often played the game. Quiet, calm, and deadly. They did not need horror-style theatrics.

"I can hear you pacing. Go to sleep," her uncle ordered telepathically.

"Did you put the extra protective spells on the house?"

Silence.

"I can't sleep if they're not there."

Uncle Stephen grunted. A few minutes later, his bedroom door opened, then the floorboards creaked as he stalked past her bedroom.

Half an hour later, he returned to his bedroom and slammed the door. *"Go to sleep!"*

"Thank you."

An hour later, her astral form stood in the Matusa's hospital room again, the portal glowing brightly.

His face was contorted with pain and his cheeks flushed with fever. She touched his forehead, and he opened his eyes. They grew round.

"You have to close the portal, Matusa."

Uncomprehending, he stared at her.

She motioned to the portal. "You have to close it. It keeps bringing me here." She hadn't meant to say that. She guessed she was so tired, that her thoughts were too jumbled to think straight. Then a weird thought crossed her mind. Demons couldn't open portals. How did he manage to do so?

If they could now open it at will, the human population was doomed.

5

"Today, so you don't wake me again in the middle of the night to add protective spells to the house, we'll work on some. Besides, I can't afford for you to break any more of my dishes, so we'll forgo the levitation practice." Uncle Stephen showed no emotion as he stood before Alana in the living room.

Was he truly upset with her? Her mom would have been.

"*You* were the one who insisted on using breakable objects. We could have levitated pillows." Alana raised her chin.

Ignoring her comment, her uncle started the new lesson. "First, you weave the spell with your hands thus and so, and say the chant at the same time. This will fortify a brick house into a walled castle. Though anyone will see the house as a brick two-story home, unless he attempted to break in, then he will see an impenetrable stone castle."

"How will I know if I cast the spell right?"

He gave her a small smile as if she were a kindergartner. She couldn't help it that her mom wasn't big into protective spells. "You will see whatever spell you cast."

She practiced several times, the first time only getting half a stone wall, the rest in shambles as if a cannon had blown it to smithereens. The next time the wall went up in the form of bricks, not stone. Exasperated, she tried a few more times and finally got the spell right.

"Next, we'll try growing briars to cover the walls. The thorn tips are poisonous, causing severe itching, swelling, and burning. No man or beast can get through that stuff."

"But it's not real."

"Ye of little faith, Alana. If we cast the spell and someone gets into it, they'll feel it."

Without any trouble, Alana grew brambles all over the castle walls, making an impenetrable barrier. She smiled at her uncle.

"Good, it appears you have an aptitude for plants. You may make an outstanding healer."

Great. What she needed were fighting skills if she was to protect herself from the Matusa.

"The other is a water barrier. We will surround the castle with shark-infested water. Again," he quickly added when she opened her mouth to speak, "to the intruder, he will suddenly be immersed in the briny sea, and believe me, the shark is very real to him and a great deterrent."

It wasn't exactly what she had in mind as far as an attack spell, but for protection, it might come in handy. After several attempts, she finally managed a small, reed-filled pond. No sharks though. Not even a tiny water moccasin for show. This was hopeless.

Her uncle shook his head. "You're not a water mage."

Weren't teachers supposed to be supportive? What kind of encouragement was that?

After practicing the protective spells, they took a break to have lunch. After cutting up the pepperoni pizza, her uncle slid a spatula under one and dropped it on Alana's plate. "How do you feel about your training? Are you learning anything worthwhile?" He sat across from her at the long oak table.

"The protective spells will help. But I want you to keep on guard. I'm afraid a Matusa or even a couple of the Dark Ones will be after me before long."

"While you're living with me, I don't want to hear about this."

He would hear about it, whether he believed her or not. She wanted her uncle to know what they were up against. "One Matusa demon hurt another, although I didn't think they ever fought one another." Alana lifted her pizza off her plate. "He's in the hospital."

Her uncle shook his head and poured parmesan cheese on his slice of pizza.

"Why don't we run over there and check it out?" she asked cheerfully, hoping her uncle would at least humor her.

"How do you know a demon is at the hospital?" he suddenly asked, his blue eyes spearing her.

She shrugged. "Somehow my mind transports me there. I don't know how, but I think I know why. Every time someone summons a portal to the demon world, I find myself standing near it, but only if the portal is close by. Anyway, the demon was burning up with a fever and kept opening the gateway by accident, I think."

Uncle Stephen stroked his red beard. "If you're done with your lunch, we'll practice personal protection spells."

"What about the demon?"

"What about him?"

"Shouldn't we go see him? So you know I'm telling the truth?"

"Several hospitals are in the Dallas area. Do you know which one he's at? Do you know his name?"

She grabbed her plate and her uncle's and shoved them in the dishwasher. "No. All I know is what he and his room look like."

"Then we'll return to our lessons."

"You don't believe me, do you?" She couldn't help the way her voice elevated, her temper rising. She missed being able to talk to her mother about this. Even though her mother didn't have any good advice as to what to do. At least she didn't act as though Alana was crazy.

"I haven't seen your eyes turn red once."

"I haven't gotten angry enough." If her uncle kept it up, she was certain she could show him flaming red eyes enough to convince him.

When they moved to the living room, her uncle asked, "Do you know how to cast the repel spell?"

"Yes, basic witch spell to keep a bully from manhandling us."

"Another is more aggressive."

"An attack spell? All right!"

"We don't learn attack spells. This is strictly for defense."

In disbelief, Alana stared at her uncle. "What do you mean we don't learn attack spells? What good are protection spells if a Matusa demon wants to kill me?"

"Witches and warlocks do not need attack spells. If they learned them, someone could anger them to the point that they might kill the individual without even thinking. We use protective spells only. Or other spells that help us in our work or daily lives. But nothing of an aggressive nature."

This was not going to work. If she couldn't learn any attack skills, she didn't figure she would live more than a few minutes in the Baltimore demon's presence. As far as she knew, they left no witnesses alive.

"This spell is a combination of repel and push. Not only is the threat repelled like two positive sides of magnets that can't touch, it gives an extra shove, so the would-be assailant will be pushed back a few feet. Several, depending on how strong your aura is in that field. The spell can be quite effective. Believe me, if a mugger tries to grab your purse and you use that on him, he'll think twice about trying it again."

"I doubt the Matusa demon will find it that frightening," she mumbled under her breath.

For the first time, her uncle had her cast the basic spell to see how strong she was. When she attempted the advanced spell, she heard the whoosh of the portal to the demon world opening. Before she could block the astral displacement, she returned to the hospital room where the sickly Matusa was still confined to bed.

He grinned at her, his eyes sparkling like the devil, but his cheeks were still flushed with fever. "See?" He turned to another boy she hadn't noticed until now.

His hair was long and dark and his eyes the same color as the shell of a Brazilian nut, but he wasn't a Matusa. He stared at her in awe.

"I told you, Jared. All I have to do is open the portal, and she's at my beck and call."

She whipped around and glowered at the Matusa demon, certain her eyes glowed red now.

JARED LOOKED the Kubiteron female up and down. "She's not here, physically." He glanced down at his laptop. "That's why I can't see her signature. I've never heard of anyone doing something like this. But she looks as real as you or me."

"She's a Kubiteron demon, right?" Hunter asked, aggravated that they couldn't figure her out, though some of his anger resulted from the pain slicing through his body.

"Yeah, she is."

"A Kubiteron?" Her green eyes widened.

Jared's gaze shifted to Hunter. "Why wouldn't she know what she is?" Before Hunter could comment, Jared shook his head and considered the girl again. "She's talking. I mean, just like she was here."

"Yeah, I told you she talked to me before." He groaned when another ripple of torture coursed through his nerves.

"You're an Elantus," she said, staring at Jared.

"Yep." He took a small bow.

"Where is your summoner?"

The smile faded from Jared's face. "Kubiterons are supposed to have innate healing capabilities, Hunter. You're a Matusa. Make her heal you."

She folded her arms. "I won't heal one who would kill or enslave me."

"He's not the enslaver type, and he has only killed two Matusa demons in self-preservation," Jared said defensively.

She turned her attention to Hunter. He clenched his teeth against another wave of pain. Knowing the wickedness of full Matusa demons, he assumed the poison the other inflicted on him would make him live a lingering, painful death.

"How did it happen?" she asked.

"He was trying to send the demon back to his world," Jared answered for Hunter.

"So that he had no competition in this world?"

Hunter grunted. "She will not help."

"Force her to, Hunter. If I could, I would. You're all this world has for protection if we're going to fight against the Dark Ones."

"Ha! *He* is one of the evil Dark Ones!"

"That's why, Kubiteron, he is needed here."

"You would defend him to the death, being that you're his slave."

Jared shook his head. "Make her do your will before you're too sick to compel her to do anything."

Hunter took a deep settling breath. The only time he'd forced a lesser demon to do anything was to break the bond she'd had with her summoner so he could send her back to her world and freedom. Her screams and sobs still made him doubt himself to this day.

But this was different. The urge to live precluded any other reasoning. "You will use your abilities to heal me, Kubiteron." He reached his mind out to coerce her to draw closer. His mind hit a barrier and in the next instant, he flew from the bed and landed on his backside on the cold linoleum floor nearly making him pass out.

Jared ran to help Hunter. "What happened?"

"She used some kind of protection spell," he spit out. Hunter's body burned like he'd been dumped into a pot of boiling five-alarm chili and renewed streaks of pain shot through his arm.

Once Jared helped him back to bed, he punched away at his keyboard. "No, no demon can cast a protection spell that powerful against a Matusa. That's what it says."

"Well, she did! You don't think I fell out of bed on my own, do you?" Hunter growled.

Jared snorted. "You flew from the bed. You didn't just fall."

"What..." Hunter watched the girl move closer to Jared.

"What's she up to?" Jared tightened his hold on his laptop.

"What powers does a Kubiteron have?" she asked, peering at the monitor.

Hunter gave a harsh laugh and winced when that pained him. "She has got to be kidding."

She flashed him a deadly look, her eyes flame red. Total turn-on for another demon.

Jared studied her. "I don't think she's kidding."

Hunter rubbed his throbbing temple. "Maybe she was summoned when she was a baby. All right, here's the deal. You heal me, and Jared will let you read about the Kubiteron." Hunter raised his brows to punctuate his statement, but even that hurt.

Her attention returned to the laptop, then shifted to Hunter. "Then you'll kill me."

"I don't terminate good demons. Only the ones who are out to murder me."

She pursed her lips. "I don't know if I can do this."

"Try."

She moved closer. Then she stopped. "Tell me what hospital you're in and what your name is."

"Why? As for the other, you already know my name."

She gave him an annoyed look. "Your *last* name."

"Don't tell her. She's got something in mind, and the way she tossed you from the bed as sick as you are, it can't be good."

"Yeah. I can see it in her eyes. Heal me, and Jared will let you look at the data he has compiled on your demon type."

She wavered.

Why was it so important for her to know where he was located? Did she know someone who might try to terminate him? In his present state, he imagined even the weakest of demons could easily finish him off.

She drew closer. Even though his sense of smell was no better than a human's now, her lavender fragrance reached him, and he took a deep breath to breathe in the sweet scent.

She reached out to touch his arm, and he cringed, waiting for the increased pain to kick in. Her gaze met his. "I can't do anything for you like this."

Jared objected. "It says here, of all the demons, the Kubiteron are best in the healing arts."

"I'm not really here now, am I? Tell me which hospital you're at, and I can come to you in my physical state." She turned to the portal. "And close the gateway!"

"If you close the portal, she'll leave, won't she?"

"She seems to be able to leave anytime she wants. Opening the portal draws her to me."

"To the portal, not you," she snapped.

He smiled smugly, and Jared chuckled. "I'm at..." Before Hunter could say anything more, the girl vanished.

Jared's jaw gaped. "What the...?"

Annoyed beyond reason, Hunter closed the portal. "Maybe her

summoner caught her unaware. I'll bring her back and tell her where I am."

"If she doesn't want to help? Demons are notoriously devious, you know."

"Yeah, except for you and me." Hunter gave a dark smile. "I don't see that we have any other choice."

~

"THANK GOD YOU'RE BACK." Uncle Stephen held Alana's hand with a reassuring grip. Nearby, another man she didn't recognize stroked his long silver beard, his blue eyes studying her. "This is my mentor, Yolan. I called him when you went into your catatonic state."

"What?"

"Do you remember what happened, Alana?" Yolan asked, his voice deep and reassuring.

"You wouldn't believe me any more than my Uncle Stephen does."

Her uncle's face blanched. Was he afraid the family secret would get out? That she and her mom were certifiable?

Yolan drew closer. "Tell me what has transpired. Leave no detail out, no matter how seemingly inconsequential."

Alana took a deep breath and told the truth. "I'm half demon."

6

A lana didn't say anything more, just waited to see how her announcement that she was half demon set with her uncle's mentor.

Yolan's blue eyes darkened, but he didn't say a word.

She explained how she came to be, why she thought a Matusa demon would be after her, and about her encounter with the other at the hospital. Once she was done, Yolan and her uncle left her alone in the living room and spoke privately in the kitchen. Because of her enhanced demon hearing, she made out most of their conversation.

"I told you it was crazy," her uncle said.

"Yes, Stephen. But her mind was drawn somewhere, of that I'm certain. Whatever is calling her is stronger than just the spells you used to try and block it, and then bring her back. In fact, the one I used to shield her mind is the strongest I know. I need to research this further, check some of my sources, and call in a few experts. I've never seen anything like it. I fear her mind may fracture under the pressure."

"What about this nonsense with the demons?"

Silence.

Then Yolan said, "The demon is in her mind, but I fear a rebel warlock has gotten through to her somehow."

She fumed. How could he be so...so dense?

"He has found a vassal to manipulate. If he's as strong as he appears, our protection spell won't last long, and he'll call her back to him. We must find out who he is and destroy him," Yolan added.

So her uncle did know attack spells after all. Her uncle's library! But first things first. She had to find Hunter. She had to help him.

She closed her eyes, waiting for Hunter to open the portal and draw her back to reveal the name of the hospital. She could still envision his lips moving when he tried to tell her the name before Yolan dragged her away from the astral excursion. But no portal opened, and she felt a kind of peace, her mind wrapped in a cloak of tranquility, dark and comforting.

Her uncle touched her forehead, and she opened her eyes.

"Alana—"

"Uncle Stephen, teach me some really good healing spells."

He exchanged looks with Yolan standing slightly behind him.

"He wants her to heal him," Yolan said, his eyes narrowed.

Of course, that's what she'd said, hadn't she? That he was at a hospital, and she needed to help him?

"The warlock must have been injured," Yolan added. "Why would he pick Alana, if she isn't already trained in the healing arts? Does she have the aptitude for it?"

Warlock? *Demon!* Why couldn't they get it through their thick skulls she needed to help a demon!

"I'll call her mother. I'm sure Alana knows the basic skills, but I doubt her mother brought in a specialist to train Alana in more advanced skills. Her witch's education has been at best minimal. My sister prefers to live among humans, doing as they do."

"Yet she uses her witch's training in her job, ridding the world of poltergeists." Yolan shook his head. "I'll return as soon as I discover anything new." Yolan vanished in a puff of pale blue mist.

Yeah, and whose fault was it that her mother lived among humans? Well, her mother because she fooled around with a demon. Beyond that, magic users were narrow-minded bigots if they couldn't allow those not of pure blood to associate with them.

"Would you prefer to sleep here on the couch or return to your bed?" Stephen asked her.

"It's too early to go to bed." Yet she felt as though she could barely stay awake.

"It *is* late, but the protection spell Yolan cast on you can also induce sleep."

"Great."

"Your mind needs to rest."

"All right. I'll go to bed." She didn't remember retiring to her room, but when she heard her uncle speaking on the phone downstairs, she realized she was tucked in, still wearing her jeans shorts, and T-shirt.

She fought the protective mind spell and attempted to break through, which only wore her out more. Then she stumbled out of bed and found her way to her uncle's library. Maybe, she could reverse the mind spell and learn about some attack spells, too.

As long as she didn't get caught.

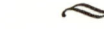

"You've got to try again, Hunter. Don't give up," Jared coaxed.

With the fever raging, Hunter's head pounded. Every effort both exhausted and pained him. "Isn't there any way you can locate her signature?"

Jared shook his head. "No. It's the oddest thing. I can track any demon within a fifty-mile radius, but I can't see anything concerning her. Maybe she's beyond my scope."

"I've opened and closed the portal fifteen times, and it hasn't drawn her back."

"Maybe she learned how to stop you from commanding her."

Exasperated, Hunter finally relented, though giving up was not part of his demon heritage, and that nearly killed him as much as the sharp pains racking his heated body. "Then we have to think of alternatives. Who else do we know might be able to counteract a demon's poison?"

"No one I know. What about your father?"

"What about him? He's not aware I'm a demon any more than my mother is. He's a doctor, sure, but..."

Jared gave him a disgruntled look. "I meant your *Matusa* father."

Hunter shot him a seething glare. "I told you. I don't want to ever see him."

"I've heard demons are very attached to their offspring."

"Right, Jared. That's why yours abandoned you." As soon as the words slipped out of Hunter's mouth, he regretted it. Jared's face fell, and Hunter knew he couldn't have shoved a dagger any deeper into his friend's heart. "Sorry. I know you've been searching for them for years. I shouldn't have spouted off."

Jared gave a nonchalant shrug. "You're sick, not yourself. The point I'm trying to make is your father is a Matusa. He might be able to get some medicine for you from the demon world to counteract the poison in your system."

"And if he's like the other murdering bastards?"

"He didn't murder your mother."

Not wanting to feel anything good about his real father, Hunter yanked his covers higher. He never wished to discuss his mother, either.

"She was pregnant with a demon child. You can't blame her for wanting to give you up for adoption. Me, that's different. Both my parents were demons. I can't understand why they dumped me with a human family."

"For your safety. I've always told you they did it to protect you."

"Then why not come back for me?"

Hunter refused to share his real thoughts on the matter. What if they'd died? That's the only reason he could think of. "Maybe they were sent back through the portal. They can't come and go as they please. They have to be summoned."

Jared slumped in the chair. "All right. Enough about me. You need help, the kind we can't get in this world. What's your father's name?"

"I don't know his name so I couldn't summon him even if I wanted to." And he never cared to learn it.

"What about your mother?"

Hunter couldn't squash his vexation. "I don't know hers, either."

Jared's brows lifted in a hopeful expression. "Ask your dad."

"No. My human parents have been good to me. I don't want them to think I care anything about my birth parents."

Scowling, Jared rose from the chair, stalked across the floor, then motioned to the wall. "Fine, I'm all out of ideas. Try summoning the girl again."

"WHAT ARE YOU DOING IN HERE?" Uncle Stephen asked Alana sharply, advancing on her in his library.

Her heart leaped into her throat. Sitting half hidden in the dark, reading by low light, she hadn't thought he would notice the scant illumination under the door. Never having seen his face so red, she shrank back in his plush chair.

His icy gaze pivoted to the book in her hands. "What are you reading?" he barked. He jerked the book from her hand. "*A*

Compendium on the Healing Arts." He took a deep breath, and she wondered if he'd worried she was looking into attack spells.

She had to heal the demon, learn about her own demon kind, and *then* research attack spells.

"I couldn't sleep." Which was true. "I thought I would get a head start on learning something about the healing arts."

He discarded the book on his desk and led her back to her room. "You need to sleep. Tomorrow, we'll work on the mind protection spell so you can see if you can use it yourself."

"Can you?"

Uncle Stephen shook his head. "Mine isn't half as strong as Yolan's. That's why I called him, but maybe you'll do better at it than me."

"Have you heard back from him?"

"No. He said he would get in touch with me in the morning." Uncle Stephen left her in her room, his look concerned. "I'm sorry that I didn't believe you."

"About the demon?" she asked, her hope rising.

"We believe the warlock is making you think he's a demon to intimidate you. Get a good night's sleep. We have much to do in the morning."

She wanted to scream! How could a master warlock be so dense?

When her uncle closed her door, she lifted her shirt and pulled the book out that she'd tucked behind her back.

Advanced Protection Spells.

She flipped it open to the table of contents. Spells, spells, reversal spells. *Okay, here goes.*

After working the reversal spell, she felt different, her thoughts freer, her mind less tired.

But the portal didn't open. Two hours later, she woke and found herself still in bed. For a moment, she felt disoriented. Where was she? She spied the bluebonnet paintings on the walls, and the lava lamp's blue blobs of wax glowing as they gently flowed up and down in the water like lava. Her uncle's guestroom. And a Matusa demon was dying in a hospital room somewhere in Dallas because she didn't know where he was exactly.

"Hunter," she called out to him telepathically, not sure she could connect that way with a demon. *"Hunter! Open the portal!"*

❧

HUNTER WOKE WITH A START, smelled the sharp odor of antiseptic and remembered where he was...the icy hospital room. "Did you hear something?"

Sprawled out in a pea soup vinyl chair against one wall, Jared opened a sleepy eye.

Thankfully, the nurses hadn't bothered Hunter of late. Jared's ability to cloak himself invisibly whenever he needed took a lot of energy. His clothes were rumpled, and a shadow of dark stubble covered his taut jaw. "Huh?"

"Did you tell me to open the portal?"

Running his hands over his mussed-up hair, Jared blinked. "I was finally sleeping, dude."

"I swear you told me to—"

"Hunter, open the portal! Hurry!"

Hunter stared at his friend, then scanned the room. "Did you hear that?"

"No. Are you sure you're not delirious?"

His heart hammering against his ribs, Hunter quickly said the spell to open the portal. The Kubiteron stood before him, her green eyes tired, her blond hair disheveled about her shoulders. She wore a pair of pink flannel pants covered in green frogs wearing golden crowns and a green T-shirt pronouncing: *Forget the prince, save the frog! Green Country Environmental Project*

She was a demon all right.

"What happened to you?" he asked, unwilling to curb the darkness in his voice. He could have died. And would still if she didn't hurry.

"Where are you? Hurry, tell me before they stop me again."

They? Her summoners. He would take them to task—once he was well enough. "Medical City, room 410, Hunter Ross."

"I'll be there as soon as I can find a way."

"I'll pick you up," Jared offered, jumping out of his chair.

She studied him but didn't say a word.

He frowned at her. "I'm Elantus. We don't hurt a soul."

"But you're under *his* control." She jerked her thumb at Hunter. "And his kind *does* kill. Then he would know where I lived."

Hunter couldn't decide whether to be amused or angry with her accusations. But the fact she had to find a way to get here made his adrenaline surge. "Jared will take you."

Jared's eyes glowed red. "I'm not under his spell."

"Ha! Matusa don't have demon friends who are beneath them."

Now Hunter was amused.

Jared gave a smart-aleck smirk. "He has made an exception in my case."

"Thanks, but no thanks. I'll find my own way." She vanished.

Hunter swore under his breath. "Stubborn-headed..." Hunter took a sip of water, but it didn't soothe his dry throat or cool his fevered body. "She doesn't have any way of getting here. What does she think? She can just fly?" He took a painful breath. "But you can track her signature once she has been here, can't you?"

Jared's eyes sparkled with demonic pride. "Most assuredly. Once she's here in the flesh, I'll have her signature and can locate her anywhere she goes next. Why?"

Hunter leaned back against his pillow. "To free her and return her home. Who would be powerful enough to prevent her from coming here? She referred to her keeper as they, so there must be a couple of summoners."

"We don't even know any demon who can do what she does. But I imagine her summoner forced her to return." Jared retook his seat and crossed his arms. "We will have to destroy them if they won't release her, and then we can set her free to return home."

"*I'll* have to set her free. *Remember?* Elantus don't kill."

Jared's ears tinged red, and he lifted his hands. "We don't *always* kill, except when warranted. What self-respecting demon wouldn't?" He gave a sinister laugh.

7

Alana climbed out of bed, determined to get to the hospital, but she had no idea where it was or how she would get there. If she could slip her uncle's Mustang out of the garage, maybe she could make it. She pondered casting a sleeping spell on Uncle Stephen, just in case.

If he realized what she attempted to do, she would be in a world of trouble. Still, her only other alternative was to let Jared come get her, but she didn't trust him or Hunter one bit. Demons couldn't be believed. That much she knew.

She changed into jeans and a T-shirt, then slipped into the virtually barren garage. The smell of fresh paint lingered in the air and she noted not a cobweb anywhere. Even the sound of her shoes squeaking against the freshly swept concrete floor seemed to echo off the walls.

Too bad her uncle was such a neat freak and wasn't like most people she knew whose garages were left best unseen by friends and family, stacked to the ceiling with stuff, all of which would help to muffle the sound.

So far so good. Starting the car's engine without a key was no problem. Would her uncle hear the garage door going up though? She didn't know how light a sleeper he was, or if he could even hear the garage door from his bedroom on the other side of the house. She could, but that was because of her demon hearing.

Taking a deep breath, she pushed the garage door button. The door rolled up, grinding all the way, shattering her nerves. She jumped into the car and stared at the stick shift. It wasn't an automatic? She groaned. The only time she'd attempted to drive a stick shift, she nearly drove it into another car on a used car lot. Chill bumps trailed her arms from the memory.

Then she spied a bicycle. Growling, she left the car and grabbed the bicycle. Some rescue job and she still had no idea where the hospital was. Then she remembered how she'd talked to Hunter telepathically. Could he communicate the same way with her?

"Hunter, I'm having trouble getting transportation."

Silence ensued.

She got onto the bicycle and rode down the quiet residential street. *"Hunter, if you can hear me, I'm riding a bicycle and, well, I have no idea where the stupid hospital is."*

She cleared her throat. Normally resourceful, she wasn't familiar with Dallas, and she feared any minute her uncle would wake up and find her missing. It wouldn't take long to find her, either, while she made her escape on a bicycle.

"Hunter, can you communicate with me?"

She guessed demons couldn't communicate telepathically, that her witch's genes gave her that gift. Yet, she assumed since he opened the portal when she called to him the first time, he could understand her but couldn't figure out how to speak to her in the same way. Or he was asleep or too sick to respond. The latter thought made her stomach clench.

She rode the bicycle to the nearest service station a mile away and asked for directions. The attendant gave her a goofy grin. His long-spiked, blue-streaked hair made him look as though he'd fallen out on the wrong side of the bed and bruised his hair. "Sorry," he said, "I just moved here, and I don't know the area."

"Do you have a local map?"

He rummaged around in the map stand. "Nah, not one of the city. Got one of Texas though."

"I need a city map," she ground out. *"Hunter, I'm at..."* She turned to the attendant. "Where is this service station located?"

"Three-ten Garland Road."

She took a deep breath, hoping the next thing she said wouldn't be the stupidest thing she'd ever done.

JARED HOVERED over Hunter's hospital bed. "Well, what did she say?"

"She's riding a bike and doesn't know how to get here. Why doesn't she have a phone?" Hunter had to acknowledge that she had escaped her summoners and was attempting to come to his aid. But on a bicycle? He growled under his breath. Why didn't she just take Jared's advice and ride with him?

"Maybe she does have a cell phone, but you didn't give her either of our cell numbers." Jared shook his head. "So she's lost in the city of Dallas on a bike. Really smart move. Should I add that to the data on Kubiteron demons? Not very bright?"

"Shh, I'm still trying to tell her we'll try to help her. But we don't know all the roads to the hospital, nor how to guide her here without a map." *Kubiteron...* He mentally chastised himself. At the very least he could have learned her name. *Kubiteron, where is your present location? Can I have Jared meet you somewhere and pick you up?*

"Is it working? What are you saying?"

"I asked her where she was and offered to have you pick her up. If we don't get to her soon, I'm afraid her summoner will discover her missing."

"And?" Jared fisted his hands on his hips. "Any response?"

"None. I think she doesn't hear me. I don't know how to communicate back to her."

"Hunter, tell Jared to pick me up at a service station at 310 Garland Road. Pronto. If he's not here in twenty minutes, I'll assume you can't hear me, and we'll have to make some other arrangements later."

Immediately, Hunter's whole being lifted despite being riddled with pain. "That's it! She wants you to go to the service station at 310 Garland Road. You have twenty minutes. Hurry or she'll leave."

"Twenty minutes."

"Virtually no traffic at this hour."

"Easy for you to say. Be right back." Jared bolted out of the room. A nurse screamed, then scolded him for being there after visiting hours.

Dressed in scrubs decorated with teddy bears, the nurse rushed in to see Hunter. He hoped he wasn't in the pediatric ward.

"I was afraid the boy had done something bad to you, the way he tore out of here."

Hunter feigned a yawn. "He fell asleep and when he woke, he realized his mother would be worried about him."

Not. They were on a world cruise and figured Jared was old enough, capable, and responsible enough to take care of himself. Though sometimes Jared wished they would be more concerned about him. Hunter shook his head. If they knew what he was really up to…

The nurse checked Hunter's pulse. "Way past visiting hours. I don't remember him being in here."

"He probably had taken a bathroom break. I've been sleeping most of the time."

"Hunter, I hope you got my message. Seventeen minutes left on the stopwatch."

Stopwatch? Since when did a lesser demon time *him*? He let his breath out in exasperation. Since he needed her help so badly.

The nurse left him alone with his morbid thoughts. If the girl didn't help him, he wouldn't be responsible for how angry he could get. If he lived long enough.

~

Pacing down the convenience store aisle, the combination of chocolate and brewing coffee scenting the air, Alana finally walked to one of the big glass windows and stared out at the dead street. She'd never felt so overwhelmingly frustrated in her life. Glancing at her watch, she found fifteen minutes had passed. Sixteen, sixteen and a half, sixteen and three-quarters. Any minute her uncle could arrive! She was only a mile from his house.

The clerk turned up his hip-hop music and bounced around on his stool, giving her a lopsided grin.

"Three minutes left, Hunter."

A misty haze cloaked the area in a foggy gloom, overhead lights making the vapor even ghostlier. A rusted pickup pulled up to the station, and the clerk immediately lowered his music and sat alert.

A dirty-looking guy with oily, long hair filled up the pump, while a slightly younger man with a chin full of whiskers sauntered into the store, real cool-like. He looked her up and down like she was something on display. Curbing her annoyance, she reminded herself she'd taken her contacts out and didn't want to show her real self to this clown.

The guy leaned over the counter. "How's about a pack of cigarettes."

The clerk sat up straighter. "Got some ID?"

The greasy teen gave him a long, searing look, then one lip lifted, but his brown eyes remained flat. "You want to see some ID?"

Alana didn't like the tone of the guy's voice, menacing, taunting, trouble.

"He asked for ID. You're obviously too young to buy cigarettes."

Alana knew she should have let things go. No sense in stirring up trouble when she needed to get out of there pronto and help Hunter. Yet, she'd faced her share of bullies in school, and she knew the best way to deal with one was to deal with him and never let him walk all over her.

"Why don't you just mind your own business?" he asked, whipping around. He reached underneath his jeans jacket. "Better yet, why don't you come with us for a little ride?"

"I have better things to do with my life, thank you very much."

"Okay, done being nice. I ain't asking. I'm telling ya." He jerked out a gun, and she didn't hesitate to react.

With a spell, she sent the weapon flying across the store. His mouth gaped wide.

The clerk must have hit a silent alarm because the sound of a siren headed their way. She had to get out of here *now*!

The guy with the truck honked his horn, and the one in the store raced across the floor to get his gun. When he reached where he thought it was, he couldn't see it. Courtesy of a mind-illusion spell. "Where did my gun go?"

The truck honked several more times.

The guy suddenly ran toward Alana and grabbed for her wrist, but she quickly put up her aggressive barrier, and he flew backward into a rack of chips, hit his head, and slid to the floor dazed.

"Wow, martial arts. Cool," the clerk said.

Yeah. Thank goodness she was so quick; he couldn't see that she hadn't used her hands and legs as death-defying weapons.

The man from the pickup slammed his door and dashed for the store.

"Lock the door. Hurry!" she said. Then she spied Jared pulling into the brightly lit service station in a neon yellow Jeep. "Wait! I see my ride."

"The guy has a gun," the clerk warned.

"Can't wait. Got to go."

She rushed to the door and bolted outside, but the man from the pickup seized her arm, his dirty nails digging into the skin. Gritting her teeth against the pain, she cast her propel spell and hurtled him to his truck. He slammed his back into the pickup with an oof, and it made her back hurt just thinking about it. He landed on his butt and cursed.

Jared pulled his Jeep into a parking space. His mouth hung wide, his eyes shifting from her to the pickup driver.

Great, just great. No way did she want Jared to see her using any of her witch's powers. Her attention shifted to her uncle's bike. There was no place for it in the Jeep. Why couldn't he have had more of a demon-sized vehicle? She figured Hunter would.

She seized the door to the convenience store and jerked it open. "Can I leave my bicycle here for a few hours?"

The clerk grinned. "Yeah, sure, lady. I'll watch out for it. You bet." He turned his music on louder and began dancing to the beat.

Alana jumped into the Jeep and wrinkled her nose at the smell like something was burning.

"Leaking heater core," he said when he saw the expression on her face. "No time to fix it."

"Get a move on. You're five minutes late."

Jared gave a short laugh. "Like you would notice when you were so busy beating up a guy."

"Yeah, well, if you'd been on time, you could have handled them for me like a good male demon should."

"Them?"

She gave him a superior look, though deep inside she was chastising herself for making the slip. "The other's taking a nap inside."

"I'm rethinking your demon type. I'm not at all sure you're a Kubiteron."

Her heart took a dive. "Why not?" She hated hearing the doubt in his voice. Finally, glad she might learn more about her demon side, the thought Jared didn't truly know what she was gave her a fit of depression.

He whipped out of the service station parking lot and headed down the street, passing the two police cars, their lights flashing, illuminating the night like a disco club. The lightweight Jeep didn't have a lot of power, but it felt like it was moving fast at least. But the way it was burning, she had serious doubts they would make it.

"Truthfully?" he asked.

She took a deep breath. "Yeah?"

"I don't think there's a name for your kind."

She glowered at him. If he hadn't been driving, she would have slugged him. "What's *that* supposed to mean?"

"Nothing, except you don't fit the pattern for any of the demons I have data on."

She tilted her head to the side. "Maybe you've stereotyped us too much?"

His mouth turned up a hair. "I should say I know of no demon that can do what you can. It has nothing to do with stereotyping. Who knows? Next, you could sprout wings."

"Like an angel." She glanced out the window and was glad Jared seemed to know his way to the hospital.

"More like a fire-breathing dragon. That would make you different from every demon also, which would have nothing to do with stereotyping." Jared grew quiet, then finally let out his breath. "Can you save Hunter?"

"You like him, don't you?" She couldn't believe it. No lesser demon liked a Matusa. Unless he said so because he was too afraid Hunter would find out how he felt.

"What's not to like?"

She stole a look at the Elantus. "He's a Matusa."

"He's one of the good guys."

"Ha! Matusa come in all shades of bad. Not one of them is good."

"Well, I like him. So, can you save him?" His tone of voice came out more of a threat than a question.

"Are you his slave?"

"For the hundredth time, no!"

Alana paused and inhaled deeply, contemplating. If Hunter truly had a redeeming side, would he be willing to defend her if the Matusa from Baltimore came for her? He was most likely the only one with the strength to take on a demon of his own kind. The thought of asking him for help irked her. She never asked strangers for assistance, let alone a Matusa.

She scoffed quietly at the idea.

"Will you?" he asked.

"Why do you think I've tried to get to the hospital?"

"To kill him."

She stared at him in disbelief. "Why would I kill him?"

"You're afraid of him."

"If we don't fear them, we're stupid."

"You're right about the other Dark Ones." He pulled into the hospital parking lot. "But know this, Kubiteron, if you try to hurt him, I will terminate you myself."

She smiled and she figured her expression was pure evil. "You can try." Climbing out of the Jeep, she added, "I thought the Elantus didn't kill anyone."

"I lied."

As soon as Hunter heard her voice, he knew it was the Kubiteron. Though her voice had a sweet allure no matter the state of aggravation she was in, he could tell she was arguing with Jared. He'd hoped his friend would put her in a better mood, and she would be more agreeable to help. From the words the Kubiteron and Jared were having, they dashed any hope Hunter had that she would be, well, *gentle* with him.

When the girl stalked into the room, her green eyes were dagger sharp. She had no smile for him, and she appeared to be there strictly for business's sake. Good, he had no desire to do anything more than get well, free her from her summoner enslavement, and send her packing to the demon world.

"What about the nurses at the nurses' station?" Hunter asked, worried they would call security because no visitors were allowed at such an ungodly hour.

Jared gave the girl a scathing glance. "The Kubiteron took care of it."

"Can we know your name?" Hunter realized how degrading it sounded to continue to call her by her demon type and not her given name.

With a firm shake of her head, she closed the distance between them and concentrated on his injury.

Jared gave him a shrug. "She's hostile? What can I say?"

Hunter scowled at the impudence of the girl, and then Jared's earlier comment registered in his fever-fogged brain. "How did she take care of the nurses?"

"Ask her. She does things no demon should. I'm rethinking that she might not be a Kubiteron after all, and she doesn't like it."

"That she's not a Kubiteron?"

"No, that I'm having doubts she's one."

Hunter frowned at Jared. Did he have to upset her *before* she tried to heal him?

Her hand glided over Hunter's arm, hovering but never making contact. Her lips were moving, but no sound came out, as if she was speaking to him through telepathy.

Watching the care she took, her eyes glowing brighter green, her brow furrowed, he thought she was the most beautiful creature he'd ever seen. "I have no doubt she's one of them."

She stopped chanting and looked at him. "Why?"

Jeez, now he had done it. Get back to the healing process, he wanted to command her. He figured it would have the opposite result. Demons worked that way.

He cleared his throat. What could he say? The truth? That Kubiteron females were known for both their inner and outer beauty, more so than any other demon? Matusa demons often wanted to enslave them. He felt the same strong pull even though he fought it, but he couldn't reveal this to her.

Jared folded his arms and grinned at him. Yeah, Jared had told him the reason. So why was he now thinking she wasn't a Kubiteron? Because she and he didn't get along?

"The other Matusa recognized you were one right away. So did I. So did Jared when he first saw you. We go by our first instincts. Everything else is a delusion. You're a Kubiteron, but I would still like to know your name."

She studied Hunter, then seemed to accept his word and returned to her chanting. She worked on his arm, moving up to his head. But she would not tell him her name! The fever seemed to abate some, though his blood was sizzling with annoyance that she would defy him.

Once she went to work again on his arm, his fever raged out of control. He tried to calm his tension by tightening and loosening his muscles so that he could let her do her healing work, though he couldn't help glowering at her through most of it. She was supposed to be a healer. Why couldn't she heal him?

After two hours, her eyes misted. "I'm sorry."

Sorry was not what he wanted to hear. He'd never seen a demon grow tearful, except the time he'd torn the one away from the summoner, and she'd wept real tears. "You can't heal me."

He realized he was going to die. Not that he was afraid of death, but he feared leaving the humans alone to face Matusa demons on their own, especially his human family and Jared's. They would never survive.

Slapping his fist into the palm of his hand, Jared paced across the floor. "We have to do something."

"Take her home."

Jared spun around and faced him. "No. She's a healer. Some of what she did helped."

"Then it stopped working. She's not powerful enough. This isn't any of her affair."

"We have to find your father, Hunter. He might know of an antidote for the poison."

"In Seplichus?" Alana asked her voice nearly a whisper.

"Yes." Hunter said to Jared, "I told you I don't know who my father is."

"But we can find out who your mother is, and she might know," Jared argued.

Alana looked from Jared to Hunter.

Hunter shook his head. "I would have to ask my parents, and you know how I feel about that."

"We could tell them the truth, that we need to locate your mother because she might have some antidote in her blood that would save you. Then we'll see your mother and—"

"No. And that's my final word."

Jared stormed out of the room.

Alana stared at the empty doorway.

"Go with him. He'll take you home."

"You're living with human parents?"

"Yeah. It's not so odd. Jared also lives with some."

Alana tucked her hair behind her ears. "Your mother was a demon?"

"No."

She took a deep breath. "You're only half demon?"

Not liking what she was getting at, he ground his teeth.

"Me, too," she said softly.

His jaw dropped. "You're not a full demon?"

She shook her head. "Now I see why you're not a killer like the other Matusa."

Oh, he was a killer all right, but he hoped he would only be forced to kill the Matusa murderers.

She licked her lips and swallowed hard. "What can I do to help?"

8

Alana hurried out of Hunter's hospital room, stopping briefly only to wake the nurses, then she headed for the elevator, with a new mission in mind. In the lobby downstairs, a housekeeper waxed the floor with a lemon fragrance, while Jared paced nearby. Seeing Alana, he stopped abruptly and jammed his hands in his pockets, his face wearing a scowl.

"I want to help you find Hunter's birth mother," she said, joining him.

"And?"

"What do you mean, *and*?" she asked, her voice elevating.

"What do you hope to get out of it?"

"I want to help, no hidden agenda."

Jared took a deep breath. "You can't look at the data on the Kubiteron until you've healed Hunter."

"That's not why I want to help."

"Why then?"

"Maybe..." She bit her lip. "Maybe he can help me later if we can make him well."

"How?"

"I witnessed a Matusa murder a woman. He saw me. He'll come for me."

Jared stared at her, then cursed under his breath. "He'll kill us all if we try to protect you and Hunter's not well enough. *Just super.* We pick a healer who can't heal, and now we learn she's on a Matusa's death list. Terrific." He glowered at her. "You just wanted to help—no hidden agenda, right?" He stormed out of the hospital.

She hurried after him, trying to keep pace with his long stride. "Are you half demon?"

"No, full."

She gave him an irritated look. "Figures."

"You're only half?"

"Yeah, I guess that's why I want to help Hunter, too."

He gave a dark laugh. "Figures." He stalked out to the Jeep, and she shadowed him. Then he turned to her, his brow furrowed. "So, if you're only half demon, what's the other half? It can't be human."

Though her blood sizzled, she disregarded his remark. "Can't you find anything about his birth mother on your laptop? The internet or something?"

"No, I looked, despite Hunter telling me not to. I figured he could get angry with me later."

They climbed into his Jeep while Alana pondered the news. "But you had no luck."

"No. The best way to go about this, I assume, is to get hold of his birth mother."

Great, as if that would solve all their problems. "She might not know who his father was."

Jared's expression was somber as he quickly looked at her, and she could tell he was a bit taken aback.

She shrugged. "My mother didn't know my father's name."

"That's all I needed to hear. Can you possibly think of something more upbeat?"

WHEN THEY ARRIVED at Hunter's home, the one-story house was shrouded in dark, except for a single security light hanging from a lamppost in the yard.

Jared shoved his hands in his pockets and stared at the door.

Alana glanced at Jared when he didn't knock on the door. "Well? You have to be the one to approach them. I don't know them."

"I know, I know."

When he still didn't react, she rang the doorbell.

He glowered at her. "Why aren't you wearing contacts?"

"I took them out, so I could show my uncle I'm half demon." She tilted her chin up.

He shook his head. "And here we're always trying to hide the fact we are."

"Me, too. Normally." She rang the doorbell again.

"Coming, coming," a gruff male voice said.

"Hunter's father. A mortician," Jared said.

"Gruesome."

The front door swung open, revealing a dark-haired man with bleary, dark brown eyes. Jared and Alana stood on the threshold, and she felt like an intruder in the man's world.

He was not as tall as Hunter, with a larger, more hooked nose and darker skin. He did not resemble Hunter's birth father at all. The man's gaze flicked over Alana before settling on Jared, a question in his eyes.

"What's going on?" he asked, his voice hoarse and rough.

Jared took a deep breath, steeling himself for the confrontation that Alana knew would come. "I'm here to talk to you about Hunter," he said, his voice steady and firm.

The man's eyes narrowed, suspicion and mistrust clear in his gaze. "Why should I talk to you about my son?" he asked, his tone defensive.

Jared held out a hand, palm up, a gesture of peace. "We need to find Hunter's birth mother. Her blood might contain an antibody that could help him."

Mr. Ross frowned. "No one from the hospital has said anything about this to me."

"He seems to be dying, Mr. Ross." Alana's words were tinged with anger. "This might be his only chance."

Shaking his head, he started to close the door. "If the hospital calls me and tells me what you have, I'll consider it. Not before—"

Clenching her teeth, Alana quieted her rising temper. "You want to tell us her name."

"Crissie Carruthers."

Jared glanced at Alana, his eyes saucer sized.

"Where does she live?"

Mr. Ross shook his head but waited obediently for her to release him.

"Thank you, Mr. Ross. You don't remember us coming here tonight. You don't remember giving the name of Hunter's birth mother to anyone. You may go back to bed and have a nice sleep."

Mr. Ross shuffled back into the house and closed the door.

Jared cursed under his breath. "How did you do that? No demon can use mind control."

"Must be my other half." She pointed at his laptop. "Can you find her address in there?"

TWENTY MINUTES LATER, Jared pulled up to a small stone house, and Alana took charge. A petite blond peered at Alana through navy drapes, her electric blue eyes worried. Alana was still concerned that the demon wouldn't have told the woman his name. Then what?

Alana knocked on the front door. "I'm here to speak to you about your son, Miss Carruthers, Crissie. I have to talk to you. Please, open up."

The door remained shut like a castle barricade between them. "I don't have a son."

Great. Just great. Alana hadn't thought of that scenario.

"You had a son." Alana looked at Jared to help her out. "How old is he?"

"Eighteen," Jared said.

"You or someone summoned a demon, and you became pregnant," Alana said to the woman.

The woman opened her door to Alana and Jared. She looked like she was about to collapse, and Alana helped her into the living room. "Does anyone else live with you here?"

Crissie shook her head.

"Did you ever marry?"

"No one could ever be like him."

Alana's heart nearly stopped. Her mother had spoken nearly the same words. "But you gave up your baby."

Crissie's eyes filled with tears. "My father was ashamed of me for having a child out of wedlock. He forced me to give my son up when he was born."

"Who summoned his father?"

The woman swallowed hard.

"Did you summon him?"

She nodded.

Alana didn't sense the woman had any magical abilities. She must be like the Goth women she'd seen, just experimenting in the realms of the unknown. "Crissie, this is so important. Your son's name is Hunter, but he was trying to send an evil demon back to his world. The demon tore Hunter's skin, infecting him with some kind of poison. We think the only way to save his life is if we find his father. He may know of an antidote."

"Can I see him?" Crissie asked, her voice no more than a whisper.

"Hunter?" Alana wasn't sure if his mother wanted to see her son or the man she had loved.

"Yes, my son."

Now what? Hunter didn't want to see his birth mother. But she couldn't deny his mother the chance to be with him. Especially when he might still die.

Jared shifted from one foot to the other.

"Yes. We'll take you to him."

Thankfully, Jared didn't contradict her, but he gave Alana a look that could kill her. Good thing *he* was wearing contacts.

"So who was his father?" Alana asked as they climbed into Jared's Jeep, though she feared Crissie wouldn't know, just like her mother didn't.

"Bentos."

Relieved, Alana took a deep breath. "Thank you."

"What will you do?"

"Try to summon him to the hospital room."

Crissie ran her hands over her lap, smoothing her jeans. "Will Hunter hate me?"

Probably, if he were a full demon. Maybe not, being half-human. Alana didn't answer her. His mother would have to learn the answer for herself.

WHEN THEY ARRIVED at the hospital, Alana quickly put the nurses at the station to sleep, but Crissie was so eager to see Hunter, though she incessantly wrung her hands, she didn't seem to see what Alana had done. Jared, for being a full demon, looked a little spooked when Alana used her magic on the nurses. Good, she felt outnumbered by the two male demons. This gave her a slightly better edge.

Now, the problem—Hunter—and hoping he didn't go ballistic over their bringing his birth mother to the hospital.

"Alana, where are you?" Uncle Stephen telepathically communicated to her. He sounded both anxious and angered.

Having forgotten all about him, she nearly had a stroke. *"Safe, Uncle Stephen, but I've got to take care of a friend. I'll be home soon."*

"Alana!"

She silenced his communication with her. The business at hand was too important to dismiss. If they weren't careful, they might unleash a new Matusa and have a whole lot of bloodshed on their hands. However, she couldn't understand how Crissie had summoned the Matusa, and he hadn't killed her for it already.

Jared went into the room first to check on Hunter.

Unable to stand Crissie's nervousness, Alana wrapped her arm around her shoulders. "My mother felt as you did. Except she kept me." She wasn't sure why she told the woman that, except she wanted to show her others were like her—in love with a demon they could never have.

The revelation seemed to surprise Crissie. "And your father?"

Alana shook her head. "My mother didn't know his name. She didn't even tell me about it until I turned seventeen."

"I'm sorry," Crissie said.

Alana managed a smile. "I love my mother. I just don't know anything about my father. Hunter's been raised by a nice family. But you're still his birth mother."

Jared came out of the patient's room and gave Alana a look that she couldn't read. But she guessed it wasn't good. "He said to go in."

Alana raised her brows.

Jared shook his head, but Crissie seized Alana's hand with titan strength and pulled her toward the room. "I can't go in alone, and you understand the way it is. You can help smooth things over."

Right. Alana was not the smooth-things-over type. She'd been angry with her mother for not telling her about her father. If she ever met him—which she *never* wanted to do—she would give him an earful, too. She'd pissed her uncle off now. Smoothing things over was not her bag.

Crissie nearly crept toward the bed; Hunter's eyes fixed on her. "I'm Crissie Carruthers," she said softly. "Your birth mother."

His eyes hardened, and his jaw ticked with rigid control.

"My father forced me to give you up. I wanted to die."

Hunter looked at Alana, and she nodded. "My grandparents forced my mother out of the house when she vowed to keep me. She struggled for years to support us. Crissie did what she felt she had to, gave you to a family who could care for you better than she could."

"Your father's name was Bentos," Crissie said. "If I can do nothing more for you, I want to help you live."

For an instant, he closed his eyes. Looking sunburned from the fever, he shivered endlessly.

Feeling they had no other choice, Alana said, "Call him forth, Crissie. Summon him."

Her blue eyes grew big. "He said he would kill me if I called him here again."

Fisting her hands, Alana feared the worse. He was a true Matusa, a Dark One. "Call him forth. Then you leave. If he sees his son, hopefully, he will change his mind." If not, she would defend him to the death, even though she feared Hunter already didn't have long to live.

"I won't leave. I want my son well again."

Hunter nodded.

Crissie raised her hands and did the incantation. The portal opened, but no one came forth.

"Why would a demon who has been summoned by name not show?" Alana asked.

Jared cleared his throat. "Maybe he's dead. Or if not that, maybe he's too far away from the portal. Like you said, you were summoned when the portal opened, but only if it was close by."

Alana felt a strange tingling all over her body. "My uncle. Ohmigod, he's trying to locate me." Panicked, she turned her attention to the portal's shimmering blue-green lights. "Before my uncle finds me and stops me, there's only one other thing we can do."

"What's that? Though I hate to ask," Jared said.

"We find Hunter's father."

"No," Hunter said. "I wouldn't want you to—"

"Too late. I'll need your help when I return. You're of no use to me half dead." She tossed him a simpering smile, then stalked toward the portal. "Coming, Jared? I'm not sure a half-demon will survive in this world. I might need your help."

"Yeah, I'm coming. I think I got me a girlfriend."

"In your nightmares." She glanced back at Hunter who winced in pain. "Don't you die on me, Matusa, or I'll wring your sickly neck when I return."

He gave her a half smile, and she winked. *Keep thinking those evil thoughts, Dark One.*

Dreading what she might find in the demon world, she held her breath and stepped into the portal.

9

A lana was not normally a clinging vine, but in the demon world, she couldn't help but cling to Jared. She wished Hunter had been well enough to come with them, his Matusa powers would have made their journey much easier. With him by their side, she assumed most of the lesser demons would have left them alone.

As she looked over the sprawling city, she wondered if she had lost her mind. How were they supposed to find Hunter's father in this chaotic and sinister place? The buildings were a mix of brick and glass, all towering toward the smoky sky. Alana couldn't shake off the feeling of being watched, and the shadows that seemed to lurk in every dark alley only added to her unease. The city streets were much like their own world but darker and more foreboding.

They made their way through the city, and Alana's footsteps echoed off the slick pavement. The buildings seemed to close in on them. The air was heavy with the smell of damp earth, a stark contrast to what she thought it would smell like. It seemed unnatural for a city to have such an earthy scent. Alana couldn't shake off the feeling that they were being watched.

"Have you ever been here before?" she asked, trying to keep the tremor out of her voice.

Jared shook his head, his jaw tight and his eyes vigilant. "Now you ask. Yeah, the Hall of Records is straight up the street. We'll search for Hunter's dad there."

Guardedly relieved, she nodded. "Tell me what I should know about my demon kind. What powers can I call on if I need them?" She swore Jared shivered. "Jared, answer me. What do you know about my kind?"

He took a deep breath and bumped her arm when a demon looked out a storefront window at them. The guy said something to another.

"Matusa," Jared said under his breath, his voice jittery. "You don't know anything about your heritage?"

"How could I? My mother didn't even know my father's name. She didn't know what kind of demon she'd called forth."

"How do you know what we are?" Jared's gaze kept shifting to the dark alleys which made Alana nervous. Jared quickened his step.

Alana nearly had to run to catch up. "Inborn trait, I guess. I don't know why I couldn't tell what I was though."

"Maybe your other half blocked your ability to recognize what you are?"

She cast him a dirty look.

Jared let out his breath. "I have to tell you that Matusa like female Kubiteron. I've heard the Matusa often will find a female they want and force them to be their mates."

She gave Jared a scathing look, not believing he would keep such a thing secret from her until they'd entered the demon world. "And you didn't tell me this before because?"

"We have to save Hunter."

"You could have told me, you jerk!"

He smiled, but the look faded when a shadow moved closer to them.

Frowning, she tried to calm the new anxiety crawling inside her. "How many times have you been here?"

"Several times, looking for my parents. Nobody bothers me, but I hadn't realized having you tag along would be a problem."

She was a problem? She was the solution! Was Jared going to find Hunter's father on his own? No siree! "Hey, I'm here to help Hunter, just like you. So why does Hunter want to return demons to their world? I wouldn't think he would care since he's a Matusa."

"He's half demon," Jared said.

"So? Not all humans would risk their necks over someone they didn't know. Especially if they had to fight a Matusa."

"He's half Matusa." Jared gave her a smug smile.

Alana cast Jared an irritated look. "That doesn't explain anything."

"Three years ago, two men summoned a portal near the pizza place where Hunter used to hang out. He'd never seen another demon, never seen a gateway to the demon world. They brought forth a female Kubiteron. She was blond and green-eyed like you. Hunter was at once attracted to her. Inborn trait. Can't be helped." Jared took a deep breath. "I'd been experimenting with locating demon signatures, trying to find someone else like me."

"So you hadn't met Hunter yet?"

"No. I'd just spotted the Kubiteron and Hunter's signature on the laptop and headed in their direction, though I'd meant to keep a low profile because Hunter was a Matusa. The summoners, fearing what they'd done, killed the Kubiteron. Hunter didn't react in time to save the girl. When I arrived, he had nearly killed one of the summoners. The other had fled the scene. Hunter was so enraged when I tried to stop him, he nearly killed me."

Alana stared at Jared. "And you call him a friend? So what happened?"

Jared shrugged. "Hunter finally realized I was a demon and could track others close by."

"So you were convenient, useful, his slave."

Jared scowled at her. "I'm not his slave."

"What about the other summoner?"

"He died from a heart attack."

"That Hunter had caused."

"Suppose so, in a round-about way. Hunter learned how to open the portal. He vowed to send our kind back when they were summoned into this world, so no summoner could harm a lesser demon again."

"So you were fourteen at the time?"

"Yeah. Hunter was fifteen."

"How come you guys knew about your demon heritage so young?"

Jared shook his head. "Everyone's different. My human parents said I learned to walk when I was nine months old. I could type complete sentences on a computer keyboard long before I could master writing my A, B, C's in cursive."

"I was reading chapter books when I was five."

"Yeah, see? Maybe for me, it had to do with my being a full demon. In any event, everyone's different. Hunter said he took forever to walk because his human mother coddled him so. Don't tell him I told you though."

She could imagine how the Matusa would hate it if anyone learned of it.

Jared bolted up stone stairs that led to a gray stone building, and Alana hurried to follow him. Strange writing was etched in the stone.

"Their equivalent of a courthouse. Birth records, genealogy information, family roots, that sort of thing," he said.

"Did you know your parents' names?"

He jerked the door open and let her go inside first. "No. I've tried to find which demons were summoned to Earth world at about the time I was conceived. Records for millions exist all over the world. I've gone through maybe a thousand, checked leads, every one of them a dead end."

"I'm sorry, Jared." And she meant it. At least she had a mother who loved her, even if she kept secrets from her. She figured it all stemmed from having a fling with a demon and her mother had to keep secrets after that. Or maybe her mother's father had been unreasonable to live with. Yeah, as much as he was mean to her over having anything to do with someone who was not a magic user, Alana could understand that.

The hall seemed to stretch forever, and the ceiling was several stories high. She wished they would hurry up and get there. Doors twice as tall as Jared were situated along both sides. "Why are the doors so tall?" Her heart fluttered. Were some demons that big? Her footsteps sounded eerily noisy against the marble floor when everything was so deathly quiet.

"Their file cabinets are tall."

She laughed inwardly at herself. Now why hadn't she thought of that?

"Do you ever want to know about your father?" Jared asked.

She ground her teeth and for the first time, she told the truth. "Yeah. As much as I hate to admit it, yeah, I do." Though why she was telling such an aggravating demon, she didn't know. Well, maybe she did. She guessed she felt sorry for him for wanting to locate his parents and having no success. "I want my dad to know I exist. I want him to know how much my mother still loves him."

"It won't make any difference to him, you know."

"That I exist?"

"No. They say demon parents take great pride in their offspring."

How could he say such a thing when his parents were both demons and abandoned him?

"They probably tried to save me from something or someone and left me in a human family's care," he responded to her questioning gaze.

"Ah."

"What I meant was your father probably wouldn't want to return to your mother. She summoned him and controlled him, and no demon likes to be forced to do anything, especially not by a human. Same thing with Hunter's dad. All we can hope for is that his dad will care enough about him to want to return and take care of him or know someone who can."

A tall, thin Elantus demon approached Jared, his gray eyes shifting to Alana. He smiled at Jared and gave a nod. "Jared."

"Treikal."

"Are you searching for your parents again today? Or perhaps for the young lady's?"

"Neither. We're looking for a Matusa."

The man's brows rose.

"Long story. We need to help a sick friend, and we're hoping his father might assist us."

"Hopefully you have a name this time."

"Bentos."

Treikal rubbed his chin, then nodded. "Come this way."

The man moved slowly along the black marble floors, his shoes never making a sound. Demons were sneaky, crossed Alana's mind. She communicated to Hunter, "*So far, so good. We're in the building housing court records.*"

"Treikal has been like a father to me," Jared said, with no effort to speak softly. "He taught me the ways of our people and helped me to build my database with information about some of the demon types, though I'm still compiling information."

"Now I understand how you know so much while you were raised by humans. How did you make a portal appear so you could come here if you're a full demon?"

"Hunter summons it for me whenever I want to cross over."

"How did you become friends? I mean, after he nearly killed you?"

Jared's expression turned grim. "A long story." He motioned to Treikal. "Treikal thinks we might be related, even if distantly. He says there's always a connection between family roots. We sense it when we meet a relative, no matter how far removed."

"Yet, you still haven't found your parents." Her curiosity about how Jared and Hunter had finally become friends garnered her real attention.

"Without names or other details, it's hard to make much headway."

Treikal nodded. "Knowing Bentos's name helps. Does the young lady also seek a parent?"

"Her father, but we have to concentrate on Bentos right now."

"She shouldn't be here, you know."

"Yes, I know."

She wondered if it was because of her human heritage. However, they didn't seem to know she wasn't a full demon. "Well, I don't know why I shouldn't be here. So will someone please enlighten me?"

Treikal's mouth curved up slightly when he heard her barbed tongue. "You're a Kubiteron. Just the other day a Matusa was expelled from the Dallas Earth city madder than, well you can imagine."

"Expelled by whom?" Jared asked.

"Another Matusa."

Alana's heart thundered harder. She knew the demon could hear it beating, too. No matter how much she tried to quiet it, she couldn't.

"You know who the Matusa was that expelled the other?" Treikal slowed his pace and motioned to a room.

"Yes, our friend," Alana guessed. "The demon cut his skin and poisoned him. We need to find a cure."

"Ah. Ferengus saw a Kubiteron female in Dallas and said he claimed her. Except the younger demon knocked him back into our world. Ferengus left a lasting impression on the younger man, who swore the other wished the Kubiteron for his own. You would not happen to know this female, would you?"

Alana's throat felt parched. "He only saw a vision of me."

"A vision?" Treikal looked at Jared for an explanation.

He shrugged. "She has strange ways. Some demon, but some... something else. Not human. She won't tell me how she does these strange things."

No matter how much Jared irked her, she would not tell him she was half-witch.

The old man smiled, his skin wrinkling under his eyes glittering with humor. "If this friend of yours did not already want the Kubiteron..." He lifted a hand toward computer screens resting on what looked to be a hundred tables or more. "She might have been yours."

She scowled at him. "I'm not the Matusa's or anyone else's."

Treikal laughed. "As I said. This system has all the data about demon families. Look at will. Mind you, the rumors will quickly spread that the young lady is here. Ferengus or some other will come for her."

Jared punched in a code into the computer. "Not in the court of records."

"They will wait on the steps outside the building where she will have no protection," Treikal warned.

"Thanks for letting me know this before we came here, Jared." She was furious with him! He was as evil as a Matusa!

"What are friends for?" He gave Alana a sinister grin.

FOR TWO HOURS, Alana and Jared sat on chairs at a terminal, searching and cross-searching records. Treikal had left them alone, but demons wandered into and out of the football field-sized room, seemingly more interested in observing Alana and Jared than in doing any research themselves. Chills erupted over Alana's skin when she caught the seventeenth demon in an hour staring at her.

None of them were Matusa, and only one was a male Kubiteron. She thought they would be one or the other. The one, because supposedly the Matusa were crazed about having a female Kubiteron, and the other because he might have been her father.

As many records as they'd already seen during their search had yielded no results, Alana couldn't help but feel thwarted. She thought their task was impossible as time was running out for Hunter. "Jared, is there a hospital we can go to that might have an antibiotic or cure for Hunter?" she finally asked, her voice heavy with defeat.

Jared shook his head, his expression mirroring her own. "Our best bet would be to get hold of Bentos. Except for the court of records, we are not demon citizens. We wouldn't have access to some places."

Jared finally leaned closer and gave her the reason for all the interest. "All demons desire Kubiteron females. You're a rare commodity. They know the Matusa wants you, and so they will look, but not touch."

"That's just great." She did not say it gratefully.

He brought up another record and his face brightened. "I think we've got our man. Doesn't he look like Hunter?"

Her heart raced. Ohmigod. Was it him? "Brown eyes, brown hair, longer than Hunter's. Same stubborn chin. It looks like him and the same name as Crissie gave us. But none of them have last names."

"Nobody has the same first name. No need to give last names."

But would he aid Hunter? Would he even know a cure? Her stomach tightened. "How can we contact him?"

Jared pushed a button. "A direct line to the person in the file."

"What if they've moved?"

"All demons are in the court of records. If they move, their records are updated at once. It's just a formality."

At the bottom of the screen, someone typed: *You seek me for what purpose?*

Jared, Elantus, seeking Bentos for the purpose of reuniting him with his son, Hunter, in Earth world. Son dying of Matusa poison, needs antidote. Can you assist us?

Us? Identify us.

Jared's face darkened and his eyes glowed. "I really hate the formality you have to use here." *Pardon. Jared, Elantus, and...*Jared turned to her. "Your name?"

She ground her teeth. "Alana."

Jared shook his head and typed in: *Elana*

She pointed to the screen. "A, not E."

"He isn't going to care how you spell your blasted name."

"Spell it right! *I* care."

Cursing, Jared retyped her name. *Alana, Kubiteron, seeks help from Bentos to save his son.*

Kubiteron female? Earth inhabitant?

Half Kubiteron, half...

Alana punched Jared in the arm when he hesitated. "Human."

He glowered at her. "You're not human, but I don't know what you are."

"Type in human," she growled.

...human. Jared clenched and unclenched his hands.

Staring at the screen, Alana crossed her legs and rocked her foot. "What's he waiting for?"

"I don't know."

Explain Kubiteron female.

"He's hung up on you instead of Hunter."

"Give me the keyboard."

"You don't know how to respond formally. If you say the wrong thing, you can piss him off, and then…"

She jerked the keyboard away from Jared. *Listen, Bentos, your son is dying. Who I am is of no consequence. He desperately needs your help. I tried to heal him but had no success. So will you help or not?*

Is this the Kubiteron speaking?

Yes!

Jared ground his teeth. "Jeez, you never end anything with an exclamation mark. Never."

She was really beginning to dislike this world. "Why do they have it on the keyboard then?"

"They like Earth-world technology."

"Well, then, they ought to learn how to deal with exclamation marks." She typed another message: *We don't have all day! Are you going to help us or not?*

Why do you want to help my son?

"What are you going to say to that?" Jared crossed his arms. "If you lie, he'll know. You can't tell him you want his son to kill a Matusa for you."

"Give me some credit, will you, Jared?" *I witnessed a Matusa kill a human woman. I need your son's protection.*

You can have mine.

Her mouth dropped open. "He can't mean what I'm thinking he means."

"That he wants you? I would say it was a pretty sure bet."

"This is unreal." She typed: *I was mistaken to think demon parents had close attachments to their offspring. Thanks for nothing!*

Jared reached for the keyboard, but she signed them off before he could react. "What now? You've just blown any chance we had at getting his help!"

"You know what, you be Bentos's main squeeze. It ain't gonna be me." She stalked out of the room, her heart in her throat. She had signed Hunter's death warrant. Now what was she going to do? Her thoughts scrambled together, and she couldn't untangle them to come up with a plan. Tears welled up.

"Wait up!" Jared raced after her and seized her arm. "Ferengus or one or more of his buddies will probably be waiting outside."

"So what do you suggest we do?" She bit back tears, hating herself for blowing up at maybe the only chance Hunter had. But no matter what, she wouldn't offer herself as a love slave to his father.

The oak door to the court of records opened. A Matusa sauntered in, his black satin hair hanging past his shoulders, his raven-colored eyes looking Jared over as if considering the weakness of the other demon, then his gaze shifted back to her.

Ferengus—he was the one who hurt Hunter. He was the one who said he'd claimed her. She expected to have to fight the one from the alley in Baltimore.

This Matusa she wasn't ready for.

10

Hunter heard male voices speaking way before the men reached his hospital room, and he quickly closed the portal.

"She has been here," one of the men said at the nurse's station, his voice anxious.

"She used a sleeping spell on the nurses." The other's voice was older, surer of himself.

Crissie looked at Hunter, but he held his finger to his lips to silence her question. He knew she couldn't hear the men's words, but closing the portal had worried her.

For a moment, silence followed, then the first man said, "We're looking for a blond-haired girl, green eyes, slender build, petite. She was visiting a sick friend."

"Yes, yes, a girl who looked like this photo came in with a boy. We told them it was too early to visit with the patient. They had to come back later." The woman yawned. "To my knowledge, they haven't returned."

"Who were they seeing?"

"The boy had been visiting with Hunter Ross all day. One of the nurses caught him staying in his room way past visiting hours late last night."

"And he's in which room?"

"Oh, 410. Right over there. Wait, are you family?"

Nobody responded to the question, which Hunter thought exceedingly odd.

"This patient of yours, Hunter Ross, is he young? Old?" an older man asked.

"Young, eighteen."

A significant pause ensued. Then the older man cleared his throat. "Is he terribly sick?"

"Very. He's not responding favorably to any antibiotics we've given him."

"Thank you for your time, miss," the older man said.

Then another thought occurred to Hunter. How had her uncle located her? Jared was right. The girl was different and now it looked like her uncle was strange, too.

Hunter wished Alana had communicated with him again, but with no further word, he feared the worst. Now, he wondered how he would manage to deal with an irate uncle, as he figured that was who the one man was. The poison felt like it was eating away at Hunter's body, and he had no strength to call on.

When a red-bearded man stalked into the hospital room with four others, Hunter tried to steel his back. Frustrated, he couldn't do anything but lie weakly against the stacked pillows. An older gray-haired man inspected the room, and then nodded. "She has been here."

Before the redhead spoke, Hunter's mother folded her arms and glowered at the men. "Unless you're family, you must leave at once. My son is extremely ill."

The redhead gave a slight bow of his head as if he were attempting to appease a protective mother. Then he turned to Hunter and said in a low voice, "Where's Alana?"

Anyone else might have shaken at the tone of his words they were spoken as darkly as any demon might, but Hunter wouldn't be cowed. Then he smugly realized he now knew the Kubiteron's name, even if she refused to give it to him. "Who are you?"

The redhead's temple wrinkled, and he fisted his hands. "Her uncle. I ask again, where is she?"

"She and a friend of mine are searching for my father. They hope he can cure my illness."

"That doctors cannot remedy?"

"Nor could your niece's healing skills."

Her uncle's eyes narrowed. "What do you know about us?"

Nothing, until now. The uncle and his cohorts were not demons, yet his question provoked more uncertainty. Hunter dared not reveal he was half demon if these people did not believe Alana was one. "I know only that Alana tried to help me with...prayer and it didn't work."

"You are not a..." The uncle did not finish his statement.

Demon? Or was there something else her uncle thought he was? *Some other dark being?* Hunter only knew of demons. Jared kept warning him Alana was half demon, but the other half wasn't exactly human. *If not human, then what?*

Hunter motioned weakly to the chairs sitting against the wall. The pain still streaked through every nerve, and his body barely responded to his commands. "You're welcome to wait for them."

Her uncle scowled. "How did you imprison her? You appear too weak to do anything."

"Imprison her?" Hunter feigned innocence, though he wasn't sure any demon, half or otherwise, could pretend such a thing and get away with it.

"She said you called her to you."

Hunter furrowed his brow, which wasn't difficult given the excruciating pain he was in. "Called her to me?"

"You know what I mean."

Crissie touched Hunter's hand, and he squeezed hers, glad—despite not wanting to meet her initially—that he finally had. She seemed genuinely concerned for his welfare. He wondered how different his life would have been if his birth mother had raised him. Though thinking of such a thing was probably self-defeating.

"You are not to take that tone of voice with my son!" his mother said, her voice almost reaching passable demon tenor.

Suddenly, Hunter's human father stalked into the room. "What's the meaning of this?"

The men moved aside. For an instant, his father stared at Crissie. Did he recognize her? Either he did, or he guessed who she might be as much as he looked both upset and worried. She stood her ground. Hunter couldn't have felt any sicker than he already did.

"Who are all these people?"

"They're looking for a friend of mine." Hunter knew whatever was said now would be the hardest for his father to hear, but Hunter could do nothing to prevent it.

Alana's uncle said, "Hunter says my niece is looking for his father."

His adoptive father looked at Hunter, hurt and indignation in his eyes. "Is this true?"

"Yes, Dad. Alana and Jared have gone in search of my birth father, hoping he might be able to provide the cure for the poison in my blood."

"That's utter nonsense."

"It is not," his mother said. "If anyone can save him, it's his flesh and blood father."

"You believe this, Son?"

"Yes, Dad. Nothing my birth father can do will change the way I feel about you, Mom, and Dara. But maybe he can give me a chance at life."

"Alana is returning here?" her uncle asked.

"Yes."

Her uncle took a seat. "Then we'll wait. I want the whole truth of the matter."

"If my son says your niece is looking for his birth father, then you can take his word for it." His father turned to Hunter. "I hope you know what you're doing. I have to get to the morgue. I'm already late. Your mother will be by later this afternoon." He gave the men a disgruntled look, slid a glance Crissie's way, patted Hunter on the shoulder, and then left.

For an hour, Hunter's birth mother ran a cool cloth over his burning temple. She talked about her life, repeating several times how a day hadn't gone by that she hadn't wondered what had become of her son and how she wished she could have raised him as her own. He felt a pang of regret that she'd wanted what they'd lost and never even married.

Through soggy eyes, Hunter watched Alana's uncle and his men cast each other annoyed looks. Her uncle crossed the floor to the hospital window and stared out, but the eldest man barely took his eyes off Hunter. Under his scrutiny, Hunter almost had the urge to squirm. *Almost*. But demons didn't squirm. Certainly *not* Matusa demons.

Worse, his hope was fading that Alana and Jared were still all right. He reproached himself for not letting her know that just hearing her words helped to set his mind at ease.

Her uncle rose from his chair again, looking like a redheaded demon, his eyes hard. "Where is she?"

The room seemed to swirl, and Hunter knew he was losing it. A sprinkling of stars flashed before his eyes; a strange humming sounded in his ears.

His mother leaned over and whispered to him, "It's him, isn't it?"

Him? Hunter thought he was dying. He stared up at her. "You felt it, too?"

Tears in her eyes, she nodded. "I think because I had you, I'm still connected to him. Do...do you want me to try and bring him here?"

Alana's uncle and the other men stood watching them, their postures tense and on alert. They ought to be. Who knew what would happen when Crissie opened the portal and called Hunter's father forth? If his mother was right, he would kill her and anyone else who witnessed the murder.

He squeezed her hand, part of him knowing he needed his father's help, part of him hating his father for leaving his mother and causing her so much pain. "Let me do it. If he didn't want you to—" His voice cracked.

His mother raised her hands. "I love you, Hunter. I always have."

"You'll need to leave," he said to Alana's uncle, but the men didn't budge.

To open the portal, his mother mouthed the words silently. The gray-bearded man tried to decipher her unspoken words. He said to Alana's uncle, "She's not a..."

The wind blew through the room, catching the door and slamming it shut with a bang. The portal's shimmering blue-green light appeared.

His mother called his birth father from the demon world. Like a mirage materialized into something solid, the man appeared.

Dark brown hair and eyes like Hunter, he saw the family resemblance at once. Bentos scanned the room like any demon would, determining the strength of his opponents. He quickly discounted Hunter, the sickly half-demon and his mother. But his focus on the men in the room lingered longer than Hunter thought necessary.

Finally, he pivoted his attention to Hunter. "You are my son."

"Where's my niece?" her uncle demanded.

Hunter closed his eyes, unable to prevent bloodshed should Alana's uncle enrage his father.

The demon looked at her uncle, his eyes as hard as crystal. "You are Alana's uncle?"

His father had seen Alana? Sure, she must have told him Hunter needed his help. Why didn't Alana and Jared return with him? He was certain there'd been trouble, and his imagination was already running amuck. "Is she all right?" he croaked out.

"Yes, I'm Alana's uncle and Hunter said she'd gone to look for you. So where is she?"

"She found me and sent me to see my son. Once I heal him, he can help me return her to you."

"What's happened?" Hunter knew he shouldn't have asked; knew he shouldn't have left themselves open for more questioning. But he had to know that she and Jared were all right.

"Nothing that we cannot fix." Bentos moved toward the bed, silently, like a panther, dark and foreboding.

"What do you mean? What's happened?" her uncle persisted.

Bentos stood over Hunter and raised his hand to silence Alana's uncle. "Calm yourself. The young lady is fine. We will bring her back shortly."

Hunter wheezed, short of breath. His father ran his hand over Hunter's chest, never touching, chanting silently, his lips moving, his eyes focused on the center of Hunter's being.

Taking his first steady breath, Hunter began to breathe freely again. His father clasped his hand over Hunter's forehead and continued to mouth words, drawing out the fever. Touching his arm, Bentos turned in such a way as to hide his demon actions from the others, then extended his claws and dug into Hunter's arm.

Hunter felt no pain, only heard his father's soothing words

spoken repeatedly. Then the streaks of red running up his arm faded. Fresh blood dribbled on the sheets, and the new torn skin looked as raw as when the other demon had sliced it to ribbons. The excruciating pain was gone just a light burning. Bentos continued to chant, running his hand over Hunter's arm until the wounds began to close.

"You are healed, Son."

"What magic is this?" the gray-haired man asked, moving in closer to see the results of Bentos's work. "Are you the one who imprisoned Alana?" He motioned to the portal. "What kind of an evil warlock are you?"

"Warlock?" Bentos gave a caustic laugh. "Come, Son, we'll bring Alana back." He glanced at Crissie, tears brimming in her eyes. "We made a beautiful son, did we not?"

She didn't say a word, just stared into his eyes.

Bentos gave her a sinister smile. "Next time, summon one who is not so dark."

Hunter could have hit his dad for being so insensitive to his mother, but he couldn't help being grateful to him for saving his life. Still, he scowled at his father, gave his mother a warm embrace, then took his clothes into the bathroom to change.

"You will take us with you to get Alana," her uncle demanded.

"The path is too dangerous," Bentos argued, his voice eerily threatening. "You would not live long."

"A boy barely off his death bed and one man is safe?"

"No, but safer than the likes of you."

Hunter jerked on his clothes, not liking the sound of the men's elevated voices. When he entered the room, he whispered in his mother's ear, "Close the portal immediately after us. Don't let them follow us or they'll surely die."

He hoped his mother could hold out against the men and not succumb to their pressuring her to reopen the portal again. Most of all, he hoped Alana and Jared were safe.

As soon as his mother reopened the portal, Alana's uncle and the other men moved toward it. The older man raised his long, bony fingers and began to chant.

What was he doing?

Bentos's eyes flared red, he growled a demonic curse, then jerked Hunter through the gateway to the demon's world.

11

"Like father, like son," Bentos said to Hunter as they stepped into the demon world, then released his arm.

The portal instantly vanished.

Hunter studied the buildings, black glass or stone facades stretching to a gray sky. Shadows lurked in darkened alleys, but otherwise, he was amazed to see the city looked like any other.

"What do you mean by that?" he asked menacingly. He wasn't a full Matusa, didn't have their dark heart, or at least his human half-tempered his own.

"You've fallen for a witch."

Hunter gave his father a glower. Anyone else would tremble at the look he cast him. His father's lips curved upward slightly.

"You should have gotten in touch with me sooner." His father led him down the narrow street.

"I didn't even know who my mother was."

"She didn't raise you?"

"No."

Bentos made a disgusted sound. "I thought she wanted a child after having summoned me." He tilted his square jaw up. "I want the Kubiteron." His father's darkened eyes revealed he meant every word.

"She can't be yours. She belongs in Earth world."

"She belongs with a Matusa. Do you know how rare it is for Matusa females to be born? We have to find mates in the other demon forms. But everyone fears us. So what do we do? We take what we want, or our lineage will die out."

Like Hunter cared. It could be the best thing for demon kind. "Why didn't you ever return to Mom?"

"She summoned me. She's lucky I liked the way she looked, took pity on her, and left her with child. However, I did not think she would give up my son. Had I known..." He gave a shake of his head. "Most summoned Matusa kill the summoner. None of us appreciate that a human thinks he or she can summon us and enslave us."

"She loved you!"

"Evidently, she still does. But it is her fault, not mine. You cannot force another to love you."

Hunter shoved his fists in his pockets. "You're incapable of love."

Bentos gave him a smug smile. "What do humans know about love? They say they will love their selected mate forever, 'til death parts them. A few years later, the one dumps the other. This you call love?"

"My parents have always loved each other."

Bentos grunted.

"I thought demon parents felt something for their offspring."

Demons of various kinds peered out shop and office windows at them, but when Hunter caught their eye, they faded into the background. Symbols that looked like Japanese were etched into the stone on all the buildings, but he didn't have a clue what they said.

"We do care about our offspring. Why do you think I came to help you?"

"You wanted Alana and thought by saving my life she would agree to have you."

Tossing his head back, Bentos laughed. "I could have her whether I saved you or not. As far as demon parents and their offspring go, a half-demon child must seek his parents. Not the other way around. In your case, you didn't want to see me until you had no other choice."

Hunter had to agree. He considered the normalcy of the city streets, darkly amused that he'd envisioned fires and molten lava, men and women chained to rocks. Unspeakable horrors. Except for the eerie shadows hovering in the alleyways and the strangely smoky gray sky, the place looked similar to Dallas.

"Surprised?" his father asked. "Not unexpected. Artists' renditions of the demon world equate it to hell. The place we live in is no more a hell than the human world. If you do not believe me, just watch CNN. Killings, muggings, famines, disease, greed. Half your politicians are more untrustworthy than the demons of this world."

"Demons are notorious liars."

"And politicians are not?"

A large gathering of Matusa hovered outside of a stone building, and Hunter straightened his shoulders, preparing himself mentally for a fight. "What's happening?

"Alana is still inside the court of records building, it appears. As you can see, several Matusa are waiting patiently to claim her."

Having never had to deal with a pack of Matusa, Hunter felt his resolve faltering. "What are we going to do?"

His father's brows rose. "*We*? I like that. Matusa normally do not stick together. They usually do not fight one another, except over a female, but they don't offer to help each other in times of trouble, either."

"Except you offered to help me."

"Yes, well, when I learned you were the one who thrust

Ferengus back into our home world over a Kubiteron, I knew you were worthy of being my son. Not all half-demon children are."

Wondering if his father had spawned more half-human/demons, Hunter stared at him. "You have other children?" He couldn't suppress the surprise in his voice.

"You have a half-brother." Bentos paused when the Matusa guarding the entrance of the stone building turned to look at them.

"In Dallas?"

"Yes."

"Is he worthy of your acknowledgment?" Hunter haughtily asked.

His father seemed amused. "He hasn't come looking for me yet, so I think not. But he's only sixteen. Maybe when he's eighteen like you, he will." Bentos lifted a shoulder.

Scanning the crowd, Hunter turned his attention to the potential threat in front of them. "I don't see Ferengus."

"He'll be inside with Alana."

His blood percolating, Hunter stormed toward the building, the other demons parting to let him pass. He figured one of them would try to stop him or kill him for the way he acted. Then again, maybe his father's presence made them show some respect.

When he shoved the door aside, he found a long black marble hall empty. Though as soon as they entered it, a tall thin man joined them from a side room.

"Treikal," Bentos said, bowing his head slightly in greeting.

Amazed to see his father acknowledging a lesser demon with such courtesy, Hunter couldn't help staring at the slight man. Like Jared, the demon was an Elantus. Powerful, but below that of the Kubiteron in strength.

"Your son?" Treikal's eyes glistened with admiration.

Bentos slapped Hunter on the back, which made his eyes heat. "One to be proud of."

"The Kubiteron is in the hall of records."

Bentos lifted a brow.

Treikal sauntered down the hallway and Bentos and Hunter followed, though Hunter wanted to race to the room, instead of crawl at a beetle's pace.

"What's she doing?" Hunter asked.

"Waiting for you and your father to rescue her."

"What about Jared?"

"Safely at her side. She tried to leave the court of records, but Ferengus stopped her. She's very clever. She returned to the records room and began searching for her father's name to buy her and Jared time."

"And Ferengus?"

"He is hovering over her. Her eyes have been glowing red ever since he came to claim her. He loves it."

"She won't be his," Hunter growled.

Treikal gave Bentos a sly smile. "Your son takes after you."

"He is worthy of being my son."

Changing the subject, Hunter asked his father, "What's my brother's name?" He didn't appreciate that anyone would say he took after his father because he'd abandoned his mother so cavalierly. And he didn't care whether his father thought he was worthy or not.

"He hasn't turned of age yet. He doesn't know he's half demon. Until he does, you do not need to see him."

"You've been checking up on him?" Hunter asked, his voice raised, irritated that his father had never checked on *him*.

"I have revisited his mother from time to time."

"And not mine?" His words echoing off the walls, Hunter couldn't contain the heat in his voice.

"Your mother was too needy. Rolling's mother is a witch, demanding and endearing." Then Bentos frowned. "Do not think I don't want the Kubiteron because of her."

Treikal smiled intriguingly and motioned to a room.

"If she's such a witch...," Hunter said, remembering the comment his father had made earlier about Alana.

Bentos motioned to silence him. "The Kubiteron is..." He shook his head. "Forget it. I want her. Leave it at that."

"You can't have her."

He laughed when Hunter glowered at him. "Today, we will fight as one."

"Not in the hall of records," Treikal warned.

A crowd of several different demon types gathered in a circle. Alana *couldn't* be in the middle of it all.

When Hunter and his father reached the circle, the demons politely moved away. Their actions made Hunter feel like a prince among his courtiers. He'd never seen more than a couple of demons together at one time and whenever he'd run into them, they'd always moved out of his path. Seeing a whole crowd of them part for him, he realized how much the lesser demons feared the Matusa. The idea was sobering.

Until he observed Alana seated at the monitor, her fingers tapping away at a keyboard, her spine tense. Jared saw Hunter first and gave him a worried look. Ferengus noticed him next, and his eyes flamed.

Alana glanced at Hunter last. Her green eyes widened, and his heart skipped a couple of beats.

At first, her lips parted, and then his name slipped off them. Her gaze suddenly shifted to Bentos. Again, her eyes rounded. Then she looked back at Hunter, leaped from her seat, and raced to close the gap between them, surprising him to the nth degree.

"Thank God you're all right!" Her firm embrace started a white-hot fire burning deep inside him. Then she quickly released him. "What took you so long?"

Before he could respond, she communicated privately to him. *Now what do we do?*

He had no idea. Every demon's eye remained fixed on them.

Even Bentos didn't seem to care for Alana's display of affection for Hunter. He sure hadn't expected it.

"Your uncle awaits you in my hospital room," he said.

She groaned. "He will ground me forever." She squeezed his hand. "I was afraid he would kill you. He said he would."

Hunter couldn't contain his amusement. "He could have tried."

She gave him an annoyed look, then turned to Treikal. "Thank you for allowing me to use your computers."

"You're welcome to use them anytime." He bowed his head to her.

"Ohmigod, why didn't I think of it?" Alana's face brightened, and she tugged at Hunter's hand. *"Open the portal! I don't know the spell, but you do. Call Jared with us, and we can go through the gateway. Only us."*

Hunter glanced at his father. Too bad he couldn't get to know him a little better, but his father wanted Alana, and Hunter wasn't about to let him have her. She was half-human and belonged in the human's world, now that he knew she hadn't been kept in Earth world by maniacal summoners.

Hesitating a moment longer, he assumed his father would frown on Hunter's cowardly way out, not fighting for the right to have Alana. But he couldn't risk losing her to Ferengus, or any of the other demons waiting outside the records building, not even his father. Then he reconsidered. Maybe it wasn't such a cowardly way, but a human way.

He opened the portal, summoned Jared to come with them, and then yanked Alana through before Ferengus could stop them. None of them could follow unless Hunter or Alana summoned them.

When they entered the hospital room, there was no sign of Alana's uncle or the other men. Crissie was sobbing, wringing her hands.

Surmising the worst, Hunter asked, "Where's Alana's uncle? What's happened?"

12

As soon as Alana saw how distraught Hunter's mother was, she assumed her uncle had come after her. "He hasn't gone through the portal?" she quickly asked, her voice shaky. "Not to the demon world?"

"Yes. The gray-bearded man with him forced me to open the portal. He didn't get physical, but somehow..." Crissie began sobbing again. "He...he just made me."

"All of them went through?" Hunter asked.

"Alana's uncle and four others, including the older man."

"Yolan," Alana said under her breath. She grabbed Hunter's arm. "We have to go back."

"No. You're safe here. You stay."

"No, Hunter, they'll rip my uncle and his friends to shreds. I have to go back."

"He made his own choice."

"To save me, right? He wanted to help me! I...we can't leave him...them alone there."

Hunter yanked her hand away from his arm. "I'll go back, but *you* will stay here. I don't want to fight the whole male population of Matusa over you."

"I can help."

He gave a haughty laugh. "You didn't even know which demon type you were or what demon powers you possess."

"I'm not a very powerful witch either, but maybe I can draw on something that will help." Telling non-magic users she was a witch was forbidden, though she figured since Hunter was a demon, he would understand it was something best left unsaid. But she hadn't wanted his mother to hear.

Hunter stared at her, and she could tell he didn't believe her.

Folding his arms, Jared cursed under his breath. "I told you she wasn't human."

She glared at him. "I am too human. I'm just a witch on top of it."

Hunter growled. "There is no such thing as witches."

"Yeah, well, there is no such thing as demons, either. But we're all in the myths and legends of every culture who bothered to write them down." She headed for the portal.

Hunter seized her arm. "You stay here."

"If you go back and force me to stay, I'll have your mother open the portal and reenter the demon's world alone. Wouldn't it be better for us to stick together?"

Hunter's eyes flared red. He turned to Jared. "This isn't your fight. You stay here."

"Not this time. I want to see what else a witch can do." Jared gave her an evil grin. "I knew you weren't human."

"I'm a Matusa demon!" Hunter moved toward the portal like a warrior bent on a fight. "Lesser demons are supposed to listen to me, cower before me, obey my every wish."

Alana grabbed his hand and Jared's arm. "Right. Lead on, Dark One. Command us all you like."

He glanced at her, his look truly demonic. "And you *will* obey."

The trouble with demons was they had this rigid pecking order.

But Alana didn't believe she was beneath any demon, Matusa, or otherwise.

Not that she didn't fear the Matusa. Most were evil to the core, and anyone who didn't give them a wide berth would soon pay. She still didn't think she was beneath them, just didn't have the strength of one, that was all.

For now, though, she hoped her witch's skills and a demon power of some sort would manifest itself, and she could help her uncle and his friends return to their world unscathed. Although she didn't even want to think about what her uncle thought of her now. However, this wasn't exactly the way she wanted him to learn she was half demon.

AT FIRST, when they entered the demon city, Alana didn't see a soul, except for the shadows moving deeper into the alleys, but when she, Hunter, and Jared approached the record's building, blue sparks flew into the street and up toward the gray heavens.

The zigzagging lights looked like a bolt of lightning hit a power transformer. Uncle Stephen, Yolan, and three other bearded men she didn't recognize cast some kind of magic at several Matusa demons. Lesser demons peered through windows, not venturing forth into the melee. The Matusa fighting the warlocks, waved their hands, motioning in their direction, but didn't seem to be having any effect. The strained expression on the warlocks' faces didn't look good.

"Uncle Stephen!" Alana screamed, running toward them. She had to get them through the portal before their strength dwindled and any of them were killed.

Everyone stopped and turned to watch her. Relief washed over her uncle's face, then he furrowed his brows. "Get back!"

"You and the others must come with us through the portal. They can't follow us there unless summoned. Hurry!" Alana responded.

The truce swiftly abated and the demons again attacked the warlocks. She hurriedly cast a protection spell around herself, Hunter, and Jared but wasn't sure if it would work.

Uncle Stephen told the warlocks, *"Fall back to the portal with Alana. Keep up the attack but fall back."*

Ferengus rushed for Alana, but Hunter threw himself in front of her. As soon as Ferengus's wicked claws extended, she hurtled her aggressive defense spell. He glanced at her and smiled. Her spell had had no effect, and she realized she'd only been able to throw Hunter from his bed when he tried to control her because he'd been so weak.

Ferengus slashed his claws at Hunter, who jumped out of his path.

Her uncle and the others were moving toward them, inching backward.

"Can you open a portal here, closer to us?" she asked Hunter.

Hunter shook his head. "I can't open two portals at once." He kicked Ferengus on the side of his knee. Even over the noise of the bolts of electricity the warlocks cast, she heard Ferengus's leg snap. His eyes blazing with fire, he cried out in pain. Bentos leaned against the stone building, arms folded across his broad chest, his gaze focused on his son. He nodded approvingly.

He wouldn't lift a finger to help Hunter? Some father!

Jared stayed out of the fracas, but she couldn't blame him. If his kind was less powerful than her kind, and she couldn't handle a Matusa, Jared didn't stand a chance.

She cast a bramble protection spell. The wicked thorns stretched across the street and up the sides of the buildings, but the demons didn't seem to see them. The spell wouldn't trouble the warlocks, but her spells seemed useless against the demons, too.

"Teach me an attack spell, Uncle Stephen! Let me help!"

"They're not bothering you. Go back through the portal!"

"No! They want me! You have to let me help you!"

He didn't respond, and she fumed, trying to think of anything else in her simple witch's repertoire. She'd never really cared about learning spells and potions, mainly because her mother had never been interested in teaching them to her. It always seemed like just more schooling. And the way that Uncle Stephen made her learn constant levitation, and other boring skills, none of it appealed.

Levitation? Would that work?

She cast the spell on Ferengus before he clawed Hunter again.

At first, Ferengus continued to hop around on one leg, trying to strike at Hunter, then dodged his swift kicks and deadly hand blows. Alena tried again, and Ferengus lifted slightly off the ground. For a moment, Hunter stared at him, then he jumped in for another kick. This time when he planted his sneaker into Ferengus's chest, the demon sailed back against a glass building, crashing right through it.

Bentos let out a bark of dark laughter, then clapped his hands in slow action.

"Cathors, Relentus, Prickenen, Chorlantus," Uncle Stephen told Alana.

She watched the way he twisted his hands, directing sparks of electricity toward two demons at once.

Hunter squeezed her hand. "We'll never make it. You go, and I'll help your people leave."

"Close the portal! Reopen it here, hurry!" Alana ordered him.

Hunter gave her a sinister look, hesitated, then dashed off for the portal.

Without Hunter to protect her, when Ferengus climbed out of the broken window, she readied her first weapon attack and hoped it would work.

She spoke the words, but nothing happened. Watching the way

her uncle and the other warlocks moved their fingers, she tried again. Nothing. "*I can't make it work!*" she shouted to him.

He gave her another spell, and she tried it, to no avail.

"*What do the Kubiteron demons have in their arsenal of tricks?*" she asked Jared.

He stared at her, probably trying to figure out how she'd gotten into his head.

"*Jared! Snap out of it.*"

Ferengus's face and hands were bleeding from the glass he'd shattered, and he barely could walk on his injured leg, but he still crept toward her like a grim-faced zombie from a late-night horror movie.

"*Jared! What can I do?*"

"I'm thinking! I'm thinking!"

"Think, faster!"

Ferengus's mouth inched up, and his eyes challenged hers. "You will come to me and be mine, as I have claimed you."

"An image! You claimed an image, not me. Hunter Ross claimed me!" She only meant to show the demon she couldn't belong to him, not submit to Hunter or any other.

Jared shook his head at her words. "Hunter will love to hear this."

She couldn't tell from his sarcastic tone of voice if it was a good thing, or bad. Ferengus's demonic pull attempted to control her mind, and she struggled to fight it. Though she couldn't repel him like she could a human or maybe a lesser demon, he couldn't rule her—maybe because of her witch's abilities.

"Water? Do you have any power over water?" Jared quickly asked.

Remembering how her uncle had said she wouldn't be any good as a water mage, she shook her head.

Jared punched up information on his computer. "Healing, the data bank says."

"Won't help here. Even with Hunter, it didn't work. Besides, I need offensive or defensive spells."

One of the warlocks sank to his knees, and Alana gasped, then tried to run to him. Yolan caught her arm and shoved her back. "Stay out of this, Alana!"

"Wind," Jared shouted, sounding proud of himself.

She stared at him. "What?"

"You can command the wind."

"How?"

"How do I know? I'm an Elantus, not a Kubiteron."

She raised her hands and tried to stir up the wind. A sickly breeze blew her hair into her eyes. "*I can't do it!*"

"Certainly, you can't, if you're going to think negatively." Jared's eyes flashed red.

She growled back at him, then turned and nearly had a heart attack when Ferengus snatched at her arm. She jumped back, stumbled over Jared, and fell on her butt. Commanding the wind, she felt like an utter fool. Of course, nothing happened.

"Are you even trying?"

"Of course, I'm trying."

"Apparently not very hard!"

Ferengus hovered over her and reached his hand out to her, his eyes willing her to agree. "Come now, Kubiteron! I command you."

She jumped to her feet, stepped back, and levitated him again.

He screamed an ear-piercing racket, and she realized then that her simple act of levitation proved more powerful than an attack spell. The demon couldn't fly, couldn't move toward her.

Hunter grabbed her arm, and she let out a squeak, nearly dropping Ferengus. Then she concentrated on her spell again.

"Come on! The portal's right behind you," Hunter shouted at her.

"Uncle Stephen, Yolan! The portal's here!" she hollered, finally feeling the wind from the gateway at her back.

"I summon you, Jared," Hunter said, but before he could pull Alana through the portal, she raised Ferengus higher, and then dropped him. He cried out in pain with murder in his eyes. So much for him wanting her for his life mate.

Quickly, she levitated the fallen warlock, bringing his lifeless body with her as Hunter drew her into the swirling blue-green light, and the other wizards ran to join them.

"You are mine!" Ferengus screamed.

Alana knew there was only one way out of this.

13

Alana's expression was stricken while she, her uncle, and the gray-bearded man crouched over their fallen comrade in the hospital room. Hunter noticed then that Alana was moving her hand over the unconscious man, like she'd done with Hunter when trying to heal him.

He closed the portal, but before he could do anything else, his mother ran to him and hugged the breath from his chest. His human side couldn't help but be cheered by her reaction, but his demon side was annoyed. He didn't need to be fussed over, particularly in front of a room full of people.

"The nursing staff was so upset when they found you missing. I said you were in the bathroom, but when they came back later, they checked it to make sure you weren't any sicker. I didn't know what to say about you not being there. Just acted dumb," his mother said.

She didn't appear to be dumb in the least bit, just very caring and oversentimental about his demon father who didn't deserve her love.

"What about him?" his mother asked, pointing at the prone man.

Alana hung close to the man. She moved her lips silently and wiggled her fingers slightly, but looked like she was trying not to let the other warlocks see her action.

Yolan raised his hands over the man's chest and spoke strange words under his breath.

"One of the demons broke through Zoros's defenses and stopped his heart," Uncle Stephen said.

Yolan touched the man's chest and spoke a different set of words, then moved his hands in a dissimilar path. Alana continued to do her healing chant, but Yolan and the others ignored her.

Mesmerized by her actions, Hunter hoped she would save the man on her own and prove to the others how worthy she was.

"We have a lot of things to discuss," her uncle suddenly said, giving Alana a harsh look.

She stopped her healing chant and looked up at him.

"Yeah." Hunter closed the gap and directed his words at Alana. "We do." Why hadn't she told him before that she was a witch?

She raised her brows at him. Turning to her uncle, Alana said, "I told you I was half demon. You wouldn't listen."

Her uncle motioned to Hunter. "What is he?"

"Half Matusa demon," Hunter said, and proud of it.

"I'm Kubiteron," Alana said, and pointing to Jared added, "he's Elantus."

"Different demon types? Never heard of them."

"You didn't believe in demons, period," she scoffed, her eyes hard, but still green.

Zoros took a deep breath and his eyes fluttered open.

"He's back, thank God." Yolan squeezed the man's gray hand.

"What now?" Crissie asked.

Hunter patted her shoulder. "Jared can take you home. I'm going with Alana."

"Like hell you are." Stephen rose to his full height like an enraged grizzly.

Yolan motioned to the other warlocks. "Take Zoros home and call one of our healers."

Hunter glowered at Stephen. "I'm going with Alana because she asked me to. A deed for a deed. She would find my father who would cure me, then I would help her fight the Matusa who's after her."

"She's safe now in our world." Her Uncle Stephen wrapped his arm around her shoulder. "She doesn't need help from your kind."

"My kind is what will come after her. The Matusa saw her watching him when he murdered a woman. Either he will want her dead if he already has a mate, or he will want her for his own, rest assured. If you care for Alana, I would think you would want anyone's offer of help to protect her."

Though her uncle's lips remained fixed in a grim line, Yolan nodded and her uncle finally acquiesced.

"What about me?" Jared sounded like he was afraid he would miss all the fun.

"One demon is quite enough," her uncle said.

Alana scoffed. "Two, Uncle, but who's counting?"

Hunter slapped Jared on the back. "Watch for a Matusa's signature. If it comes anywhere near us, let me know."

Jared smiled, but the look in his eyes reflected wickedness. "Will do."

A genius when it came to electronic gizmos, Jared could track demon signatures anywhere in the city. All he had to do was trace Hunter's signature until he found where he settled for the night, then notify him if another came into the area.

Before Hunter left the hospital, he had to check in with his human father, to let him know he'd miraculously recovered and would be spending some time with Alana's family. Thankfully, his adoptive father was so grateful the "cure" had worked, that he gave him his blessing and said he would smooth it over with Mom. Hunter had to discover all he could about witches and warlocks or

whatever they were though. Here he thought he'd known everything there was to know.

Until he met Alana.

HUNTER COULDN'T HELP but stare in awe at the overwhelmingly
large two-story, brick mansion that belonged to Alana's uncle. It
was a sight to behold, with its grandeur and opulence, making him
wonder what kind of work Alana's uncle did for a living. Inside,
every piece of furniture, from the velvet pinstriped couches to the
intricately carved solid oak tables, looked new and expensive.

The Turkish carpets covering the floors and the oil paintings of
fields of bluebonnets that adorned the walls only added to the
luxurious atmosphere. Whatever business Alana's uncle was
involved in, it must pay exceedingly well.

Alana sat on one of the plush couches, fidgeting with what
appeared to be a crystal ball on the coffee table. Hunter shook his
head, still not fully believing in this world of witches and demons.

However, he couldn't deny that if Alana's uncle and his friends
didn't possess some kind of supernatural powers, they would all be
dead in the demon world. After everything he had experienced in
the past few days, Hunter was starting to accept the existence of
witches and warlocks.

Stephen stalked back into the room, his red-bearded face grim.
He gave Alana a sharp nod. "Protection spells are in place."

"Mine didn't work against the Matusa." She sounded discour-
aged and her shoulders sagged a little.

"Wrong spells. The kind Yolan and the rest of us cast worked
until Zoros grew too weak. I haven't shown you the advanced
personal protection spells yet. That was what we were going to
work on when you woke this morning, but instead, you ran off to
the hospital in the middle of the night."

She set the crystal ball on a four-legged brass stand on the coffee table and folded her arms. Hunter distanced himself from the two, watching their actions and reactions.

Stephen cast him an annoyed look, then sat on a chair across from Alana. "Well, Alana? Tell me about your father."

"Mom told you how I came to be. You didn't believe her." Alana's voice remained on edge, though she looked exhausted for being up so late.

"Who was the father...your real father?"

"She didn't know his name."

Her uncle snorted, his brows furrowed.

"Well, don't think *I'm* any happier about it!" Alana snapped. She took a deep breath. "She didn't even tell me until I turned seventeen and only then because weird things began to happen." Alana's cheeks colored. "One day when I was driving us home from the store, a guy nearly ran me off the road. Mom nearly had a conniption when my eyes started glowing red."

Her uncle shook his head, not believing her, which frustrated her.

"That afternoon, she bought me green contact lenses. Then the strangest thing kept happening. No matter where I was—though thankfully it never happened when I was driving the car—the opening of a portal into the demon world drew me to its location."

"Like the one in the hospital room where Hunter was," her uncle said.

"Yes. But it wasn't exactly me. It's like an astral form of me or something. What's weird is now anyone in the area can see me as clearly as I sit before you. Earlier, I seemed to be invisible." She let out her breath and for the first time, Hunter noticed she looked drained.

"It's happened five times to me, not counting the times Hunter called me." She gave him an evil look, and he cast her a small smile.

Didn't she know how much her scowls encouraged his interest in her?

She shifted her attention away from Hunter and looked at the coffee table. "In four of the cases, summoners had brought demons other than Matusa forth. I'm not sure why they do it. Except thinking it's a game, or maybe just playing with what they think is the occult. Witches and warlocks, well most, know better. Mom was just bored and thought it was a game."

Uncle Stephen shook his head like *he* had never done anything wrong in his life.

"Of course, witches or warlocks might get ahold of one of these summoning books and plan to do some harm, commanding a demon to do its bidding. In the last case, I saw three Goth-looking women summoning a Matusa, and he murdered one of them. I'm sure he killed the others, leaving no witnesses. But he saw me watching him."

"Is this a demon trait? This ability to be someplace in your mind?" her uncle asked, his voice anxious.

Looking for answers, she turned to Hunter.

Hunter cleared his throat, not knowing what to think. "I don't believe so. That's why Jared kept saying he thought Alana wasn't human because they can't do that, nor can demons."

"Witches can't either," her uncle said with firm conviction. "Was it Hunter who brought you to his hospital room, Alana?"

"Yes, by opening the portal. He didn't summon me. If a portal is opened somewhere nearby, it draws me forth."

Her uncle pondered the notion and then directed the next question to Hunter. "Can you kill the Matusa if he comes for her?"

Hunter shrugged. "I can try."

Her uncle's steely gaze tightened.

"Jared said you've gotten rid of two already." Alana sounded hopeful.

"Self-defense. I was trying to return them to their world, but they didn't like the idea. Of course, I could always marry Alana, then the other Matusa would *have* to leave her alone."

"Marry?" she shrieked. "No way would I marry a Matusa who thinks he can summon me at his whim."

Hunter didn't attempt to hide his amusement at her outburst. Alana had genuinely been ecstatic when he appeared in the court of records, raised from his deathbed. Unless the demon side of her had faked her enthusiasm, hoping he would rescue her from the demon world. No, she had been thrilled to see him alive and healthy again. Not that he wanted to marry her, either. But he loved getting a rise out of her.

Hunter straightened his back. "I didn't say I *wanted* to marry you." Her cheeks flushed anew, and he loved seeing her reaction. "What demon in his right mind would want to marry a witch? Beyond that, what self-respecting Matusa would take on a lesser demon who won't obey him?"

He half expected her uncle to defend her, but his mouth curved up slightly. He let his niece respond instead.

"Lesser?" she said, her voice becoming demonically shrill. "I'm *not* a lesser demon! Maybe I'm not as strong or heartless as you, but I'm *not* beneath you!" Her eyes turned their beautiful fiery red like the blood moon on an autumn day.

Her uncle was staring at them as if he had never seen anything so unreal.

"Okay, now that we've had demonology lesson 101, start talking about this little business about your being a witch." Hunter's gaze bored into Alana's.

"Only family knows of such a thing," her uncle said. "Being that you're not family, if you learn too much, we would have to kill you." Her uncle's mouth quirked up.

A little demon-type humor? Hunter was already beginning to like Alana's uncle. He had demon potential.

"You could try," Hunter replied. "Think of me as family. You know I'm half demon. Now I know you're witches and the like. But I need to know what skills you possess that could help us against the Baltimore Matusa. I hate to mention it, but Ferengus will also probably try to slip into our world again. When a human attempts to call forth a demon in the city, I would lay odds he'll be waiting."

"That's the other thing I don't understand," her uncle said. "How are people getting the spell to open a passage to the demon world? Alana's mother is a witch and so were her college girl-friends, so I figure they might have stumbled across a book of summoning in a shop. But your mother wasn't a witch. Where are these people getting the summoning ritual?"

Hunter thought back to the summoning book in the box of trash. He had to destroy it before anyone else got hold of it, though he would ask his mother first if she'd gotten the portal spell from it. If so, where had she gotten it from? Why hadn't he thought to question her before?

Well, he was barely alive when she first came to him, which probably had something to do with it. Then he had to rescue Alana, and after that, her uncle. No wonder it had slipped his mind.

"Jared's been trying to track down the source, while he watches for signatures of demons entering the area. As soon as he locates one, I send them back. With the lesser ones, it's no problem. A human attempts to enslave one to do his bidding, so the demon is grateful to be released. I thought that was Alana's case and wanted to free her from her summoner."

She lifted a brow.

"What was I to think? In most cases, the demon is glad that I free them and send them home. The summoner is so terrified of me, that they don't attempt to summon again. On the other hand, I destroy the summoning book they've used so that helps to stop them, too, if they haven't memorized the spell. But we need to find where the summoning books are coming from."

"You said in most cases the demons are happy to return to their home world," Alana said.

"Except for the Matusa. They want to control the human populace, and no one will rule them. Which makes me think a Matusa is at the root of all these summonings. The more Matusa demons he can have brought into this world, the more havoc he can cause." Hunter took a deep breath. "There was another who didn't want to return to the demon world. She cried when I sent her back."

"Why?"

"I guess she wanted to stay with her summoner. But she didn't belong here. We're here because we're half demon. She needed to be with her kind."

Alana didn't seem convinced. "What if they truly loved each other? The summoner and the demon? What if she had a miserable existence in the demon world and her summoner offered her something better? Are *we* playing God?" She didn't say it as if she was including herself.

He would not be baited, though he clamped his teeth down to avoid grinding them.

"What about Jared?" she asked, her chin lifting.

"That's different. He's lived all his life in the human world. He's still searching for his real parents, but until he finds them, he'll remain here. He's not enslaved unless you call his adoptive parents making him take out the trash or mow the yard slave work. But I have another question for you. Why couldn't Jared locate your signature in the city?"

"Maybe because of my uncle's protection spells on the house to prevent burglary attempts?"

Hunter's cell phone buzzed at his belt, and he pulled the phone from its pouch. "Jared, what's up?"

"I've taken your mother home, but she wants to know if she can have your cell phone number so she can keep in touch."

"Sure. Let me talk to her, will you?"

"Just a sec."

"Yes, Hunter?" his mother said, her voice worried.

"Where did you get the summoning book to open the portal?"

She gave a disgruntled laugh. "My brother sent it to me as a joke for my twenty-fifth birthday. He said since I couldn't find a man that would make me happy, maybe I could summon one. He could be a real bastard sometimes. Everyone had left after the birthday party, and I was feeling morose. I couldn't sleep. So I played around with the summoning spell. Out of a whirlwind of a portal steps your father."

"Where did your brother get the book from?"

"Some weird incense shop, he said. I gave it to the people who adopted you. I told them it was your family's and you should keep it. I thought if you ever wanted to open the portal and see your father, you would need the summoning book. I memorized the spell just in case I ever got up the nerve to call your father back. I…I can't believe we've found each other. Thank Alana and Jared for making it happen."

"Uh, yeah, I will." He wasn't about to tell his mother he'd discovered the summoning book in the box of trash and that his adoptive parents had never told him about it. Though he could understand their reservations.

Alana went into the kitchen and brought back glasses of water for them.

They probably thought it was a book on devil worship. Though why Hunter's parents had kept it for so long, he hadn't a clue. Unless it was because it was so old and maybe they thought it was valuable, then changed their minds and dumped it into the trash. "You wouldn't happen to know which incense shop your brother got it from, would you?"

"My brother died in a car accident a few days after he'd given me the book, driving drunk as usual. At least he didn't injure anyone else that time. So no, I don't know where he got it exactly, and now, we can't ask him. Hunter, I...I don't want us to be strangers. I would like for us to get to know each other."

He wasn't sure how he felt. Still, a bit rejected, maybe, that she'd given him up to strangers. Annoyed that she hadn't bothered to search for him for the past eighteen years. Reserved, and not willing to give up the grudge. "Sure, we'll have to do that."

"Do you think Bentos will come back to see me again? Now that he knows you exist?"

What was he supposed to say? If he had been fully demon, he would have told her the truth.

14

Alana watched the expression on Hunter's face, first serious, then concerned while he talked to his mother over the phone in her uncle's living room. She'd never thought a Matusa demon could have any feelings of disquiet, but she guessed it was Hunter's human half showing through.

"I wouldn't get your hopes up concerning Bentos, Mom," Hunter warned. "You know what he said. He's one of the Dark Ones. You need to find someone else. I've got to go. Call me anytime."

He ended the call and glared at Alana. "Why don't you have a cell phone? If you had one, it would have made it so much easier to keep in touch with you. While we're on the subject, why didn't you telepathically contact me and say you and Jared were still safe at the Hall of Records?"

"For your information, *Dark One*, my mother didn't want a cell phone. We telepathically communicate when we need to. I wasn't sure you could hear me anyway when I was in the demon world. Besides, I was kind of distracted."

Hunter turned his attention to her uncle, who immediately looked annoyed.

"Why didn't you tell me you didn't have a cell phone? I'll get you mine." Her uncle stalked out of the room.

Alana crossed her arms. "You know, you could speak to me more nicely. And to think you want to marry me."

Hunter gave a sinister laugh. "In your dreams."

She raised a brow. "I would say it was more likely in *yours*. So, what are we going to do about this Baltimore demon?"

Hunter stretched his legs under the coffee table. "Wait for him. It's safer than if we searched for him in Baltimore. If your uncle's protection spells work—and they appeared to when they were battling the demons—we need to wait here until he comes."

Alana didn't want to wait. Her motto was to take charge and get a thing done. Never procrastinate. She sighed. She figured she couldn't do it without Hunter, as much as relying on someone else to help her didn't appeal. At least if she screwed up, she had only herself to blame.

Uncle Stephen returned to the living room. "Here's my phone." He glanced at Hunter. "You can sleep in the guestroom next to my bedroom. Don't mess with anything in there while you stay with us —I keep it clean for anyone who pops in for a visit. One further thing, I'll be using a protection spell to cloak Alana's room, so don't get any ideas." Her uncle gave Hunter a piercing look. "Why don't we all get some rest? It's already past—"

"The bewitching hour," Hunter said. "Witches, warlocks." He shook his head, but the darkly amused look he gave Alana warned her he didn't think her uncle could protect her from him at all.

THAT NIGHT after taking a shower and dressing in her favorite frog prince pajamas, Alana curled up in bed and began reading the advanced personal protection spell book she'd tucked under her pillow to get a head start on her uncle's teachings for the next day.

She felt fairly safe with her uncle's protection spells surrounding the house, Jared watching for demon signatures for the time being, and with a half-Matusa demon staying with them, too.

Halfway through trying to memorize the fourth spell, her eyelids grew heavy, and she fell asleep.

Until the portal yanked her out of her dreamlike state and cast her before Hunter in her astral form. Irritated enough to scream, she scowled at him. If she'd had the ability, she would have turned him into something slimy.

He reclined like a panther against the black velvet spread of his guest bed. Tilting his head to the side, he studied the green frogs wearing gold crowns on her pink pajama bottoms. His lips curved up, and she folded her arms.

"My uncle can put a stop to your doing this to me."

His eyes sparkled in the soft lamplight. "By casting a spell over you?"

"Yes."

"Then why didn't he before he went to bed?"

Hunter was so annoying. Yolan was the only one who'd been able to cast the protective spell around her mind to keep her from being yanked in the direction of the portal when it opened. She'd hoped she could find a spell she could use to cast on herself before someone summoned the gateway again.

"Well?" He looked so smug.

If she could slug him, she would. She could!

She left him, returned to her body, and sat upright in bed. For a second, her mind was so groggy that she couldn't remember what she had intended to do.

Then the portal opened again, and she was pulled back into Hunter's room. She would kill him. "Quit doing this!"

"I love it when your eyes flame. Did you know that?"

"Quit calling me here! I need to sleep, or you won't *even* want to see me in the morning. That's a promise!"

"I have to figure out why, when I open the portal, you're called to it. There has to be some key. Don't you agree? If demons and witches can't do what you do normally, what's making you do this? Don't you want to learn why this is happening?"

Wondering if he was being honest, she narrowed her eyes at him. "That's the only reason you opened the portal?"

"What other reason would there be?" His eyes sparkled with shady humor. "What? That I would take advantage of you? I can't touch you, can I?" He moved slowly from the bed. "I can't kiss you, can I?"

"You'd better not even go there."

"You say no, but your eyes and lips say otherwise."

He crossed the floor to her. She opened her mouth to tell him off when she felt the strong pull of another portal open somewhere else in Dallas.

"Another demon gateway," she warned, her heart racing.

Hunter's face turned stormy, then he cursed as she was yanked away.

ALANA'S astral body arrived at a rundown, single-story house where three slovenly, middle-aged men guzzled beer and chanted. All the men wore straggly beards and greasy hair down to their shoulders like a bunch of old hippies.

Flea-bitten, secondhand couches, and dead crickets entangled in gold stringy, shag carpeting decorated the place. Dim lights filtered through dirty lamp shades and the smell of beer and ciga- rettes permeated the stale air. A lone cricket chirped underneath one of the sofas.

Though Alana had it in mind to destroy their summoning book, she realized in her present state, she couldn't physically touch it. She had no idea where she was, or she would have told Hunter. She hoped the idiots didn't bring Ferengus forth.

"Next part," the man wearing three chins said.

She stepped in front of the portal, the wind from the gateway blowing her hair and her pajamas. The guys stared at her, their mouths gaping. Their eyes leered at her, and they gave her disgusting grins.

"We did it! I told you Barney said this is how he got his love slave."

Alana quirked a brow. "You brought forth the wrong kind of demon. Didn't you know how deadly some of them can be?"

"Nah, don't believe the witch. We summoned her. She's ours to do with what we please." The guy with the biggest belly that could have rivaled dear Saint Nick's, smelled like he hadn't bathed in as many years as the raggedy carpet had been in place. He stumbled toward her.

She took a step back, the feeling he could touch her with his grimy hands, making her stomach revolt.

"Stand still, witch."

If only he knew. Alana cast a protection attack spell and sent him flying back into the older man, his hair graying at the temples. And was instantly shocked that she could use that spell in her strange state. She immediately tried the levitation spell on the book which made it rise, but what was she to do with it?

"She likes to play rough, eh?" the third guy growled. He broke an empty beer bottle and headed for her.

"Some demons can't be controlled," she warned, hoping they would back off. "They don't leave the summoners alive."

The man bared yellow-stained teeth and sliced the broken bottle across her face. His jaw went slack when the bottle went through nothing but air. He backed up. "It's...it's not real."

No telling who they would conjure up if they messed with the spells again. She shoved the man against the wall, then concentrated on covering the book with brambles.

"What's she doing?" the older man said.

The big guy managed to chant another spell.

The portal shimmered and a Matusa female stepped forth, nearly giving Alana a stroke. The demon glanced in Alana's direction and sneered. "Kubiteron."

Alana's blood chilled, but she gave the Matusa an equally contemptuous look. Standing up to them was the only way to deal with them—she thought.

"You dare to call me? For what purpose, little men?" the black-haired siren asked, dragging her long nail across the fattest man's cheek. Blood dripped from the thin line she cut into the skin.

His hazel eyes went round, and his mouth hung open.

"Hmm, cat got your tongue?" Extending her claws, she ripped out his tongue and tossed it to the other men.

"Oh God." Alana stifled a shriek and tried to will herself out of the place.

The fat man passed out. The older man let out a strangled cry.

The demon turned to the one wielding the broken bottle. His hazel eyes filled with terror, he waved the jagged glass at her like a shaky dagger.

"I was busy with my mate," she said in a dark, sultry way. "Why did you bother me?"

"W-we're your masters. Y-you're our love slave," the armed man said.

Her short bark of laughter rattled the house. "You, human? You're not worthy of being dirt beneath my feet. You, my master? Ha! Kneel before me, dog!"

Trembling, the man dropped to his knees.

Alana tried to throw the demon back against the wall. The Matusa only glanced at her, the expression on the Matusa's face surprised. Whatever Alana had done to the demon, it was like with Ferengus. She couldn't stop them with her meager witch's skills.

Jared had said Kubiteron might command water. She tried to gather a storm. Nothing happened. She tried the attack spell with lightning bolts, but again, nothing came of it.

Then vehicles drove up to the house, their headlights shining into the bare windows, their brakes squealing.

The demon smiled. "Good. More company to play with."

Alana tried to distract her. "Don't you want to return to your mate?"

"I believe I'll stay awhile. Make you do my bidding. Come here, Kubiteron." The demon yanked the man's head up by his hair. "Kill him for me."

"I don't do *any* demon's bidding."

"Oh, yes you will, little one."

The door to the house slammed open and banged against the wall. Hunter and Jared stormed inside.

Alana couldn't believe her eyes, nor could she have been more relieved.

"Go, Alana!" Hunter shouted at her.

Instantly, he stoked her ire.

"Alana?" the female said. She cast a devious smile. "Ferengus is looking for you. He will be disappointed he wasn't summoned instead of me."

Hunter grabbed the woman's arm and sent her flying back through the portal. Alana would catalog the demon's look of surprise for future reference. Chalk one up for the semi-good guys.

"Go, Alana!" Hunter hollered at her.

"No! What about these men?"

"The drunken bums deserve whatever she meted out to them," he growled low.

"They said their friend has a love slave," Alana warned.

"Jared?" Hunter asked, turning to him.

"Yeah, yeah, I'm looking." He peered at his laptop. "Faint signature two blocks from here in a southwesterly direction."

"What's the address?" Hunter asked the men.

The older man croaked out, "Two-twenty-one, 1st Street. Don't kill us, please."

Hunter closed the portal and then seized the summoning book. "Where did you get this?"

"Our friend got it. I had nothing to do with it. We were just fooling around."

Alana approached the man. "You will remember nothing about demons or your friend having one." She repeated the same message to the other two, then leaned over the man with the bloodied mouth and stopped the bleeding. "Get him to a hospital."

"Why couldn't you have tried to heal me in your current state before?" Hunter asked, leading her out to his truck, his tone of voice perturbed.

"I have more power over humans even in my current *state*. How did you find me here?"

"I called Jared as soon as you disappeared. I told him you were pulled away to another portal, and he needed to monitor the area until the demon was summoned. Shortly afterward, he informed me she was Matusa. Now I want you to go home."

"I want to go with you."

He looked at her skeptically. "Can you?"

"I don't think so, unless you open a portal for me at the other man's house."

"Go home, Alana. No telling what we'll find there."

"You said the demon's signature is faint. I may be able to heal her if she has been injured."

"Not in your present state, you said."

She scowled at him. "I won't let you back into my uncle's home."

"Then I can't protect you if the Baltimore demon comes for you."

She folded her arms.

Hunter's jaw tightened. "All right. I'll call you." He snorted under his breath. "You're a Kubiteron and I'm a Matusa. That means you're to obey me."

"You mean, 'You, Matusa, me, Kubiteron?' No way, Tarzan. Go beat on your chest before some other lesser demon."

Jared quickly hid a smile.

Hunter's face turned dark. She gave him a quirky smile, then vanished.

As soon as Hunter opened the portal at the next house, Alana was pulled to the place. The smell of whiskey filled the air instead of beer. A Kubiteron female lay chained to a pillar holding up the back porch. Her face and arms were bruised and swollen but as soon as she saw Alana, her face brightened a degree.

"Guardian of the Gate," she whispered, her violet eyes sparkling with hope.

"Can you heal her?" Hunter asked.

"I'll try."

Hunter and Jared stormed into the house.

"What the..." a man shouted, then a couple of rounds of gunfire rang out.

Her eyes full of fright, the female demon glanced at the house.

"We'll release you as soon as we can," Alana said, unable to free her without being in her physical state. "*Hunter*," she said, totally exasperated.

Hurrying out of the house, he favored a bloodied arm but yanked at the rusty chains binding the woman until they pulled apart. She lay still on the cement, barely able to lift her head.

Alana tried to touch her but couldn't. "I can't help her here—I guess because she's not human. Can either you or Jared?"

"No. Neither of us has healing powers."

"But your dad—"

"It's like human abilities. Some can do some things; others have different abilities. We'll bring her to your uncle's home, then return her to the demon's world."

Alana reached for Hunter's arm. "What about you?"

"Later." He looked back at the house and hollered, "Jared?"

"Coming." Jared hurried outside. "I couldn't find any other summoning books."

"What about the man?" Alana asked.

"What man?" Hunter snarled. "He was a savage beast." Hunter lifted the injured demon off the porch, his touch gentle. "He won't be torturing anyone else from now on."

She knew Hunter had killed the man. The demon part of her cheered him for ridding the world of another sadist. The human part of her...she wasn't sure. Not after she looked at the pretty woman nearly dead from the beatings she'd received.

"Go home, Alana. Let me into the house or come out to me when I get there. I'm afraid your uncle's barriers will prevent me from entering on my own."

Boy, would her uncle be mad if he found out she'd been running around with a couple of demons again.

As soon as Hunter and Jared arrived at her uncle's front door, Alana greeted them, hoping her uncle wouldn't discover the mess they'd been in. She hurriedly went about healing the Kubiteron and was grateful her powers worked to mend even the bones she could feel broken in the slight woman's hands and feet.

Hunter nodded. "Your healing skills work on human-inflicted wounds and even on demons as I thought. It was only the Matusa's poison you had no abilities to counteract." He opened a portal and the Kubiteron quickly squeezed Alana's hand, and her eyes lowered. "I thank you and owe you my life, Guardian. I'm Tessalyn. If you ever need my help, call me."

"I'm Alana. Why are you calling me a guardian?" Though Alana had a creepy feeling she wouldn't like the answer.

The woman's violet eyes widened. "You are of Earth world?"

"Yes." Which Alana hoped would make all the difference.

"You're the one. Forgive me. My mother was also a guardian of the gate. But..." She turned and cast a wary glance at Hunter, then considered Jared. "Neither of them are Samuria."

Hunter drew taller. "What's that got to do with anything?"

"A Kubiteron gate guardian is always matched with a Samuria. They give each other equal strength to manage the return of demons summoned from our world. Since the early age of demons and humankind, some Matusa have wished to conquer other worlds. And some Earth inhabitants wish to enslave those of us who cannot fight them."

Alana nodded.

"Gate guardians are rare, but necessary to keep either from happening. The Kubiteron who possesses such an ability is highly respected by all demons but the Matusa." Tessalyn gave Hunter a dark cursory look. "The Samuria she selects will be most honored."

Alana didn't believe it for a minute because she was half-human, thank the heavens!

Jared poked away at his laptop. "From the information I have here, the Samuria are mainly politicians. I can't find what their strength is concerning other demons."

Tessalyn sighed deeply. "My father was Samurian. You would not want to see him when he was angered."

Jared looked up from his monitor. "I see you as a Kubiteron. I thought offspring always carried their father's demonic aura."

"Except in the case of the Samuria. There's always an exception to every rule," she said.

"Like having a Samuria matched with a Kubiteron as gate guardians." Hunter raised a brow, punctuating his comment.

"No," Tessalyn said vehemently. "In all the centuries they have existed, the match of demon types is always the same. It cannot be changed."

Jared looked uneasy. "Then we need to find one of these Samuria to match up with Alana. Maybe Alana and her partner could help at the site of the portals while Hunter and I can track down the summoning books."

"I must return home. If you ever need me, just summon me," Tessalyn said to Alana. "You have the power." She stepped into the portal.

When the lady disappeared, Hunter closed the gateway. Alana stared at the spot where the woman disappeared, her mind still sifting over the woman's words.

"Are you all right?" Jared asked.

"I don't believe I'm some gate guardian. I'm not even a full demon and..." Alana shook her head, then began to work on the bullet in Hunter's arm. No way was she going to pick some Samuria, politician, whatever, to become her guardian match. "I don't know anything about this. Aren't there rules? Training? Can't people have a choice as to what they want to do with their lives?" She stared at Hunter's arm. "Your wound is beginning to heal already."

"Demons heal faster if the wound is human-inflicted. But the man beat Tessalyn so frequently, her wounds never had time to heal." He glanced up at Alana. "As for having a choice in life, I have chosen what I want to do. Keeping the demons where they belong."

"I'm with Hunter," Jared said.

"You're a full demon. Why wouldn't you want to go home, Jared?"

"This is the only world I've known."

"So why not let a few of your kind in?"

Jared gave her an annoyed look.

"I thought you wanted to send them back," Hunter said.

"I want them gone, yes. But I don't want to be some guardian of these blasted portals," Alana said.

"We need to go to Seplichus and find a Samuria to help her." Jared closed his laptop. "Maybe between the four of us, we can make some progress."

She frowned. "Absolutely not. I'm finding a way to stop being summoned to these portals. I'll help in whatever way I can otherwise, but I wouldn't be some gate guardian."

"But Tessalyn...," Jared said.

"She's wrong. I bet there has never been a half-Kubiteron gate guardian ever. And what were we supposed to do anyway? Return to Seplichus and search the database for a Samuria willing to work with me?"

Jared said, "Yeah. We could check it out in the morning."

"I'm joking," she said sarcastically.

Jared looked at Hunter. "I don't know anything about these gate guardians. I could get some information on them while we're there."

"No," Alana said.

"How can you make an informed decision without knowing all the facts?" Jared said, sounding perturbed.

Hunter shook his head. "She can't go back. Not with the Matusa wanting her."

"Then I could return."

"To find out everything you can about gate guardians," Hunter clarified.

"You don't want me to locate a Samuria?"

Alana's face steamed. Didn't she already say she wasn't going to be a gate guardian?

"Tessalyn said it had to be a Kubiteron's choice," Hunter said.

"Okay. I'll bring back a list of names and profiles."

"Then *you* pick your mate from one, Jared." Alana huffed, then turned her attention to the house and tried to get Hunter and her back inside, but her uncle had locked it in such a manner she couldn't reopen it. She rang the doorbell and banged the brass knocker. His bedroom was on the backside of the house, but even so, he was a lot heavier sleeper than she thought.

Jared waited patiently for them to get safely back inside before he left.

"Is there somewhere else we can stay?" Hunter asked, and she thought she sensed he seemed a little concerned.

"Back patio? Chaise lounges aren't the most comfortable to sleep on, but the backyard is protected by a barrier," she offered.

Jared looked a little left out. "What do you want me to do?"

"Maybe you ought to hang around in case we have another summoning episode," Hunter said.

"There are six chaise lounges. Enough for a whole party of demons." Alana headed for the backyard gate, glad that Jared could watch for demon signatures that might approach the house.

"Hopefully we won't have any uninvited guests crash the party." Hunter followed her.

With his laptop under his arm, Jared trailed behind.

The night was warm and muggy, the stars glittering against a black satin sky while ornamental brass lanterns shed small amounts of light on sleeping flowers and winsome maiden statues. The fragrance of roses perfumed the air, but mosquitoes buzzed around their ears and landed on any inch of exposed skin. Alana cast a bug-off protection spell over the patio, and the three demons climbed onto the loungers for the night.

For several minutes no one said anything, and then unable to shut off her mind, Alana rolled over onto her side. "So, Hunter, what did you think of your father?"

A heated growl rumbled from Hunter's direction.

H unter rolled over on his back onto the chaise lounge and ignored Alana's query. What kind of a question was that to ask of a Matusa anyway? Even if he was half-human? How did he feel about his father? He hated him for making his mother pregnant, for leaving her, for caring for another woman more, and for having a son with her.

Bentos had even checked up on his other son, but not once had he learned how Hunter fared. Hunter stared up at the overhang above the patio. Only a Kubiteron/half-human would ask him such an irritating question.

He glanced at Jared who was watching him. What? Did he wonder, too? He growled inwardly. Jared ought to know him better than that.

"I was just curious," Alana finally said. "I try not to think about my father because Mom said he'd left her right after making her pregnant and never got in touch with her." She took a heavy breath.

Hunter watched the emotions playing across her face: irritation, disappointment, stoicism.

"Anyway, kids bugged me at school when I was little. 'Where's your dad for the Dad's Day with their Daughters?' And 'Why aren't you making a Father's Day card for your dad?' Worse, my teachers insisted I make one for some *other* male family member. Why should I have?"

He shook his head.

"Mom's dad had disowned her for getting pregnant without a husband. She was supposed to marry a nice, respectable warlock. Uncle Stephen had treated her coolly for years. Even until recently, he wasn't very accepting of me. So, why should I honor some male member of the family, I would like to know."

"So, did you make a Father's Day card?" Jared asked.

He needn't have asked. Hunter could see from her mutinous expression she hadn't.

"No."

Except for cicadas and crickets singing in the muggy breeze, and the sound of water spilling from a marble maiden's pitcher into a fountain in the rose gardens, no other sounds intruded on the night.

Then Jared asked, "Did you get in trouble?"

Hunter shook his head. He'd hoped Alana's mind had quieted so they could sleep. If he'd had a pillow, he would have socked Jared with it.

Alana offered a sinfully wicked grin.

"I take that as a yes." Jared smiled. He always found humor in the most devilish situations.

"I made a Mother's Day card and said it was because my mother needed to be honored on Father's Day for being both my mother and father."

"You got into trouble for that?" Hunter asked, though he'd been expelled so many times from school over the years himself when-ever someone hassled him, and he wouldn't let them get away with it, he couldn't understand how he ever managed to graduate this year. Though he'd wondered if they had wanted to get him out of the school quickly.

"No. One of the boys tore up my card and said I was the reason my father wouldn't come home."

Hunter raised his brows. "Good thing your demon half couldn't kick in until you were older when you could handle it better or that kid would have been in some serious trouble."

She smiled, and the look was pure evil. "Maybe so, but I had my witch's powers. Suddenly, the little creep, Jeffries—though he was a lot bigger than me—got a nosebleed. He screamed and said I gave it to him, but I hadn't touched him, *physically*."

"So how'd you get in trouble then?" Jared asked.

"The kid swung his boot to kick me in the shin, and I socked him in the eye. The teacher only saw me hit him. When he kicked at me, I'd put up a protective spell, so he didn't hurt me. The problem was I couldn't prove he'd kicked at me first. Either the other kids hadn't seen what happened, or they were more afraid of him and lied."

Jared frowned at her.

"Anyway, I got sent home, and Mom lectured me big time about not using my witch's powers at school. However, punching the kid in the eye was perfectly acceptable, according to my mother. Giving him a nosebleed wasn't."

"I like your mother, at least about the punching-Jeffries-in-the-eye bit." Jared leaned back against his lounge chair.

Alana stretched out. "After that, I always said my father was dead. And he was until I learned I have this demonic connection to him. Now, I have this weird nagging at the back of my mind. What traits might we share? Is he an early riser like me? Does he grind his teeth when he's mad? Most of all, I want to know what being a Kubiteron means. On the other hand, I'm not all that sure I want to meet him. I doubt he would care anything about me, or he would have tried to get in touch with me."

"Unless he couldn't," Jared said, "because he would need to be summoned again."

Her brow furrowed.

"Also, my father said it's up to the demon child to search for the parent. Not the other way around," Hunter said.

"Yeah, well, I've thought about it ever since my mother told me the truth about him. You know what? I was right. He's dead. Whatever I am, is me. I've been me all along without him. I'll be me the rest of my life and not give it another thought."

She sounded less convinced of that than she let on, Hunter thought. "Did you find any clues to his identity while you were searching at the court of records?" He didn't believe she wasn't interested in finding her father, even if she meant only to chew him out for leaving her mother behind.

Jared chuckled darkly. "You should have seen the way she talked to the Kubiteron she investigated. Remember I told you how you have to correspond with the demons in their world? Very cordially? Not this one. Man, she even used a ton of exclamation marks. *Exclamation marks!* I was amazed we didn't have a swarm of Kubiteron demons at the courthouse looking for blood, and I don't mean as in looking to see if they were related to her or not."

Hunter could believe it. What he couldn't believe was that she would persist in questioning him!

"What does your father do, besides rescue his poisoned son?" Alana asked Hunter, her voice not sounding in the least bit sleepy.

"What do you mean, what does he do?" As if Hunter knew or cared.

"His occupation?"

"How should I know?"

She glanced at Jared. "Do you know about the demon culture?"

"It's similar to ours in a way," Jared said. "Some areas of their world have more hostile environments, hardier demons living there. Others are city demons like the ones here. They don't have elected officials, but reigning princes instead."

"Matusa?"

"No. That's the ironic thing. The ruling princes are made up of the various demon clans. The Matusa are the only ones who do not rule. According to the records custodian, Treikal, who by the way is a ruling prince's cousin, the Matusa have too volatile tempers to preside over the rest. In that regard, they understand their limitations and leave the governing of regions to lesser demons."

"I thought they would never allow others to rule them."

"Humans, no. Truthfully, if a lesser demon tells a Matusa what to do, he has to word it in a conciliatory manner or risk the Matusa's wrath."

"So if you are related to Treikal, you could be related to a ruling prince. Wow." She gave Hunter a frosty smile.

He cast her a so-what-of-it look back. Then she closed her eyes and Hunter sighed, figuring he would finally get some sleep.

Stephen's voice suddenly boomed in their ears. "What is going on here?"

They jumped from the loungers ready to do battle. Stephen fisted his hands on his hips and glared from one to the other.

"Alana was drawn to a portal in the city. We had to send the summoned demon back," Hunter said, yawning.

"But we couldn't get back in the house, though I tried to wake you." Alana rubbed her eyes.

"If you were there in a vision—"

"I had to help heal the injured demon. Hunter brought her to the front lawn."

Enough with the questioning already. If it wasn't so important Hunter stuck to his part of the bargain and helped protect Alana against the Baltimore Matusa, he would have gladly gone home to his own bed. Though he had to admit he hadn't had this much of a hassle in a long time, and it rather perked up his life.

Stephen motioned to Jared. "What is *he* doing here?"

Looking only half awake, Alana stretched her arms above her

head. "He's the one who tracks the summoned demon's signature, so he could locate me."

"He needs to return to his home." Stephen gave Hunter a long, exasperated look. "No more leaving the house with my niece tonight."

"Yes, sir," Hunter said, sardonically. How could he stop her from leaving, if another portal opened? He slapped Jared on the back. "Call you later."

"Much later, will ya?" Jared took off for his Jeep parked out front.

Stephen led Hunter and Alana back into the house. "I'm afraid I can't get hold of Yolan at this hour. We need to see if you can learn the spell to protect your mind from this portal intrusion."

"Hunter said we should examine the reason I'm being pulled to them," Alana said, following her uncle.

Hunter expected her to mention her possibly being a gate guardian, but she gave him a look like he'd better not say a word. Ignoring what she might be wasn't the solution, and he had half a notion to bring it up. Then again, her uncle would talk longer and there would go the chance of returning sooner to bed. Self-preservation was more important.

"Good idea." Stephen stopped before her bedroom door. "Get some sleep." His voice sounded groggy and annoyed.

"Right, Uncle Stephen." She glanced at Hunter. "Night, Dark One." Privately, she said, *Don't you dare call me to your room again tonight!*

The notion was tempting; he gave her a cocky smile. "Night, Kubiteron."

&

EARLY THE NEXT MORNING, Hunter woke to the sound of Stephen scolding, and Alana defending herself downstairs. He opened a bleary eye and peered at the glare of the bold white numbers on a digital clock. *Five a.m.?* Even the roosters were probably still sleeping off the morning.

Yanking the spare pillow on the queen-sized mattress over his head, he wished his demonic abilities could put people to sleep as Alana had done to the nurses at the nurses' station. Witch ability or demonic?

Whatever. He just wished he could zap Alana and her uncle back to sleep.

Then everything grew quiet.

Sometime later, in his semi-conscious state, he heard a voice speaking to him in his mind. *Hunter, are you still sleeping? The morning's half over! Call Jared and let's get on with business. Hurry, before my Uncle Stephen returns.*

Then blessed silence. The quiet only lasted a few minutes. Suddenly, demonic pounding shook his bedroom door. Grinding his teeth, he tried to ignore it.

"Hunter! Get your butt out of bed! We need to find the shop where the summoning book came from. Now, Hunter!"

Throwing the spare pillow at the door, he glowered at the clock. Seven? Still too early.

"You never, ever want to wake a Matusa demon, Kubiteron!" he growled, running his hand over the light stubble covering his chin.

"Yeah, well, if you don't hurry and get your lazy butt out of bed, my uncle will be back, and I won't be going anywhere."

"You need to stay here. Jared and I will check it out."

"Nope."

He yanked the black velvet comforter aside, then sat up, his mind still groggy. "You really don't want to see me pissed."

"All right, sleep your life away. I'll call Jared myself."

Standing, Hunter stretched his arms toward the ceiling and yawned. "He's even grouchier than me before his first soda."

"Don't tell me you drink soda for breakfast."

"No, I drink coffee. Jared drinks sodas." Hunter grabbed his clothes and headed for the door. Yanking it open, he glared at the spitfire before him.

Alana looked like a sunshiny day, her golden hair braided down her back, her green eyes sparkling with enthusiasm, and her lips raised in an impudent grin.

"You, Kubiteron, will have to learn your limits when it comes to dealing with a Matusa."

She chuckled under her breath, and he stalked off to the bathroom. "Has your uncle got any spare toothbrushes?"

"Bottom drawer on the right. Throwaway razors, too. Despite there being only one of him, he buys everything in army-sized quantities. Mom said it was because his parents would run out of things, and he had to borrow someone else's stuff to make do until they went shopping again. Cute boxers, by the way."

He glanced down at his black satin boxers covered in red hot chili peppers, his little sister's Christmas gift to him. He tossed a glower over his shoulder. "Last female demon who got a glimpse of them, didn't live long."

She laughed out loud.

He slammed the bathroom door behind him and smiled.

HALF AN HOUR LATER, Hunter scarfed down four scrambled eggs, a half dozen slices of bacon, and three slices of toast dripping with honey, not even noticing Alana was there. Tossing down his fourth cup of coffee, he finally looked up from the table.

Alana rested her chin in her hand as she leaned her elbow against the table and watched him. "Do you always eat that much?"

"Only when I've been up half the night and had to fight demons all day. Not to mention I wasn't able to eat while I was ill." He glanced at the stainless-steel kitchen that looked like it deserved to be featured in a cooking show. "Does your uncle like to cook?"

"A hobby of his."

"What kind of work does he do to have all this?" Hunter motioned to the lavish furnishings.

"Stocks and bonds."

"Stockbroker?" He slid his plate to her.

She raised her brows, hesitated to take the scraped-clean plate, then jerked it off the table. She would not be his servant! "Investments."

Hunter leaned back in his chair while she shoved the plate into the dishwasher. "You mean he has inside information?"

She turned and frowned at him. "He's just good at what he does."

"I bet. You said your mother doesn't have a cell phone. Can't she afford it? Can't she get insider information on the stock market, too?"

"Everyone's different, Hunter. My mother can barely balance her checkbook, but she does a pretty good job exorcising ghosts, which my uncle and most of his friends can't do."

"And you?"

Giving him an impish look, Alana shrugged, and he knew then she exorcised spirits. Which intrigued him.

Once, he'd encountered a ghost and he'd always wished he could have helped the soul find peace.

"So if Casper the Ghost came to visit me in the middle of the night, you could zap him back into the netherworld?"

"We don't *zap* ghosts. We attempt to give them solace, and they depart our world."

Not believing her for an instant, he tapped his fingers on the table. "You don't mean to tell me only sweet-natured spirits are out there who nicely do as you bid." Though the one who'd come to him was one of the good guys.

"Are you ready to go? Uncle Stephen ran out to get some groceries, and though he's the most aggravatingly slow shopper—has to read every label, weigh every option, compare every price—he will probably return in the next couple of hours."

Hunter pulled his cell phone from his belt. "It's only eight. Jared will be like a Matusa this time in the morning now that school's out, and we kept him up half the night."

"Are you scared of him?"

He grunted and punched in Jared's number. While the phone rang, he turned to Alana. "I don't believe you about the ghosts, by the way."

She gave him an evil smile. "Yeah, well, my life isn't going to be an open book to you."

"Keep that thought, Kubiteron. Before long, you'll be spilling all your dark secrets to me, begging for me to know them."

Laughing, she shook her head. "Yeah, right. Do you come by this tough guy act naturally, or do you practice it?"

He grinned back at her.

Jared finally answered the phone and grouched, "Hunter? I told you to call me later. Since when is eight in the morning late?"

"If you think that's late," Hunter said, glancing at Alana, "you should have heard the Kubiteron kibitzing with her uncle at five this morning."

She stalked out of the dining room.

He chuckled. "Ready to find that shop that sold the summoning book?"

"Yeah, in a couple of hours. Call me back."

"No doing. Alana's uncle is returning in a couple of hours."

"What? Do we have to take her with us? We do these jobs alone, together, I mean. Just the two of us. She's nothing but trouble."

"Agreed. And she's going with us. *Now*. Meet you at the address the beast gave us in fifteen." Hunter pocketed his phone and then joined Alana. "Ready to go?"

She was running her hands over the crystal ball, scowling at him. "You know, my talk with my uncle is none of your business."

"Does that thing work?"

"What?"

"The crystal ball."

She laughed again. "It's a paperweight."

"Oh. Ready to go?" He didn't wait for her. Matusa didn't wait for anything or anyone. Besides, he liked having her chase after him, two steps behind, just the way it should be.

When she didn't follow him, he glanced back. She was still sitting on the couch playing with the crystal ball, her eyes green daggers as she glared at him.

"What?" he bit out.

16

"So, exactly *what* were your uncle and you arguing about?" Hunter asked when Alana climbed into his pickup.

As if it was any of his business! As high as the pickup sat, she felt like she was sitting on top of a mountain...a very plush, comfy mountain. "I *thought* you'd been sleeping." She slammed the door closed, then took in a deep breath of the smell of—she glanced up at the scented tree hanging from the rearview mirror—pines.

"You and your uncle were slightly vocal."

"It's none of your concern."

Hunter drove around her uncle's circular drive. "Let's see. Your uncle said something about you not getting mixed up with a guy like me."

She folded her arms and glared out the window. "Like that would ever happen."

"He's worried you'll fall into the same trap as your mother?"

"So why did you ask what we fought about if you already knew?"

"Lucky guess."

"Well, I'm *not* like my mother."

Slamming on the brakes, he honked at a driver, and Alana grabbed the dashboard.

"Idiot. Yield signs mean *yield*!" He turned his glower on Alana. "You and your mother are witches. You both can *exorcise* ghosts. I would say you had some things in common."

"Yeah, well she summoned Dad. I didn't summon you and—"

"No." He looked self-satisfied. "I summoned *you*."

"The portal did, not you." She crossed her legs. "So it's not the same. Plus, I'm half demon."

"And so am I."

"So? That doesn't mean a thing to me."

Hunter's lips rose in a smug smile.

"It *doesn't*!"

"Yep. I bet you tell that to all the half-demons you meet."

"Has anyone ever told you that you're insufferably arrogant?"

"My little sister does all the time. But you know what? She loves me." Hunter gave Alana a critical look. "So what does that say about you?"

"There's no..." Alana turned her attention to the shop numbers and pointed out 101 Grisholm. "There. Haggerty's Incense Shop."

Hunter pulled into the parking lot. "Do witches buy special merchandise from magic shops?"

"Get real." She yanked off her seatbelt.

"I'm being sincere. What do I know? All this is new to me."

Alana studied the bars on the outside of the windows and the way they were painted black. "Looks like a place where vampires might congregate."

"Don't tell me vampires are real now."

"Santa Claus is. I'll tell you about it sometime. And werewolves? Everything bound in myths and legends has some truth to it." She unbuckled her seatbelt. "Maybe even dragons." She gave him a sarcastic look.

"All right but vampires are going too far."

"Hey, besides the folklore, there are people who have a rare condition called porphyria which causes extreme sensitivity to light and a disruption in making their own blood cells."

"And they suck people's blood? Grow fangs?"

She smiled.

He motioned to the incense store. "So what are these shops for if they don't sell to witches?"

"People who like incense? How do I know?" She started to climb out of the truck.

Hunter grabbed her wrist. "We wait until Jared gets here."

"A Matusa demon can't handle this?" Alana expected macho man's eyes to flare, but he only smiled at her.

"I'm smarter than you give me credit for. I would never barge into a situation without knowing the odds."

"Except when you were willing to help rescue my uncle and his friends."

"I already knew the odds." His eyes sparkled like the devil.

"Oh?"

"Yep. We were outnumbered."

That sounded just like a Matusa. Jared drove up beside them and gave Hunter a perturbed look.

"Showtime. I guess I couldn't convince you to stay in the truck, could I?" Hunter looked half-hopeful.

She climbed out of the vehicle. "Sorry. I'm not a wilting flower type."

"I didn't think so." Hunter joined Jared while his friend punched in stuff on his laptop. "What do you see?"

Jared closed the laptop. "Just the three of us. No other demons nearby."

"All right, let's do this."

Hunter led the way as if he were in charge, which suited her fine since he was supposed to be Mr. Macho. He pushed open the glass door, and bells jingled their arrival.

Inside, bittersweet incense filled the store, and the smell of burning candle wax added to the smoky environment. Shelves rested against three walls filled with dusty books, glass vases, and brass containers covered in verdigris, looking like they could hold the genie of one's dreams.

Alana halfway expected to see preserved body parts floating in murky jars, or skulls hanging from the ceiling. Instead, a chandelier of lighted candles cast shadows across the dimly lit shop. Except for tons of books, containers, a bunch of incense burners, spicy incense, and moody music piped in overheard, the place looked benign.

"Where's a clerk?" Alana whispered.

Hunter pointed to a backroom behind a counter, then he walked over to the closest bookshelf. "Look around for the books."

"I guess they don't have a card catalog index," Jared groused under his breath. He pulled out a copy of a book and crossed the floor to join Hunter.

He quickly examined it and nodded. "Yeah, this is the one."

"Fascinating, isn't it?" a woman's husky voice asked, coming out of the backroom, but though she tried to sound cheerful, her tone was much sullener, withdrawn. "Sorry, I didn't greet you earlier. I was pricing merchandise, and sometimes people like to look around without me bothering them. So, did you need any of the items that make the experience more real?"

The woman had Goth written all over her from her black hair coiled on top of her head in a strange, spiked fashion, the body piercings, black dress, and combat boots, same colored lipstick, eye shadow, and her skin made paler by the white foundation.

Hunter turned his back to the clerk and whispered to Alana, "Is she a witch?"

Alana cast him an irritated look. "Goth."

"Where did you get the book?" Alana asked the woman. "Do you have any others?"

"I have two. They're expensive so not many customers are interested in paying that kind of money. Usually, groups buy them and split the cost." She raked long, black fingernails over the counter. "As for my source, it's private. If I let you know who sold them to me..." She lifted a shoulder. "I could be out of business."

Hunter turned to Alana and whispered, "Is she telling the truth?"

"How would I know? I don't read minds," Alana said telepathically to Hunter. She turned to the woman. "Tell us who gave you the books."

For a moment, the woman resisted Alana's hypnotic command. Then she took a deep breath. "A man came here three weeks ago. He said he had these great demon-summoning books, and they were all the rage in New York City. He told me they were the latest for New Age parties. I pay ten dollars for them and sell them for a huge markup. He suggested the price of one-fifty. I've already sold two and made more money on them than I have in combined sales for a month."

"Who is he?" Alana asked.

The woman squinted and stared at the countertop, then shook her head. "He didn't say his name."

"What did he look like?"

"Oh, that's easy. Handsome, charming, the most beautiful silvery blue eyes, and hair my color, only natural, and milky white skin. He wasn't dressed in black as I expected. He was all in white, a shirt and jeans. Except for his feet. Tan cowboy boots, fancy trim. No cowboy hat though. And charming. Did I mention that? He knew the way to a woman's heart right off."

"Is he returning anytime soon?"

She nodded vigorously. "As soon as I sell these books, I'm supposed to call him."

"We're buying the books," Alana said, as Jared set them on the counter. "Call him."

The woman hesitated.

"*Call...him.*"

Lifting the phone off the hook, the clerk punched in a number. "This is Rhiannon from Haggerty's Incense Shop. I've sold the last of my summoning books and need more."

"*You have customers waiting on three more,*" Alana told her.

"I have customers waiting on three more." The woman frowned. "Tomorrow?"

"*Today, if possible. The women are just passing through, and I'll lose the sales.*"

Rhiannon repeated Alana's words verbatim to the man. The clerk smiled. "That would be great. Thanks. See you soon." She hung up the phone. "He'll be here within the hour."

"We'll be back." Alana gave her thirty dollars for the books. "This is the amount you asked for."

"Yes, that was the amount I asked for." Rhiannon deposited the money in an antiquated cash register.

"When the person arrives with the books, you will thank him and set them underneath your counter. You will give them to only one of the three of us."

"To one of the three of you."

"Yes. Then you'll forget who the person was who sells them, his phone number, and everything about the books."

"Everything," the woman parroted.

"Have a nice day." Alana hoped the demon wouldn't sense what had happened here and terminate the woman.

"Have a nice day," the clerk responded.

Jared grabbed up the books and he, Hunter, and Alana walked out of the store while he kept shaking his head. "She's dangerous."

"The clerk?" Hunter asked.

Jared glanced at Alana. "No, her. Have you ever seen anyone control minds like she can? It's scary. No telling what she would make us do if she got mad enough."

Hunter laughed. "She wouldn't dare try, but beyond that, she couldn't control us. I'm sure it has to do with the clerk's weak will." He studied Alana. "You don't have blood-sucking urges, do you? An aversion to sunlight?"

Jared looked from one to the other. "What am I missing?"

"Nothing," Alana said. "For your information, Matusa, you might not be as strong as you think when it comes to my will."

"Try me."

Jared seemed eager to see what would happen, but Alana wasn't about to see if her abilities would work right now. It was best to try them out when they least expected it.

"We're not leaving, are we?" Jared asked as they headed back to the vehicle. "What if we return later to find he has left more books off and we've missed catching him?"

"You're going to watch for his signature. You'll locate where he goes after this. We'll find his lair and make sure there are no others with him," Alana said, not waiting for Hunter and Jared to come up with a plan.

"They say sometimes a mating between demons can transfer some of the abilities of the mate to another." Hunter's line of reasoning completely threw Alana off.

Jared stared at him as if he didn't know what Hunter was getting at.

Hunter took the books from Jared and stacked them together on the ground. With a flick of his wrist, he set them ablaze. The blue flame grew white as it completely devoured the books.

"Impressive. Why didn't you use it against Ferengus?" Alana asked.

"I can only use it against inanimate objects."

"Oh. Great for cookouts," she said, sarcastically.

"So what did you mean about the mating of demons and sharing abilities?" Jared asked.

Hunter shifted his gaze from Jared to Alana and gave a wicked smile. "I wondered if witch's abilities would transfer, too."

Alana gave her head a shake. "Sometimes abilities are enhanced or transferred between witches and their warlock spouses. Never between a witch and a human though. Who knows about a witch and a demon? But you would have to find one who's agreeable."

"I have." Hunter kicked the pile of smoldering ashes around, stirring them up so that the breeze carried them away.

Jared grunted. "You can't mean her."

Hunter's smile broadened, but he didn't respond.

Jared pulled out his laptop from his Jeep. "Now what? We don't just sit here in the opening awaiting his arrival, do we? Wouldn't we be conspicuous?"

Hunter pointed to a seedy-looking bar next door. Though it was morning, three dented and rusty vehicles were parked in front.

"We're all underage," Jared said.

"Alana will take care of it."

"How many do you think I can handle?"

"At least three," Jared said, walking toward the bar. "That's how many nurses you knocked out at the hospital."

"Yeah, I could sure use some abilities like that. Especially when people wake me up too early in the morning." Hunter pushed the door open.

Inside, the bar was even darker than the incense shop. All the windows were covered in black boards and a dim light barely illuminated the place. It reeked of beer and body odor.

Six men turned bleary eyes toward the newcomers.

A bearded bartender leaned against the bar and gave them a hard look. "Kiddie Pizza World is three blocks over."

"Serve us bottled water and make it quick," Alana said.

The men at the three tables looked from Alana to the

bartender, watching for his response. Their jaws gaped when the man pulled out three glasses of water. "That'll be twelve dollars."

Alana turned to Hunter. "I'm all tapped out."

Jared yanked the money out of his wallet. "Robbery. Whoever heard of paying so much for water?"

Hunter grabbed two drinks and carried them to a table on the other side of the room.

"Couldn't you just—" Jared started to stay.

"Make him give it to us for free? Yes, but I don't want to do it in front of all the other men," Alana said to him privately.

They took their seats, and then Jared opened his laptop.

For an hour and a half, they sipped their water and watched the monitor.

"How did you ever design software to pick up our signatures?" Alana was impressed.

"He's a genius when it comes to computer stuff." Admiration was evident in Hunter's voice.

"I wonder," she said, giving Hunter a simpering smile, "if Jared's abilities would transfer to a witch."

Hunter's expression was darkly amused.

"There!" Jared pointed at the monitor. "It's an Elantus. Why would an Elantus be doing this?"

"A Matusa has to be behind it." Hunter stood.

"The demon's inside the shop."

"Okay, we wait here until he or she moves."

"You can't tell which it is?" Alana couldn't help sounding disappointed.

"That's my next job. I haven't been able to manage identifying sex yet." Jared rubbed his chin. "The Elantus is still in the shop. Now it's leaving."

"We take my truck, leave your Jeep here. I'll drive; you give me directions." Hunter led them outside to his pickup.

"What do I do?" Alana climbed into the truck.

"Look beautiful like Kubiteron females are supposed to and stay out of the way." Hunter cast her an evil smile.

She slugged him in the arm, and Hunter laughed. "That's the first step."

Jared slammed his door shut. "First step for what?"

"The selection ritual between demons."

Alana didn't believe it for a minute.

Jared snorted. "Yeah, so I've heard."

Hunter drove out of the parking space. "I don't think she believes us. Maybe you ought to read up on our culture before you do something you're not ready for."

"So arrogant." She jammed her seatbelt in place. Yet she wondered what other demonology there was that she didn't know about. How did *they* know? *Jared.* She guessed he'd done the research in the demon world and relayed the information to Hunter. She glanced over the seat at Jared's laptop. He was bent over the monitor.

Maybe she could get him to make her a copy of his information for her flash drive. Or not. She hated to ask him for anything and knowing what little she did about him, he probably wouldn't give up anything anyway unless she bribed him again.

Feeling anxious, Alana tapped her fingers on the door. "Do you think she has seen us?"

"No, I think wherever she's staying isn't close to the store." Hunter smirked. "What? You don't think *I* can be a super sleuth? The demons don't expect any others to be cataloging their movements. I've never had any problems in the past."

"None?" Alana didn't believe it.

Jared chuckled. "Maybe Alana's a mind reader also."

Hunter gave her a sharp look. She grinned. Of course, she couldn't read minds. Though she wished she could. Telepathic communication was as close as she got. She wouldn't let Hunter and Jared in on all her abilities or lack thereof if it kept them on their toes.

The Elantus led them across the city and into the Dallas suburbs when Jared said, "A Matusa. Straight ahead." After a few more minutes, the demon drove into a driveway and parked inside a triple-car garage.

The place was huge, sprawling with a park-like setting out front with a statue of Atlas holding the weight of the world on his back right in the middle of the front yard. Ironic that a Matusa would have claimed this house? Or had the statue been the reason for his choosing it?

"A Matusa is in the main part of the house," Jared warned.

Hunter parked a couple of houses down from the white stone home. "Can you get a fix on who owns the house?"

"Looking into it already."

Jared might not be as strong physically as a Matusa or Kubiteron, but he made up for it in smarts. She had to admire him, despite how he annoyed her most of the time.

"Harold Weaver, bank vice president of First Texas, out of the country on hiatus."

"Dead, more likely," Alana said, her stomach clenching. "Would he have summoned the demon?"

"Maybe. Or maybe not. Anyone could have summoned him, then he picked a home he wanted and set up shop, killing the occupant," Hunter said.

"Yeah, he liked Atlas," Alana said.

"What?"

"You know the story of Atlas carrying the...," she started to say, but Hunter gave her such an incredulous look, that she shook her head. "Forget it. I guess you two have never read anything about folklore to know much of anything."

"Different strokes for different folks. I bet you're not into demon lore." Jared pointed to the house. "The Elantus is in the same place as the Matusa."

She let out her breath. "I would be into demon lore, but it seems the only kind I could read was ancient cultures' perceptions of demons, and I doubt any of it comes close to the real thing. Now if I could see what the demons really say..."

"You can check out Seplichus's main library. They have a ton of literature on it." Jared continued to watch his laptop and the movement of the demons inside the house.

"Folklore, too, or the real thing?" she asked.

"They are the real thing." Jared gave her a small smile. "Of course, I could share the information I got if the price is right."

She knew it! "Does it say that Elantus are money-grubbing—"

"Traders and barterers from ancient times."

"Let's make a house call." Hunter jumped out of the truck, ending their bickering. Glancing at Alana, his look willed her to stay behind. She ignored him and Hunter let out an exasperated breath. "You know, you could be more cooperative sometimes."

"Ditto," she said.

When they reached the house, a man and woman's voice reached her ears, but she couldn't make out the words.

Hunter twisted the brass doorknob with care. Alana held her breath.

17

The door to the bank manager's house clicked open. Hunter hesitated. The talking inside the house continued.

Alana tensed, and she struggled with self-doubt that froze her in place. After the experience with the Matusa battling her uncle and the rest of the wizards and because Ferengus had injured Hunter so badly, she wasn't sure they would manage.

She got a whiff of a burning odor and a trace of smoke greeted them.

Without another second's hesitation, Hunter slammed the door open and rushed into the living room filled with massive oak furniture. The Matusa male and Elantus female turned, their eyes wide and mouths gaping. The slender, brunette female backed away from the Matusa, her blue eyes anxious.

Immediately, Alana wanted to rescue her, and a sense of strength and resolve replaced her insecurities.

The Matusa's amber eyes flamed red, and he turned his attention to Hunter, the strongest demon in the room. "If you're barging into my house unannounced and unwelcome like this, I assume it's not a social call."

"It's not your house. What did you do to Mr. Weaver?" Alana asked, trying to stall the inevitable since none of her companions were jumping in to say anything. She hurriedly said to the Elantus, *"Run this way and get behind us!"*

The woman stared at her, but Alana quickly spoke again to her telepathically, *"Hurry! We'll get you home as soon as we can."*

Dashing across the room, the Elantus slid in behind them.

The Matusa shook his head at her, then pointed to the charred remains near the fireplace in answer to Alana's question. "Mr. Weaver played with fire and got burned." He glowered at the Elantus. "If any of you think you're going to live—though..." His mouth curved up slightly and he bowed his head to Alana. "...on second thought, I'll take the Kubiteron, thank you very much."

"He's a fire demon," Jared warned, noting the obvious.

Instantly, the Matusa cast a fireball at Hunter.

Without thinking, Alana erected a wall of water, dousing the ball of blue-orange flames. The fire sizzled, and the Matusa quickly cast another.

The hot flames pounded against her protective barrier, and she prayed it would last until Hunter did something. What in the world was he waiting for?

Hunter watched the other Matusa but didn't react at all.

Jared shouted encouragement to her as if he were her one-man cheering crowd. "Great job, Alana. I knew you had water abilities."

Maybe the other Elantus was helping her. Maybe that's how she could manage. No matter what, she had to concentrate. Sweat beaded on her brow as the heat and humidity in the room increased, making it feel like a sauna. The Matusa appeared tireless while he propelled another volley of flames at her blue water shield. Steam hissed. Beyond the wall, the Matusa seemed to waver.

Wanting to shout at Hunter to do something before she gave out, her whole body trembling with exertion, she bit her tongue.

Concentrate. She was certain he would do something soon. Jared didn't seem worried, and he'd known Hunter longer than she had.

The wall of water began to thin. The heat of the fire made it boil. Bubbles rose through the wall, blurring the image of the Matusa.

Suddenly, the demon clutched his chest.

The bubbles in the wall grew smaller and disappeared. The water began to cool. Still holding his chest, the demon's eyes rolled into the back of his head, and he dropped to his knees.

Not trusting he wouldn't jump up and cast another flame their way, Alana held the water in place, her breathing hard, her shirt soaked with perspiration.

The Matusa choked out something inaudible, his face turning gray, and then he collapsed on his face.

"Is he dead?" the Elantus asked, her voice worried.

"You can put your protective spell away," Hunter said.

"Are you sure?" Alana asked.

"He's dead." Hunter walked through her wall of water and checked the Matusa's pulse. Lifting the demon's limp wrist, Hunter repeated his verdict. "Dead."

Alana dropped the water spell and would have collapsed from exhaustion if Jared hadn't caught her.

"Thank you," the woman said. "Mr. Weaver brought me through the portal and decided he not only wanted a free house-keeper slave, but a man to do his yard work also. Except he made the mistake of bringing a Matusa through."

"What do you know about the summoning books?" Hunter asked.

"Five Matusa—well, four now—are in this world, spreading the summoning books to stores. They have a pact to make the North American continent theirs. Europe is next on their agenda."

Hunter growled. "Do you know where the others are?"

"One was in Dallas. Ferengus, I think his name was, but he

fought another Matusa over a Kubiteron, who sent him back to the demon world. Ferengus planned on taking over the West Coast."

"Ferengus. Do you know the other demons' names?" Hunter asked.

"Indigo was to take over the East Coast, but another Matusa demon was called forth and is now in Baltimore. He and Indigo are already fighting over territorial possessions."

"The Baltimore Matusa isn't one of the original five?"

"Well, no. Originally there were four, but the Baltimore Matusa makes five. Well..." She glanced at the one dead on the floor. "... four now."

"So that leaves one more. Any idea where he is?" Hunter asked.

"Florida, but not sure where."

"I guess you shouldn't have sent Ferengus back to Seplichus, Hunter," Jared said.

"You're the one?" the Elantus asked. "He killed ten people at the hotel he was staying at. They had it on the news this morning."

"I won't make the same mistake twice. Time for you to go back home." Hunter opened the portal for her.

"Thanks for helping me with the water spell." Alana sat on the floor, her strength gone.

"The only water ability I have is to make a light rain shower in a compact garden when we're having a drought. I can't make walls of water like you can. Really impressive."

"I told you so," Jared said. "You just have to believe in yourself, and it'll work."

"You do want to go back, don't you?" Alana asked the woman.

She nodded. "I don't belong here."

Hunter gave Alana his superior look. "You're free to go," he said to the woman.

"Thank you. All of you." She slipped through the portal and vanished.

Alana motioned to the dead Matusa and the banker's charred body. "What do we do about them?"

Hunter closed the portal. "Leave them. The police will discover the Matusa had killed the banker and was using his house and money, and then the demon died of a heart attack."

"Is that what happened to him?" Alana asked.

"The blood vessels constricted, lessening the flow of blood to his heart and ultimately his brain. I've got to search the place for summoning books." Hunter stalked off.

"Are you going to be all right?" Jared asked Alana.

She nodded, though she felt she needed a few more minutes before she could stand.

"Just sit here, and I'll help you to the pickup as soon as I've aided Hunter." Jared stalked off.

What? No thanks for saving their butts?

She wanted to get up and search for the summoning books, too. But she felt like she'd been drugged, her legs shaky, and her heart was still beating on overdrive.

"Good thing I finally was able to summon a spell that could help us," she muttered under her breath. "What would you have done without me?"

Drawers opened and slammed shut in other rooms in the house.

Alana grabbed the back of the sofa and tried to help herself up. The dead demon's face was planted in the ultra-plush, beige carpeting. Thank God.

She wobbled toward him, her stomach roiling, hoping it was only from the effects of using a spell she'd never conjured up before.

"I found some summoning books in here, Hunter," Jared hollered from down the hallway. "Cases of them."

What? Did she not count?

After she reached a writing desk against the wall, she pulled open one drawer, then another, unsure of what she might find. At least she wasn't just sitting on the floor, not helping.

Nothing. Okay, so she was barely standing and not helping.

"I found a garage full of cartons of books and more in an empty room," Hunter shouted.

Alana headed for Jared's location when she spied an office. A kaleidoscope of colors splashed across a monitor's screen, drawing her to it.

Collapsing in the desk chair, she moved the mouse and brought up the email. It appeared to be a message the Matusa demon was writing before the Elantus female arrived after delivering the books to the incense shop. Which reminded Alana, they needed to confiscate those, too.

"I don't know what we'll do with this carton loads of books." Jared stalked down the hall toward the garage.

"Stack them in the bed of my pickup. We'll have a bonfire out in the country. Where's Alana?"

Now Hunter noticed she was missing?

Alana read the email: *I'm afraid my Weaver cover will soon come to an end. Syg.*

Alana punched in the new message received. *Get out before they discover the identity theft. I just learned a Matusa threw Ferengus back into our world. Know any more of the story? Gryndal.*

Yeah, Gryndal. Will have to get back to you. Tila just returned from delivering some more books. Business is brisk. Later. Syg.

"Much later," Alana said.

"Hey." Hunter's sharp tone made her jump. "Didn't Jared tell you to stay put?"

If she'd been a dragon, her breath would have shot flames. As it was, her eyes flared, fiery red flames reflecting in his brown eyes.

He offered a small smile, which made her blood heat with annoyance even more. "He didn't tell me to do anything. Nor would he have." She considered Hunter's still-wet clothes from walking through her wall of water and smiled.

"Did you find anything?" he asked, peering at the monitor.

"Just that one of the other Matusa is named Gryndal." She searched through several more messages. None that revealed anything. Then a note from Ferengus.

A cold knot formed in the pit of her stomach.

Don't tell me when to leave here, Syg. I'll do it in my own good time. Ferengus.

Keep the killing down to a minimum. Until we have our people in place, we don't want to alert the populace that we exist. Syg.

I'll deal with this the way I see fit. Ferengus.

"I don't think they get along. Where's Jared? Maybe he can locate this Gryndal," Alana said.

"Jared!" Hunter hollered next to her.

The sound left a ringing in her ears. "Jeez, Hunter, do you think you could yell any louder?"

"Yeah, I can. I'm sure you don't want to hear it."

Jared came running, nearly out of breath, his eyes anxious as he zeroed in on Alana. "I loaded about half of the cartons in the truck."

"Is it already full?"

"No. You hollered, and I thought something was wrong with Alana."

Hunter glanced at her, and she gave him a simpering smile.

"One of the demons was corresponding with the guy we killed," Hunter said, brushing off Jared's comment. "See if you can locate him."

"Sure."

Alana rose unsteadily from the desk chair, not believing she could feel this weak, though when she was sitting down, she'd felt fine.

Jared grabbed her arm. "Are you going to be all right?"

She leaned against his strength. "Yeah, maybe you could help me to that chair so I can wait while you look for this guy, and Hunter can carry out the rest of the boxes." She gave Hunter a scathing look.

"Hurry it up, Jared. We've got to get out of here." Hunter turned on his heels.

Alana got the final jab. "Slave driver."

Hunter gave her a backward grin, which was not what she had intended, and then he stalked out of the room.

"I am *not* his slave." Jared's words were coated in acid.

"Matusa don't know how to have true friends." Alana closed her eyes and listened to Jared tapping on the keyboard, but the sounds, the smell of lemon wax on the desk, the touch of the velvet recliner she curled up in, all disappeared.

THE NEXT THING Alana heard was her uncle's worried voice. "She'd never been in any trouble before until she got involved with the two of you."

"Excuse me, but I am not the one who summoned her in the first place. I mean, I am, but I'm not the only one who does. The Matusa are trying to expand their powers in your world. In ours, their ruling powers are limited. They're feared, but they're outnumbered by the lesser demons. So they conform for the most part."

Her Uncle Stephen nodded.

"In Earth world, they'll fight each other for power, no doubt, but they'll run everything. Humans won't stand a chance. No more elected officials. You wouldn't want to see what becomes of humans who don't obey them," Hunter warned.

"I got a good indication in your world," Uncle Stephen said.

Alana still felt guilty when she considered how her uncle and his friends could have died when they came to rescue her. But did anyone listen to her? Still, she got chill bumps when she thought of Zoros's heart stopping and how close to death he'd been.

"There are five of them. *Were.* One is back in the demon world. One is dead. Another we've got a lead on. Two are in Baltimore, but one will probably kill the other. We've got a list of stores carrying the books, all off-the-wall places, none of the major chains."

"You'll need more help," Stephen said.

Hunter nodded. "If you could get some of your people to confiscate, then destroy them, Jared and I will track down this demon, Gryndal, in Florida."

"And me," Alana said.

"No," her uncle countermanded. "I can't believe you used such a powerful spell without any previous training. I don't recall ever seeing such a spell. I'm proud of you, but until you've had more practice, you can see how fatigued you can become."

"Where exactly is Gryndal?" Alana asked, irritated with herself that she had to ask.

Hunter exchanged looks with Jared and gave a shadowy smile. "You need to stay here like your uncle says."

Alana scowled at him, wishing she hadn't passed out before she'd found out from Jared about Gryndal. Without Hunter's coercion, she was certain Jared would have told her what she wanted to know. Fine, she would explore her uncle's books on attack spells while the boys were playing chase. Next time she had an encounter with a murderous demon, she would be prepared.

When she had a chance, she would sneak back to the bank guy's house and search his computer for information concerning Gryndal's whereabouts. Maybe she could play a little chase, too.

"WHAT DID your parents say about you flying to Orlando?" Jared asked Hunter over the hum of the jumbo jet's engines.

"I'm eighteen, I reminded my mother, who was most adamant about me not leaving. I told her my birth father gave me information on an uncle I had to look up. What about your parents?"

Jared shrugged. "You know what they're like. Loads of money. Always off on one trip or another. No real home life as in Mom, Dad, and family get-togethers. They expected me to tour Europe all summer like they did between their junior and senior year of high school. So when I mentioned Orlando, they seemed surprised and a bit dismayed. Anything is better than me hanging around Dallas all summer."

"With me," Hunter reflected.

Jared laughed. "They think you bring me out of my geek role and are a good influence."

Hunter couldn't contain a smirk.

Jared ripped open his complimentary package of pretzels. "Do you think we should have brought Alana?"

"No."

"She was sure pissed."

"That part doesn't bother me." Hunter stared out the window at the dark thunderclouds boiling up thousands of feet into the atmosphere. "It's when she gets quiet and agreeable that worries me."

"You don't think she'll learn where we're going and try to follow us, do you?"

Hunter faced Jared. "In her place, what would you do?"

18

Alana had put her contact lenses in to conceal her eyes, knowing fully they would be red, as angry as she was that Hunter and Jared left her behind. Resting on her uncle's couch, she felt fine. She was fed up with her uncle for making her take it easy. She needed to learn all the spells she could to protect herself, Hunter, and Jared if need be. Hiding in her uncle's house while everyone did all the work was unacceptable.

"Alana, I've got to meet with Yolan and some others about this business of canvassing the States for those demon summoning books which will take several hours. Will you be all right?" Uncle Stephen asked, stalking back into the living room.

"Sure." Alana lowered *The Beast Within* that she was pretending to read and gave her uncle a bored look. "You're not teaching me anything anyway. So go have some fun."

"It's business, and you need to rest. By the end of the week, I should be able to work with you on some more spells. I still can't believe you could create a wall of water when you couldn't even make more than a pond before."

"Maybe my life has to be threatened."

Her uncle gave her a dark look. "I would rather you learn some more skills before you have to face a life-and-death situation." He patted her shoulder. "See you later. Just call me if you need anything. The fridge is stocked full, so eat lunch when you like."

"Thanks, Uncle Stephen."

As soon as he left the house, Alana bolted from the couch. She was certain her uncle would get over being mad at her after a while. Hunter would not leave her behind. What if he and Jared needed her defensive spell again?

Intending to locate the demon on the dead bank vice president's computer as Jared had done, Alana called a taxi this time. She didn't want to repeat the bicycle fiasco, though after her uncle had returned it home, she'd been grounded from riding it again.

When the taxi neared the banker's house, she had the driver park a couple of houses down. She paid the driver with some money she'd found in her uncle's quick cash reserve and sent the driver on his way before she headed for the house. When she reached the front door, she twisted the knob and to her relief, found it still unlocked. Already, the demon's body was beginning to decompose just like a human's, and the stench of rotting flesh was nauseating.

Her heart beating hard, she ran down the hall to the office. She turned on the computer, then quickly connected to the internet and checked Syg's earlier emails. And then she found it.

The Sunshine State is the place to be, Syg. Bikini-clad women, the heat and humidity, remind me of Chaladon. I'll be in Orlando for three more weeks, and then I'll hit Miami. Keep me posted on how it's going there. Gryndal.

Yes!

A new message had arrived earlier that day, and Alana clicked on it to open it.

I know we don't agree on a lot of things, but that's our way. I was just summoned back to Dallas. I'll be visiting you before I leave for Oregon. I need help locating a Kubiteron here in the city. Ferengus.

Alana's heart stopped cold.

The front door opened with a squeak. Scarcely breathing, she rose from the desk chair, trying not to make any sound. Whoever walked into the house didn't say a thing. If it had been a human, she was certain whoever it was would have screamed or cried out at the sight of the charred banker's remains and Syg's decomposing body. And then ran out of the house in horror.

It couldn't be Ferengus. But if it was and he caught her now, no telling what he would do to her. As quietly as she could, Alana bolted for the office door, closed it, and locked it. Dashing back across the floor, she unlocked the window sash. When she shoved it up, she was sure the whole world would hear the grinding noise. Her heart thundered, and her legs and arms shook while she climbed out through the window.

The doorknob twisted, and she raced across the backyard. Glancing back, she saw Ferengus peering out the window in the opposite direction. *Go! Go!*

She dove through a towering juniper hedge into the neighbor's yard, the branches scratching at her arms and legs. Her breathing hard, her chest hurting, she kept running until she was several blocks away.

Crouched beside a tall hedge of flowering white oleander, she punched in the number for the taxi company. Speaking low, she called for a cab, hoping Ferengus couldn't hear her if he was following her.

Every sound—a door squeaking open, a cat scratching in a flowerbed nearby, a water sprinkler turning on—made her jump. A car rolled in her direction and she kept hidden. The car continued leisurely down the street. She peeked. Black and old, crushed right rear fender. Was Ferengus driving? She couldn't tell through the tinted windows from this distance.

If only she had Jared's laptop so she could monitor Ferengus's movements. She still couldn't believe someone had summoned the demon back to Earth world. But she imagined he was furious that the Matusa woman had been summoned first before he had the opportunity to arrive.

Seconds seemed like hours since she'd called for the taxi. Where was the blasted cab?

The rumbly engine was headed back her way. Oh God, Ferengus had to be driving it. And he was looking for her! Could he hear her heart pounding?

She cast a spell of protection, wishing she could make herself invisible. The car passed by at the same tired speed. When the sound of its engine faded, small footsteps headed her way, and she jerked her head around.

A redheaded, pig-tailed girl with freckles dotted across her nose, grinned at her. "Are you playing hide and seek?"

Alana's mind was racing. She had to get rid of her before Ferengus spotted the girl and Alana. The monster he was, he wouldn't hesitate to kill the child.

"Kind of. Can you watch for a yellow taxicab and let me know when it arrives?"

The girl poked her head through the oleander branches. "One's coming down the street now."

"Any other cars?"

"Yeah. A black one's behind it."

Alana had a bad feeling about this. "Thanks." She was torn between waiting for the taxi or exposing herself to danger if Ferengus was driving the black car, but she had to get the girl to safety. "Run inside your house in case the guy in the black car is a bad guy, okay?"

The girl's eyes rounded. "But..."

Just go, already! Alana envisioned a big black snake wriggling toward the girl and transferred the image to the girl's subconscious. "Dangerous snake! Go inside your house!"

With a high-pitched squeal, the girl dashed off to the front porch.

Keeping low, Alana used the high hedge to shield her from the street but peered out to see if the driver was Ferengus. The man had the same long, dark hair. She couldn't see his face. But she was pretty sure it was him.

Alana dashed off to the next block and heard a vehicle honk in front of the house where she'd been. Probably the taxi, but it was too late now.

She spied a little blue sports car parked in a driveway. Stick shift or automatic? Steal it and make a fast getaway or...

The faint rumbling of the black car's engine headed her way. It was now or never.

HUNTER STOPPED PACING, glanced out the window of their hotel overlooking the theme park, and then began walking across the same stretch of carpeting again. The place didn't hold the kind of magic he thought it might. He wondered what all the fuss was about.

Seated on a jungle print-covered sofa, Jared searched on his laptop for the signature of a Matusa anywhere in Orlando or the surrounding area. "You know, I won't find him any sooner with you wearing track marks in the carpeting."

"Alana's got me worried."

Jared tapped on his keyboard some more. "Her Uncle Stephen will keep an eye on her."

"What if she's drawn to another portal?"

"She's not physically there. If a Matusa crosses over, he can't get her."

"What if Ferengus manages to be summoned?"

Jared continued to monitor his screen and didn't respond.

Hunter couldn't curb the nagging frustration he felt where Alana was concerned. Yet, he didn't want Jared to think he had any interest in the Kubiteron. She was more like a sliver in his finger, annoying and not wanted. But he'd promised to keep her safe.

He let out his breath. Ever since he'd seen his dad, another question kept swirling around in his brain. "Do you think demons who are related recognize they are?"

"Treikal, who is head of the court of records, said so. Did you feel something between you and your father?"

"Yeah. At first, it was just the family resemblance and the look of recognition in his eyes. I was too near death to sense anything else. But then, well, yeah, there was something. Like a sense of familiarity when I'd never met the man before in my life." Hunter stared out the window, watching the monorail gliding by like a long snake on steroids. "Do you think there's something like that between..." He paused.

Jared glanced up from his laptop. "Between?"

Shaking his head, Hunter shoved his hands in his jeans pockets.

"Between you and Alana?" Jared asked, his tone amused.

"I can't help feeling like she followed us here."

"Open the portal." Jared concentrated on the computer monitor again.

"What?"

"It worked before. If she's nearby, you'll draw her to it. Then you can give her hell." Jared gave a sinister smile.

Hunter snorted. "She wouldn't be that foolish. And her uncle wouldn't allow it."

"Or that resourceful?" Jared asked. "Open the portal and see. If I could, I would, just to satisfy my curiosity."

Hunter opened the portal, the blue-green light illuminating the whole room, but Alana didn't appear. He felt a mixture of relief and disappointment. Which was ludicrous. Yet, he couldn't help wishing she was with them, so he could keep an eye on her.

"See?" Jared said. "She's not here and now you know it for sure."

"Unless she has figured out a way to block my summoning her."

Jared laughed. "She has gotten under your skin. Who would have ever thought?" He pointed at the monitor. "I see one Elantus demon north of the city, but no one else."

"Gryndal has to be a Matusa."

"Maybe he's out of town. Do you want to send an Elantus demon home?"

"You got it." Hunter headed for the door with Jared on his heels.

"We make a pretty great team, don't we?" Jared asked as they jogged down the five flights of stairs.

"Yeah." Sometimes, Jared could be a royal pain like when it came to his comments about Alana, but he was a good tracker.

Hunter led the way to a yellow rented Mustang parked in the tower. Ever since he and Jared had hooked up, though Hunter hated to admit he needed anyone, he was glad to have found a friend in him. Who else could understand the demonic side of him better than another demon?

"She's *not* here, Hunter." Jared jerked the car door open. "Quit worrying."

"I'm not worrying."

"Yeah? Why is the Marianna Trench dug into your temple then?"

"Jared, just direct me to the Elantus. All right?"

But Jared was right. Hunter couldn't quit worrying. Alana was too compulsive obsessive for her own good, and he was certain she would follow them if she could.

A MAN BOUNDED out of his house and headed straight for the blue car Alana had targeted to *borrow*.

She hid behind a massive elm, then watched until the black car with the rumbly engine skulked by. Peering around the tree trunk, she saw Ferengus behind the wheel, looking at the man getting into his car. Ripples of dread careened through her. She took a deep breath, memorized the black car's license plate, cloaked her uncle's cell phone number into something untraceable, and punched in 911.

"Hello, I need to report my parents have been murdered. The man who did it is driving their black car, license plate KUW-321, and is driving down Whitaker Street, near house number 310. Hurry! He's armed and dangerous."

Before the 911 operator could ask any questions, Alana ended the call. Even if Ferengus only stole the car and didn't murder the owner, she figured the police would give him enough grief for a while.

She headed back up the street to the next block and saw the black car idling at the curb, but no Ferengus. Where was he?

She saw him searching around the oleanders where she had hidden before. Had he smelled her scent?

Then she had another idea. Not a good one, but she would take her chances. Running on the outside of the hedges, she headed for his car. As soon as she yanked the door open, Ferengus howled.

She jumped into the driver's seat, slammed the door, and hit the gas, thankful he'd left the keys in the ignition, though she knew a neat trick to start a car without keys—courtesy of her witch's abilities. It worked wonders when either she or her mother misplaced their car keys. Racing down the street, she knew she had to dump the car before the police spotted it, but at least for a few minutes, she could distance herself from the demon.

Until he stole another vehicle.

Either the police didn't believe her emergency call, or they were all tied up with more important matters, but she managed to drive to the Dallas-Fort Worth Airport without any trouble. Not worrying about parking the car, she pulled up to the terminal doors and left the vehicle unattended. Someone would quickly report it to the police.

Before long, she settled on a plane headed for Orlando, wishing she'd worn something warmer for the chilly air on the plane. Good thing her witch's power of persuasion allowed her a free flight anytime she wanted though. First class, too.

She left a message for her uncle on his answering machine. "Hi, Uncle Stephen, Ferengus, a Matusa demon who claims I'm his, has been summoned back to Dallas. He must have been too far away for the portal to call me to it. I'm afraid he may come for me. Be safe, Uncle Stephen. I'll contact you later."

He wouldn't like it, but he couldn't keep her safe like Hunter could. She closed the phone and when the hostess asked her what she wanted to drink, she asked for a soda and a package of peanuts. Hopefully, Jared and Hunter would not get into trouble with Gryndal before she had the chance to help them.

When the plane finally began its descent into Orlando, Alana mentally prepared herself for her next big problem. Where in Orlando had Hunter and Jared gone?

NOT KNOWING what they might find, Hunter and Jared arrived at the apartment complex situated next to the University of Central Florida. Fountains shooting towers of water heavenward could be heard just a little way away and the scent of jasmine floated on the hot, humid breeze.

Hunter shook his head. "College kids?"

"The apartment is leased to two girls."

"Demon signature?"

"Third floor on the right."

Hunter and Jared raced up the stairs. When they reached the apartment, they heard blaring music and a couple of women laughing. Hunter twisted the doorknob and found resistance. He twisted harder until he broke the lock. "Ready?"

"Yep."

They stormed into the house and found two women drinking wine and laughing hysterically. The Elantus, a male teen, looked relieved to see Jared but quickly stepped back when his gaze diverted to Hunter.

Hunter cast the portal spell. "Return home."

"Hey!" the darkest-haired girl screamed at Hunter. "We summoned him. He's ours!"

Angered that the women thought they could own a demon, Hunter couched his darker emotions. He turned again to the demon. "Go!"

The demon trembled but didn't wait for another order from a Matusa and leaped through the portal.

Before Hunter could shut the gateway, the woman with burgundy hair grabbed the summoning book and began a chant to call forth another demon.

Jared shoved into her, knocking her to the floor, and clamped his hand over her mouth.

The other shrieked and tried to yank Jared off her friend.

Hunter closed the portal and then grabbed the summoning book. "Quit playing with the ladies, Jared. Time to go."

When he turned, he nearly ran into Alana. Not Alana, but the vision of her, and he cursed out loud.

"She's here," Jared said, still trying to defend himself without hurting the women.

They're witches, Hunter. Get out of there before they cast some kind of hex on you! Alana warned.

Hunter grabbed Jared and yanked him out of the apartment.

"What about Alana?"

"Forget about her. She just warned me these women are witches."

"Oh."

Hunter and Jared nearly flew down the stairs and burst out of the apartment building. A bolt of lightning flashed through the third-floor window, sending electricity sparking along Hunter's skin, but the force of the bolt hit the pavement with a resounding crack.

Jared raced after Hunter headed for the car. "Maybe we should have brought Alana with us after all."

Hunter gave him an annoyed look.

"We've got to have her join us. She's not safe on her own. *We're* not safe on our own."

"Where are you, Alana?" Hunter asked, unable to curb his irritation. He knew she would try to join them.

19

Jared pointed to his laptop and said to a fuming Hunter, "There's a Kubiteron signature at the airport."

"Forget it, Alana. We know where you are. *Stay put* and we'll come get you."

Hunter jumped in the car, his head pounding with frustration. The girl was the most exasperating demon in the world—either world. "I knew she would come."

"So, what do we do about the sleeping arrangements? The hotel was booked solid for weeks because it's summer." Jared cleared his throat. "Why did we get the Majestic Hotel anyway? Couldn't we have gone anywhere in Orlando?"

Hunter gave him a cross look meant to silence his questions. He'd never been to Holiday World and wondered what all the fuss was about. But he didn't want to explain his reasons to Jared.

"It's a suite. Living room sofa folds out into a bed."

"I know *that*," Jared said, his voice on edge, "but you already claimed the bed, and I was supposed to sleep on the sofa. Does that mean you want to share the king-sized bed with me?"

Hunter gave him a get-real look.

"Well, I'm sure you wouldn't mind sleeping with Alana." Jared smiled.

Ten more minutes and they would be at the airport. Ten more minutes of this insane discussion.

"We can get a roll-away bed or whatever they're called," Hunter said.

"The sofa folds into a double bed. She could sleep with me." Jared raised a brow.

Hunter hadn't wanted to show any emotion one way or another, but the notion Jared would be with Alana... Hunter ground his teeth. The demon side of him *wanted* her. Well, so did the human side.

But the Matusa in him demanded that the Kubiteron be his. Jared had told him about the strange attraction the Matusa had for the Kubiteron, but he'd never believed it before he'd met Alana. Even so, the girl was too aggravating to be the one for him. When he decided on a girlfriend, she would adore him and everything he did, not always give him guff.

When they arrived at the airport, Alana stood outside, wearing jeans and a silky shirt. No matter how much he didn't want to show any interest in the Kubiteron, every time he saw her, his heart surged. To make up for his annoying physical reaction to her, he glowered at her.

She returned the same look. Which only added fuel to the fire burning deep inside him. "Don't you have an overnight bag?" he growled.

"Why? I hadn't planned on staying overnight. I came to help you get rid of the Matusa, then return home."

"He's not here."

"What?"

"We may have to stay a few days. Your uncle is going to be incensed."

"What about *your* parents?" she asked, as he stalked off to the parking lot.

"*I* am eighteen." He gave her a sharp glare.

She looked at Jared.

"My parents were thrilled I was taking a trip."

"But *you* are underage *and* a girl," Hunter growled.

"Considering we've been through a couple of life-threatening situations, and I came out of them just fine, I would say that evens the odds. Besides, you're supposed to be my bodyguard. How can you guard me when you're here and I'm in Texas? For your information, Ferengus managed to return to Dallas while you were enjoying your vacation in Orlando."

"Hunter worried about that," Jared agreed.

Hunter gave him a look that could disintegrate a body into a pile of ashes, except Jared ignored the warning. "How do you know Ferengus had returned?" He climbed into the car.

"I had to revisit the banker's home. Ferengus came shortly after I discovered Gryndal was in Orlando."

Hunter stared at her, then shook his head and pulled onto the street. "Did he see you?"

"He knew I was there. He didn't catch me, but I figured that part is rather obvious."

Hunter blew out his breath. "You're trouble. But then I suspect you already know that. Tell me about this witch's thing."

"Witch's thing? What do you want to know?"

Hunter's electric brown eyes pinned her. "Try everything. Like how come we didn't know you existed?"

"You've heard of the Salem witch trials, right? People shouldn't know about us. Makes non-magic users nervous."

"Besides, you can sneakily use your powers." Hunter paid for parking and left the airport. "Like your uncle dabbles in the stock market?"

Alana glowered at him. "My uncle, for your information, is

good at what he does and doesn't need to use his magic to get him anywhere. When it comes to figuring out which companies might be coming out on top, he has a sixth sense. Plus, he studies the market constantly." Now, her mother, who wasn't that interested in magic, did use hers in her business. It was the only way to success-fully exorcise ghosts.

Alana folded her arms. "You don't even know what I'm capable of. What if I could shrivel your big head to half its size? Or could curse you to silence? You ought to be more respectful of us."

Jared chuckled.

Hunter grunted. "So what does your mother have against her kind? Your uncle said she hasn't trained you properly. Why not?"

"She's not the homeschooling parent type?" Alana shrugged.

"There's more to it than that."

"How would *you* know?"

Hunter jammed on his brakes at a light. "Blasted signals." Glancing at Alana, his mouth turned up a hair. "You get more defensive than usual when you know something you don't want to talk about. Your uncle says she also doesn't want to live near your kind. What's that all about?"

"What business is it of yours?"

"If you want me to protect you, I need to know what you're capable of. Maybe you did something terrible when you were little, not understanding your powers, and your mother decided to drop out of the witch's world."

"We don't begin to get any abilities until we're around thirteen. Supposedly, that's because we might hurt when we're younger and don't understand our powers. I was nine when I had my first ability —giving that kid a nosebleed when he said things about my father not coming home to see me because he didn't like me. Before I turned thirteen, Mom lectured me about how serious being a witch could be. I thought she was going to tell me about dating boys!"

"And she said?"

Alana glanced out the window at the city, remembering how serious her mother was when she'd told her the facts of life for being a witch. Torn between hating that she was different, and thrilled she could use her "powers" to her advantage—whatever they were—she hadn't known how to feel.

"She told me how dangerous it could be if a non-magic user found out. She gave the standard lecture on the Salem witch trials and other examples of 'witch' burnings or drownings all over Europe in the early days, whether the individuals were truly witches or not." She sighed.

He frowned. "All right."

"It made quite an impression on me. Even though we have the innate ability to use magic abilities, we need to train in them, just like learning to sew or learning math—one simple step at a time, building on the spells until we master the advanced ones."

"You still haven't explained why your mother didn't train you."

"She did when it proved useful. I've helped her with a few ghost-busting jobs. She doesn't have any patience when home-schooling me. Uncle Stephen makes me do something over and over again until I get it right. Mom gives up if I don't get something down by the second time. Then I would have to keep practicing on my own to prove to myself I could do it. She drummed it into me not to let anyone know I had witch's abilities, so I never wanted to learn them."

The look of disbelief on Hunter's face made her amend her statement. "Well, and the fact I'm a late bloomer."

"Late bloomer? I thought you'd given the kid a nosebleed earlier."

"Yeah, it was a fluke. After that, I never was able to do anything more. Just like I wasn't interested in boys."

"Wasn't?"

She flashed him an annoyed look. "Am not. How many girl-friends have you had that can deal with your demonic side?"

Hunter pulled into a parking lot, and she raised her brows when she saw the hotel. "The Majestic Hotel?"

"Why did your mother not live near other magic users?"

"Haven't I said this is none of your business?"

"It's because her parents denounced her for having you out of wedlock, isn't it?"

She figured her glower could have melted Antarctica, but Hunter only seemed a trifle amused.

"Isn't it?"

"Yes! That and because a warlock she'd met and fell in love with wanted her to give me up for adoption. He said I was the mistake in her life, and if she wanted to move in the proper magic user circles, she had to get rid of me. For Mom, that was it. Of course, I didn't learn until a couple of weeks ago when I turned seventeen how big a mistake I was."

"It doesn't sound like your mother thought so."

Alana was certain a flicker of hurt flashed across Hunter's eyes, but he quickly hid any sign of discomfort with another hard look as they left the car and walked toward the hotel.

"No. But she conveniently didn't tell me about it until my eyes flamed red. Then when portals opening nearby began to pull me toward them, she grew worried and finally told me more of the story."

"So how did you know to use the water spell you conjured up if you'd never done that before?" Hunter asked.

"A defensive mechanism? Like shutting your eyes if something is about to strike them? It's the only reasonable explanation I can come up with. Maybe it's part of my demon heritage, too. What about you, Hunter?" She considered the opulence of the hotel lobby, chandeliers, tapestries, oil paintings of jungle scenes, waterfalls spilled into tiled pools, and jungle music played overhead. She looked at Hunter. "When did you become aware you were half demon?"

She let the silence stretch between them as he led them to an elevator, but then Jared said he would be along in a minute and headed to the check-in counter.

Why should she answer Hunter's million and one questions and not get a few of her own answered about him? What dark secrets did he have to hide?

"So, when you met Jared was that when you learned the truth about your demon heritage? Or do Matusa know from birth because they think themselves so superior?"

Hunter didn't answer her but punched the elevator button for the fifth floor. "I want to know about these magic user circles you mentioned. Because both your parents weren't magical users, would you be excluded?"

"You know, it's *really* none of your business."

When they reached the living suite, Alana's mouth dropped. "Who's paying for *this*?"

"Jared's parents."

"Wow."

Hunter lifted the phone and offered it to her. "You'd better call your uncle and let him know where you are."

"No way. If I tell him, he'll have one of his warlock buddies, who lives here in Orlando, pick me up pronto and send me straight home. I'm helping you guys. Heck, those witches would have skewered you with lightning bolts if I hadn't saved your butts."

He shook his head. "Fine. *I'll* call him. You're not staying here. What's your uncle's phone number?"

She laughed, then walked over to the balcony window and peered out. "Wow, the monorail! This is too cool."

"What's your uncle's last name?"

She smiled at him, then opened the balcony door and stepped outside. "I've never been here. Mom always said it was fake magic and didn't measure up to the real stuff."

"Forget it. I'll have my mother run over to your uncle's house, and she can give him the good news about your whereabouts."

"Ohmigod! Where's Jared when we need him? A Matusa's down there, heading deeper into the park!"

When Hunter joined her on the patio to investigate her claims, she whipped around and hurried for the door. "I'll follow him. You wait for Jared, and he can lead you to him unless he's managing to cloak himself from Jared's tracking device."

She opened the door and gave a small scream. Jared grinned at her and waved a bag in front of her. "I got you a complimentary toothbrush and toothpaste at the front desk."

"There's a Matusa in the park," Hunter said, scowling. "Get your laptop. We've got to find out where he's going."

Jared tossed the bag onto the couch and opened his laptop. The three hurried to the elevator. "Jeez, I take a break from it for a minute and all hell breaks loose."

"What in the world would he be doing at a theme park?" Alana asked, wondering out loud as the three of them ran down the stairs.

20

"Why would a Matusa come here? He likes rides?" Jared asked, with a grin and shrugged.

"Tons of people. The Matusa can easily lose himself in the crowds." Hunter led them outside and stalked across the park.

Jared monitored his laptop. "He has stopped beyond that building."

Alana held her head as she felt the strong pull of a portal. "He's opening a gateway."

"No, he can't. He must be directing someone else to do it." Hunter glanced at Alana. "She's not with us. Grab her hand."

"She's like a rag doll." Unable to get Alana to walk at their rapid pace, Jared lifted her over his shoulder. "I hope nobody stops us."

When Hunter reached the edge of the building, he found a teenager chanting to bring forth a demon. The redheaded Matusa beside him concentrated on the portal and Alana's astral form stood slightly behind him.

She glanced at Hunter. *I don't know what to do!*

He shook his head and motioned for her to stay still. Then he lunged for the Matusa.

A new demon stepped through the portal, his blond hair curling about his ears, his green eyes wide. When he saw Alana's astral form, a shimmer of recognition appeared.

Jared set the real Alana on her feet. He shouted, "Samuria, return to Seplichus!"

The demon glanced at him, then looked at the human teen whose mouth hung wide.

Hunter slammed into the Matusa again, knowing if he didn't terminate him, he would be back. But Hunter couldn't kill him, not in front of the crowd gathering to watch the "Holiday" show.

The Matusa hissed and clawed at Hunter, but he kept out of the demon's path. Then with a final kick, he sent him through the portal.

The crowd cheered.

"Return to Seplichus," Hunter ordered the Samuria.

The demon's teeth glistened in a broad grin. "The Kubiteron guardian has called me forth. I am her guardian. I am her match."

"Like hell you are." Hunter grabbed the Samuria's arm, but he quickly shook loose.

Hunter tried again to gain the upper hand, but the Samuria moved like the mist.

"You must return."

"I am the Kubiteron's match."

"Tell him to return to Seplichus, Alana!"

"You must do as Hunter says," Alana responded, and then she slipped into her physical form. "Return home."

The Samuria's smile grew, and he bowed his head. "You have called me forth. The match cannot be broken."

"This kid called you!" Alana quickly wiped the teen's and the other spectators' minds. Then she fed them a line about free ice cream being given on the south side of the park. Turning her attention to the Samuria, she said, "I'm not a gate guardian. I didn't call you. You're free to go."

He didn't budge.

Exasperated, Hunter closed the portal. The Samuria would not fulfill his claim to Alana. "Fine. Stay, but keep out of our way."

"Samson is my name. I will go where Alana goes."

"Oh, no you won't." Alana stalked back to the hotel, her back rigid.

"Why would the Matusa call forth a Samuria?" Jared asked, sounding puzzled.

"I think Gryndal was trying to call forth a Matusa," Alana tossed over her shoulder.

Samson cleared his throat. "Ferengees he called out."

They looked at him.

"I am Ferengees Samson, but I go by Samson."

Alana frowned at Jared. "I thought you said demons only have *one* name."

"That's what Treikal taught me."

"We do, except some were getting me mixed up with a Matusa because our names were so similar." The demon had a round jovial face, and he did look a little like a politician.

"Ferengus?" Alana asked.

"Yeah, that's him. Sour Matusa."

Hunter shook his head. "So the boy mispronounced the demon's name. It makes sense that Gryndal was trying to call Ferengus forth since he's in on this with the others. But if he's in Dallas, how could he be close enough to be summoned?"

"He couldn't be summoned if he's already in the Earth world," Alana said. "Gryndal must not have known Ferengus had made it to Dallas, but he knew Gryndal would be in Orlando. So he planned to meet with him through a portal to the demon world here. "So now what do we do?"

"Locate the one in Baltimore. Or we could go back and take care of Ferengus in Dallas. But the Baltimore Matusa will be unaware of our intentions if we go after him. I bet Ferengus will be warier. So I say we go to Baltimore and get rid of him first," Hunter said.

"All right," Alana said. "I want to check on my mother."

"What are you supposed to do as a gate guardian, Samson?" Jared asked.

Samson shrugged his broad shoulders. "The Kubiteron must teach me everything she knows."

"Great. She doesn't *know* anything," Jared said as they walked into the hotel lobby.

"What if you learn she's up to something you might not be ready for?" Hunter asked.

She glowered at him.

"Just warning you, but I need to get you home, Alana." Hunter punched the elevator button. "We've gotten rid of the Matusa here, but you need to return home for your own safety."

"You said you would protect me from the Baltimore Matusa."

"*I* will protect you from now on. No Matusa will get near you." Samson gave Hunter a disparaging look.

"See?" Hunter waved at Samson. "You have your own personal bodyguard. He can return to Dallas with you."

"You know, Matusa—" Alana said.

Hunter flipped his phone open and punched in his mother's number. They rode the elevator to the fifth floor, and when there was no answer, he scowled and shoved his phone in his pocket.

"No one home?" Alana asked, unable to keep from sounding amused.

"As soon as I get hold of my mother, she's letting your uncle know you're here."

"But Ferengus is there."

Hunter didn't respond.

"Fine. Can I use your phone?"

"What for?" he asked.

Jared unlocked the door to their suite.

"To call *my* mother. She's supposed to be phoning me at Uncle Stephen's house today, but no one's home. I don't want her to worry."

They walked into the living room.

"Where's your uncle's cell?" Hunter handed her his.

"The battery died."

"Why don't you talk to your mother telepathically?" Jared asked.

"We're too far away." Alana punched in numbers, but after a few seconds, she shook her head. "No answer. The answering machine's full." She called the number for information. "I need the number for the Holloway Mansion, Baltimore, Maryland." Then she called the number. "May I speak with the manager?"

Jared said to Samson, "There's not enough room for you to sleep here. You'll have to find another hotel room."

Samson folded his muscular arms across his chest. "I stay with the guardian."

"Hello, Mrs. Johnston? I'm Alana Fainot and I'm looking for my mother, Caroline Fainot. She's not there? But she was supposed to be. She never arrived? Thanks."

Alana's brows pinched in a worried frown, and she punched in information again. "I need the number for Trendy Donuts, Baltimore. Thanks." She poked in the number.

Hunter motioned to Jared's laptop. "While we're here, keep monitoring for other demons."

Jared gave the Samuria one final glower, then sat on the sofa and opened his laptop.

Alana paced. "Yes, I'm Alana Fainot, and I'm calling to see if my mother, Caroline, has been there." Her gaze shifted to Hunter, and he could tell the news wasn't good.

"Thanks." She snapped the phone shut. "I'm going to Baltimore."

Jared looked up from his laptop.

Hunter took a deep breath. "We stay the night and leave first thing in the morning. You keep trying to reach your mother in the meantime."

"What if the Baltimore Matusa learned where I live?"

"Then it's already too late."

She cast Hunter a chilly glare. "You *could* be more sensitive about my feelings."

"If you wish to go now, I'll stay with you," Samson said.

Hunter glowered at him. "I'm Matusa. I give the orders. So if you want to stay, keep that in mind."

The Samuria smiled. "I only take orders from the guardian."

"Right." Alana collapsed on the loveseat. "That's why you didn't go home when I told you to."

"I can't obey *that* order. I must stay with you because we'll work as a team."

"You may get your wish, Samson. The same Matusa or another is here," Jared warned.

"Where?" Hunter asked, not believing another could have arrived as if the place was churning them out wholesale.

"The same location in the park."

They looked at Alana. She was wearing her astral-dazed expression.

Samson yanked the door open, and Hunter and Jared raced after him, but Hunter suddenly stopped. "Stay with Alana, Jared, in case he gets past us. Don't let her out of the room."

He nodded. "Will do. Do you want the laptop?"

"No, too cumbersome. Make her stay put!" Hunter dashed after Samson, and when the two arrived at the portal in the park, they found the same scrawny teen trying to summon a demon as Ferengus coaxed him.

Where had he come from?

Alana waved her hands as soon as she saw Hunter and instantly an impenetrable forest surrounded them, shielding them from everyone else in the park.

"The boy is a warlock who cloaked his identity from me earlier," Alana warned Hunter. "He's in with them and I hadn't wiped his mind as I thought."

Ferengus moved toward Hunter, his eyes burning with hatred. "The Kubiteron is *mine*."

Hunter spun around and kicked Ferengus in the chest.

Before Samson could attack, the warlock cast a spell and the demon's hair and skin turned ice blue.

Alana cast a spell at the warlock, but in her astral state, the spell didn't work against the magic user.

The warlock snarled at her. "You're no match for—"

She returned to her physical form in the hotel room before he finished his threat. Alana jumped up from the couch.

"You're back," Jared said, sounding surprised.

"They're outnumbered or will be once the warlock brings Gryndal back from wherever Hunter sent him. I've got to stop the guy." She dashed for the door, but Jared blocked her. She growled low. "Get out of my way or you'll see what the other half of me is capable of."

He hesitated.

She raised her hands.

He shrugged. "I think you're scarier than Hunter any day."

The two flew out of the room, dove down the stairs, and raced out of the building.

We're coming to your rescue, Alana assured Hunter and hoped they weren't too late.

When they reached the shelter of trees, she made an opening for Jared and her, then they entered the center, and she sealed up the opening. Everyone, Hunter, Samson, Ferengus, and the warlock were gone, and so was the portal.

"What happened?" Jared asked.

Alana stared at the spot where the portal had been. *"Hunter, where are you?"* She turned to Jared. "See if there are any demon signatures nearby."

"None." He took a deep breath. "They must be in the demon world."

"We have to help them."

"No. Hunter wouldn't like it if I took you back to Seplichus. He already said so."

"He didn't know he would need our help there."

"He said no."

"Okay, cowardly lion. You wait here while I search for him." She opened the portal.

Jared grabbed her arm. "Hunter will kill me, but you give me no choice, Miss Dorothy of Oz. Next, you'll want a pair of ruby shoes to take you home."

"Yeah, well, I already said I wanted to go home to Baltimore, but nobody would listen to me. Now look at the mess we're in."

They stepped through the portal and into a steamy jungle.

"Where's the city?" Alana whispered.

"We can only get to the city we previously visited through a Dallas portal. I've never been through a portal at Holiday World. It figures we would end up in a seething jungle in the demon's world."

"But Samson wouldn't have been in the jungle, would he have?"

"Maybe he's from a small city nearby. The closer the portal is to a large established city, the more stable it is."

"Great." Alana cast a bug protection spell when the mosquitoes the size of dragonflies buzzed around their heads. "What else do they have in a place like this?"

"Snakes, crocs, poisonous spiders, and frogs, just like Earth, from what I've read. But bigger and meaner."

The scum-covered water rose to their ankles, and Alana grimaced. "How did you manage to stay in Hunter's hospital room without the nurses kicking you out?"

"I can cloak myself."

Just as she'd assumed. "Do it."

Jared stared at her. "Why?"

"Something's following us. Don't you hear it sloshing in the water behind us? If it can't see you, maybe you can gang up on it before it attacks us."

"So now you want *me* to play the cowardly lion?"

She smiled. "Yeah and watch my back." She closed the portal, shutting out the light and wind.

Jared vanished. Her stomach tightened. Though she knew Jared stood next to her, she couldn't quash the feeling of dread that she was alone to face whatever monsters lived here. "If we need to get out of here quickly, I can open another portal where we stand. But Hunter said he couldn't open more than one at a time."

Jared's invisible hand grabbed her wrist, and she swallowed a shriek.

"What?" she whispered.

"To your left. A body floating down in the water."

Alana drew closer. "Oh...oh, it's the warlock. He's...he's dead."

"How? What killed him?"

"How would I know?" She quickly cast a protection spell around her and Jared. "But he wasn't as powerful as he wanted me to believe."

"*Hunter, Jared and I are trying to locate you. I wish you could let us know where you are,*" Alana telepathically communicated.

They squished through the muck, but splashing nearby drew their attention. They stopped and listened.

"I thought Samson wouldn't ever leave you," Jared whispered.

"I left him. The warlock froze him, and I couldn't help Hunter or Samson. I had to return to my physical state. What I don't understand is how they all ended up here."

"Probably Hunter was pulled into the portal when he tried to send the Matusa back."

Alana headed for the splashing, but Jared grabbed her arm again, and she gasped. "Quit doing that!" she said harshly under her breath.

"Why are you heading for trouble?"

"Maybe it's Hunter or Samson."

"Why didn't I think of that?" Jared opened his laptop. "Three Matusa and a Samuria straight ahead and to our right."

"What's following us?"

"Nothing demon that I can track, but it might be something just as sinister. The demons who live in the wild are more animal than human, for lack of a better term. The ones in the cities are more evolved like us. So except for Hunter and the others, we won't find much out here that we'll want to meet."

Whatever splashed in the water a few feet behind them, gained on them.

"How far are the demon signatures from here?"

"About a half mile to our right."

"Let's hurry then."

"Not out here. One false step and you could be over your head in quicksand."

A branch snapped to Jared's right.

Alana peered in that direction. Nothing but cypress and sycamores, vines climbing to the jungle ceiling, and green scum-covered water up to their shins.

"Ahh!" someone screamed from behind her, then a thump.

"Jared?" she whispered.

She flailed her hands through thin air, trying to locate him but couldn't feel him. "Jared?"

Heart thundering against her ribs, she backtracked to where she heard the sound and stumbled over something solid. With shaking hands, she reached down and felt a body. "Jared?"

He was still invisible, but the form she touched rested on a raised bit of ground, felt human, and was wearing clothes.

Reaching farther up, she touched his face. Blood soaked her fingers. "Ohmigod, Jared."

She opened the portal, then elevated his body and summoned him into Earth world.

A family of four nearly ran her over at the park, and she quickly surrounded herself and Jared with a high stone wall covered in vines. "Jared, wake up. Make yourself visible so I can heal you."

He didn't move. Pressing her ear against his chest, she heard his steady heartbeat. She ran her hand over his face, concentrating on the blood oozing out of a gash on his forehead, and stopped the bleeding.

He stirred.

"Jared? Make yourself visible."

He appeared before her, his face pale, his eyes dazed, the gash in his forehead swollen and already discolored as he lay on his back on the brick walk.

She held his hand. "Jared, can you hear me?"

"I..." He closed his eyes and whispered, "The laptop."

"Oh God." She glanced back at the portal. "You must have dropped it. I'll...I'll get it."

Jared didn't answer and she reached over and touched his cold cheek. "Rest. I'll return and help heal you, but your demon curative powers will aid you in the meantime. I'll get the laptop."

Opening the portal, she rushed back through.

Reentering the demon jungle took nerves of steel and right now Alana's felt like pieces of dental floss. She lunged forth, then reached around in the muck, feeling for the laptop, hoping that the water wouldn't have ruined it. Then she saw it sitting on the raised ground. The demons' signatures glowed on the monitor, maybe a quarter of a mile away now.

"Jared, rest. I have to try and reach Hunter and Samson," Alana relayed to him one last time and closed the portal so she could open it later if she needed an emergency exit. Trudging off in the

swamp, she hoped whatever had taken a swipe at Jared wouldn't get her next.

As soon as she began to move, she heard something following her. Despite Jared's advice, she quickened her pace. Either it was attracted to her movement or maybe her scent, neither of which she had any ability to cloak.

"Hunter, I'm coming."

21

Hunter would wring Jared's neck if they even made it safely back to the world of fun and games at the theme park. How could he let Alana follow him here into a world as deadly as any prehistoric one could have been?

In the jungle heat, Samson had quickly recovered from the effects of the severe frostbite the warlock had cast on him. Hunter could still envision the boy's wide eyes when some kind of reptilian swamp creature came out of nowhere, blending with the trees and vines, and broke the warlock's neck, then sank into the swamp again.

The creatures kept their distance, maybe sensing how dangerous the Matusa could be, maybe figuring a warlock wasn't anything to fear. But when Ferengus pulled Hunter into this world, he hadn't expected a jungle. Though he knew Gryndal had to be somewhere here also since he'd kicked him through the portal earlier.

Neither Matusa could return to Earth unless summoned, but Hunter had every intention of destroying Ferengus and Gryndal before he left the jungle. A heavy mist had separated all of them, and he didn't think he could even locate Samson. Then Alana's telepathic message reached him, and he knew he couldn't do anything but find her and get her back to safety. *Jared.* Didn't Hunter tell him to keep her in the hotel suite?

A DENSE FOG filled the swamp and unable to see anything, Alana stopped. Whatever was following her, quit moving, too. She glanced at the laptop. A Samuria demon moved toward her, but the Matusa were scattered still about a quarter of a mile away.

"*Samson, can you hear me? I'm opening the portal, and I'll summon you through,*" she communicated. Then she opened the portal and called to Hunter. "*I'm attempting to bring Samson through the portal, Hunter. I'll close it, then you have to open a portal near you and return. Jared's back in Earth world. He has been injured.*"

She opened the portal, watching the Samuria grow closer, though she couldn't hear him sloshing through the swamp like she should have. Eerily on edge, she drew closer to the gateway.

"*Samson?*"

He materialized next to her making her gasp, and he grabbed her arm. "Summon me through, Alana."

"*Hunter, we're going back. If you don't follow, I'll return for you alone. So get your butt in gear and get back here.*"

She summoned Samson through the portal and closed it, though leaving Hunter behind with two Matusa preyed on her. As soon as she led Samson back to Jared, she would do just what she promised and go back for Hunter. And kill him for making her return to the hostile jungle.

She rushed for the stone wall surrounding Jared. "What happened, Samson?"

"Someone froze me."

"The boy. He was a warlock."

Samson growled. "I don't know how I ended up in Swarly Swamp when I expected to be in my village of Mondoon, but the next thing I knew, the heat had defrosted me, and the warlock was dead, floating face down in the muck. I searched for Hunter and the two Matusa, though I thought maybe the boy and I got knocked through the portal, and I was stuck there alone."

They approached the stone wall, and Alana made an opening, then once they were inside, she sealed it back up.

Jared was sitting, leaning against a wall, his expression dazed, and his cheeks flushed. Alana handed the laptop to Samson and crouched beside Jared. Running her hand over his forehead, she began to do a healing chant.

"I heard the portal open, so I headed for it, hoping it was you. Then I changed to mist to cloak you in case you had entered the swamp."

She looked up at Samson. "Mist?"

"Yeah, it comes in handy sometimes. Is Jared going to be all right?"

"Yes, he'll be fine." She glanced at the monitor. "See if Hunter's back here." Then she began her healing chant again.

"Just our three demon signatures are here."

Alana squeezed Jared's hand. "*Samson will stay with you.*" Alana rose and reached for the laptop. "You stay with Jared. I'll be back shortly."

Samson smiled, but the look was purely sinister. "I watch out for you. You're not going back into the swamp after Hunter."

If the Sumaria thought he would dictate to her, he was sorely mistaken.

"I hate to do this, but..." It worked for the warlock. She cast a freezing spell.

Samson shifted, turned to mist, gathered about her, reformed, and pinned her to the ground.

Her demonic shrieks of anger echoed across the park.

HUNTER ATTEMPTED to concentrate on locating one of the Matusa when a demon cried out in pain. But the worry Alana would return to the swamp alone to rescue him nagged at him. *Kubiteron.* A Matusa did not need rescuing. And he wanted to get rid of both Gryndal and Ferengus in the swamp before they could stir up more trouble on Earth world.

Gryndal cursed and Hunter headed straight for him. When he located the demon, he found him favoring a bloodied arm and a lizard-skinned, half-human-looking creature lying dead at his feet.

The fog had begun to lift, but Gryndal was still concentrating on his wound and gloating over his dead attacker.

Hunter wielded his power at the Matusa, attacking the demon's blood vessels, shriveling them, and blocking the flow of blood to his heart and brain.

Gryndal clutched at his chest, but it would take several more minutes before enough damage could be done. Still, the Matusa's arm was bleeding, weakening him.

Splashing water behind Hunter warned him something was closing in fast. But he wouldn't give up his prey. Gryndal had to die.

The splashing suddenly stopped, and Hunter sensed it wasn't a swamp beast. A bolt of lightning lit up the sky, then slammed into Hunter, but the electricity charged through the water and struck Gryndal.

Gryndal grunted and collapsed.

Hunter sank to his knees, the jolt nearly stopping his heart. He opened the portal and with the last bit of strength he could muster, he crawled through. He heard Ferengus's curses, and Hunter regretted not silencing him first.

"Hunter," Alana said, hovering over him like an angel, her astral form drawn to the portal.

The devil was more like it. No Kubiteron told him what to do. She closed the portal and ran her hand over his chest. "I'll come for you once I get that Samuria off me."

Hunter's blood heated with anger, but he couldn't form any words to ask what she meant. Then she disappeared. A small crowd gathered around him. A man yanked a cell phone off his belt. If Alana didn't hurry and stop what was bound to happen next...

The crowd parted, and Alana and Samson pushed their way through to him. The crowd suddenly dispersed.

"Carry him to our room," she ordered Samson.

He looked disgruntled, but Hunter was certain the glower he shared with the Samuria could stop *his* heart.

"I'll get Jared. Go, Samson!" Alana commanded.

WHEN HUNTER WOKE, night cloaked the hotel suite in darkness. Jared slept soundly beside him on the sofa bed. Samson was sleeping on a roll-a-way bed. Alana got the king-sized bed in the master bedroom?

Hunter rubbed his sore chest, the effects of the jolt of electricity to his heart finally healing to the point he felt more human.

Samson opened one eye, then the other. "Pizza is in the fridge if you're hungry."

Hunter ran his hand over the stubble on his chin. "What did you do to make Alana so mad?"

"I kept her from returning to the swamp for you."

Hunter took a deep, settling breath. He didn't like that anyone would get physical with her, but he was glad the Samuria prevented her from following him back into the swamp. Though he was certain in part, the demon didn't want her rescuing a Matusa and it wasn't solely to keep her safe.

"What happened?" Samson disappeared into the kitchen.

Hunter closed his eyes, his body still not wanting to respond to his command to leave the bed. "Gryndal's dead." He wasn't about to tell him Ferengus killed him.

"After he zapped you?"

The microwave timer beeped. Samson returned with a plateful of pizza and gave it to Hunter.

"Ferengus got the upper hand."

"You were outnumbered. I'm glad you got the other one first."

Hunter ate the pizza, surprised at how ravenous he was. "How's Jared?"

"He ate some, then went back to sleep. Alana said the creature that gashed Jared's head infected him with bacteria. She worked for several hours isolating it until Jared's system could fight it." Samson sauntered back into the kitchen. When he returned with a soda, he wore a quirky grin. "If you wonder if she neglected you, she didn't."

"I didn't need anyone's pampering."

"Your heart stopped twice. I couldn't tell if she was beating on your chest purely to get your heart started, or if she was getting you back for dying on her." Samson chuckled darkly. "She probably left some good bruises."

Hunter's mouth turned up. He knew Alana had the hots for him. A sure demon sign.

THE NEXT MORNING, Alana made it to the bathroom ahead of everyone else, though Hunter vaguely remembered feeling her cool hand on his forehead and worried green eyes peering into his face. Even on the best of days, Hunter wasn't an early riser and often when he was in school, he missed his first hour or two of class. He faulted school officials for having them so early.

He glanced down at his bruised chest and smiled. The mark of love. Then he realized he only wore his boxers again. He stretched. The Kubiteron was his.

Samson yawned. "The Guardian is hogging the bathroom."

"Yeah. First, she got the master bedroom..."

Samson furrowed his shaggy brows. "You would not have made her sleep out here with us."

Hunter got out of bed. "I'm Matusa." He sauntered into the kitchen and opened the fridge. *Empty.* "Where's the food?"

Samson joined him. "You would not have wanted her sleeping with us."

"You're right. She would have stayed with me." Hunter gave him a smug smile.

Samson shook his head. "I am her match. She wouldn't have stayed with you." He grabbed the phone. "I'll order room service."

The shower shut off, and Hunter headed for the bathroom. He knocked on the door. "Hey, there are four of us. Quit hogging the bathroom."

He expected a smart aleck reply but when she didn't say anything, he pounded harder on the door. "Alana?"

Jared moaned. "Can't a body sleep in mornings? It's summer vacation."

Samson charged out of the hotel room.

"Alana! Jared, check the laptop," Hunter shouted. He twisted the doorknob until the lock broke.

Wrapped in a bath towel, Alana stared blankly at the fogged-up mirror.

"Where is the portal, Jared?" Hunter hollered.

"Downtown Orlando." Jared was already jerking on his clothes. He glanced back at the bathroom. "Is she..."

"Pulled to the portal." Hunter yanked on his clothes. "Samson took after her, but I don't know how he'll find her."

"He's her match, remember?"

"Yeah, but she beats on *me*."

Jared raised his brows in a questioning glance.

Hunter headed for the door. "I have the bruises to prove it."

"Those on your chest? When did she do that?" Jared shook his head. "Demon selection process."

"Yep. Samson doesn't stand a chance. Wait. You stay here. This time do *not* let her leave the hotel room. What kind of demon was summoned, by the way?"

"Elantus."

"Good. See you soon."

ALANA COULDN'T BELIEVE it when she stood dripping wet, wearing only a bath towel before a shimmering portal in front of three witches and three warlocks. They looked as shocked as she felt.

"What...what's a witch doing here in a towel?" one of the witches finally managed to sputter.

"We were supposed to summon Satan."

"Satan? You idiots. You're summoning demons and some of them would rip out your hearts and eat them for breakfast," Alana said.

She felt a hand on her shoulder. Her heart in her throat, she turned. An Elantus female looked at her with the most woeful brown eyes. "*I'm the gate guardian. Go back through the portal,*" Alana said.

The Elantus smiled and bowed her head, then ducked back through the gateway.

"What was that behind her?"

Alana closed the portal. "*Hunter, are you on your way? Three witches and three warlocks summoned the portal. Make sure you and Samson come prepared for battle."*

"Hey, open the gateway back up," one of the warlocks said. "And get rid of the naked witch."

A witch cast a lightning spell at Alana, but it disappeared right through her. She offered a sinister smile. "I'm a little more than a witch. If you want to piss off a demon, go right ahead. If you must know, I hate having my morning routine interrupted." And she hated standing wrapped only in a towel in a room full of witches and warlocks. This gate guardian business wasn't her bag.

She assumed, though, that she couldn't wield any power against them in her current state just like she couldn't do anything to the warlock who froze Samson. The others began casting other spells at her, and she frowned at them. "You call a demon forth and then what? Try to destroy it?"

The mist started filling the building.

"Ohmigod, what's she doing? It can't hurt us, can it?" one of the women said.

"Why isn't anything we cast killing her?" a warlock asked.

She didn't imagine the mist could do anything but cloak her and Samson. What powers could Samson yield that would help her? She didn't think they made a good match at all.

"Open another portal!" one of the women shouted.

"No. If we can't control this one, no way should we call another," one of the warlocks said.

Footsteps scurried away from Alana.

Then Hunter shouted, "Alana, go home! I'll take care of these vermin. No one calls forth my mate when she's taking a shower."

Conceited Matusa. *"Be careful, Hunter. They're magic users. You could still be weak from yesterday's experience."*

"Wrong thing to say to a Matusa."

"Another thing, Hunter, if you call me your mate again, you'll end up with worse than bruises."

Hunter smiled, and then he seized one of the warlocks by the throat and banged him against a wall. Hunter released the terrified warlock and targeted a witch. She shrieked.

What was Samson doing? *Nothing?* If he didn't help Hunter, Alana was firing his butt.

She could hear everyone breathing hard, separated in the pea soup fog.

"Whatever hit me, nearly stopped my heart. Whose idea was this anyway?" a warlock asked, moving against one of the walls, trying to reach the doorway to freedom.

"*Twyla*. Call Satan, she said, and we could learn more of the dark arts," one of the warlocks said.

"Satan?" the mist breathed. "Satan would no more bow to your small minds than any of us."

"Ohmigod," one of the witches shrieked. "How many did we bring forth?"

"Enough to terminate the likes of you if we wished." Hunter headed across the floor.

A door opened, and someone ran outside. Another followed.

"Crichton! Don't you dare leave me behind, you cowardly bastard," a woman screamed and stumbled on the floor. Someone cursed as they tripped over her.

"Who has got the summoning book?" Alana asked.

"I've got it," Hunter said. "Return home, Alana!"

The rest of the summoners scurried outside, and Samson formed next to Alana. He raised his brows as he considered her in the towel.

She gave him her fiercest scowl and vanished.

Reappearing in the hotel room's bathroom, she dressed and then stormed out.

"Jeez, it's about time. I have to use the bathroom, but don't you dare leave!" Jared said.

She glanced at the cart filled with food and one of the plates sitting on the table and half-eaten.

Jared glanced at the cart. "Samson ordered breakfast."

"I'm not going anywhere. Mission accomplished." She peeked under the steel covers looking for the breakfast that would appeal. No cinnamon rolls? It looked like Hunter had ordered a breakfast of eggs, sausage, bacon, and tons of toast, enough for an army of demons.

When Hunter and Samson arrived back at the hotel, Alana was microwaving a cinnamon roll and the spicy scent filled the air.

"Smells good, Alana. Did you get one for me, too?" Hunter asked.

She grunted. "You already have a ton of food to eat." She glanced at Samson, who was stabbing a fork into a sausage link. "What exactly are your powers? You have to do more than become mist or create fog or whatever."

He smiled. "Separating your foe disorients and alienates them. It's one of the simplest, most effectively disturbing spells I can cast."

"But Hunter was doing all the work."

Samson cast an annoyed look at Hunter who wore a satisfied smile. "The witch fell when I became more of a solid form. The warlock tripped over her. I create panic without hurting anyone too much, except maybe their pride."

Samurias were often politicians, Jared had said. So, that meant they would use the art of persuasion to get what they wanted. Yeah, right, like he tackled her to the ground when she wanted to find Hunter in the swamp. Maybe with her, Samson just wanted to get close and personal. She growled inwardly, still furious with him for knocking her flat on her back and keeping her pinned down until a half-dead Hunter opened the portal again to the park.

Finishing her roll, Alana licked the sugary cinnamon off her fingers. "What about you, Hunter? You stop hearts but what if you need something that can work faster than that?"

"He uses his martial arts," Jared said, defending him.

"I mean, in demonic powers. What about you, Jared? Even if you're not as strong as others, what are your abilities?"

He pointed at the laptop.

"No. What demon powers do you possess?"

"I can cloak myself."

"And?"

He shook his head, but his gaze shifted to Hunter, and she swore the two were keeping some of their abilities secret.

"What about you, Alana?" Samson asked.

She shrugged. "You've seen some of what I can do. I'm learning as I go. I don't seem to have much of an ability to cast offensive spells at demons, but I can levitate them and do some defensive spells while others don't work against them. Unfortunately, it's all trial and error."

"Maybe it's your witch's half that makes your abilities unpredictable," Hunter said.

She scowled at him.

He smiled. "Ready to catch a flight to Baltimore?"

Jared grabbed his laptop and backpack. "Yeah, all of us demons can use our abilities, and they'll work the same way every time. Must be your other half that messes you up."

Alana rolled her eyes. "I want an aisle seat."

"Are you afraid of flying?" Jared asked.

"No."

"Are you afraid of heights?" Hunter guessed.

She gave him a scathing look.

ALL THE WAY TO BALTIMORE, Alana tried to get in touch with her mother to no avail. When they landed, Jared signed up for a rental car. With a sinking heart, Alana climbed into the car with the others and directed them to her house. She couldn't help thinking the situation was bound to get worse before it got better.

As soon as they arrived, Jared pointed at his laptop and made an announcement that shocked Alana. "A Kubiteron is inside your house."

"My father?" Alana couldn't imagine it could be anyone but her father. But why had her mother disappeared, and why was her father here?

She threw open the car door, and with shaking legs, she hurried for the front door.

22

As soon as Alana rushed into the living room, she saw a Kubiteron flipping through the family photo album. He was blond like her with green eyes. That much was the same. And tall like Hunter. But she didn't like the fake smile he presented or the way his eyes darkened upon seeing her. Angry with her? Or something else?

Yet, she was the one who should have been angered—furious he'd broken into her mother's home and was invading their privacy. And where was her mother?

He glanced at her companions, but no disquiet reflected in his eyes when he saw Hunter. Everyone felt some discomfort initially when they faced a Matusa, except maybe Treikal. Nobody seemed to ruffle the Elantus who oversaw records in the demon world.

"I'm Tarn, your father," the Kubiteron said and motioned to the floral couch. "Can... we talk?"

Alana stood her ground. "Where's my mother?"

"She opened the portal to call me. When I arrived, she'd already left."

That explained how he got into the house. But not how the gate closed.

"Then she must have closed the gate from outside the house. In any event, I think she wanted me to be here when you came home," he said before she could question him.

"My mother didn't know I was coming home." Suspicious of his motives and not liking that her mother wouldn't have gotten in touch with her—unless she was with some warlock, she didn't know what to think.

Tarn shrugged. "I don't know why she called me then."

Other questions came to mind, and her skin prickled with unease. "She didn't know your name. How could she have summoned you?"

Tarn smiled, but again the expression still didn't reach his darkened eyes. "She knew my name. She told you she didn't?" He took a seat on the couch. "She opened the portal, and I was drawn to it."

"She didn't summon you?"

"No. A gate guardian cannot be controlled by a summoner," Tarn said.

"You're a gate guardian? But Mom said you made her say a spell to return you to Seplichus."

He shook his head.

"But she called you forth."

"The portal called me forth."

Just like for Alana. "You were already in our Earth world?"

"Can you give us a moment alone?" Tarn asked her companions.

Hunter glanced at Alana, and she nodded.

When they walked outside and shut the door, Tarn rose from the couch, then closed the gap between them so suddenly, Alana's heart rate sped up. The notion flickered across her mind that she hadn't felt any connection to her dad. Wasn't that what both Jared and Hunter had said? She would feel some kind of genetic bond?

Before she could react, Tarn seized her wrist. "Connor, open the portal! Now!" A warlock about her age, hiding in the adjoining dining room, rushed out and cast the spell.

Tarn couldn't open the portal! He wasn't a gate guardian!

"You're not my dad."

"I'm taking you to see him."

"No!" She attempted to wrest her arm away from the demon's steel grip and cast an ice spell, but it didn't work.

"Hunter, he's not my dad!"

Then Tarn jerked her through the portal. The warlock followed them and closed the gateway.

STEEL GRAY CLOUDS wept icy tears and a wind whipped waves into frothing torrents against a stone wall protecting the demon city. Gray buildings blended in with the bleakness hardly distinguishable from the clouds hovering low, and the chilly rain pelting Alana, soaked her silky shirt and jeans to the skin. A distinct fishy odor permeated the thick air.

What concerned her more than the fact the Kubiteron held her hostage with rigid determination—his hand clamped so hard on her wrist he was cutting off the circulation—was the way the other demons quickly moved out of their path. When she looked at her captor, she saw his demon type had changed and her blood chilled.

"The Baltimore Matusa," she said, her voice betraying her astonishment when she saw his long, dark hair and sharp black eyes.

"Tarn is still the name." He gave her a wicked smile. "A few of us can disguise our demon type."

"Where are you taking me?"

"To a safe place."

"Safe for whom?"

"Ferengus wants you for his own. Gryndal wants you dead."

Then he didn't know Gryndal was dead. *Good.* "And you?"

"You're a gate guardian—a dangerous prize. I haven't decided yet."

"What about my mother?"

"She knew better than to hang around until I located you. Smart witch."

"She's in hiding?"

"Apparently. For being a half-Kubiteron, you sure have stirred up a whole lot of trouble." With the warlock shadowing them, Tarn forced her inside a brick building. "Maybe it's your witch's half that's the reason." He shoved her into an elevator. "I figured your dad had some reason to target your mother to create a new gate guardian."

"He picked her?"

"Of course." He ran his hand over a panel, and the elevator shot upwards. "He and I have had a running battle for eons."

"With my *father*?" Alana held her stomach as she felt like it had stayed on the first floor when the elevator took off for the fortieth. "Why my mother? Why not any other witch?"

"You tell me."

She glanced at the warlock, young, impressionable, a vacant expression revealing nothing of what he thought, blond like Samson, but wiry and narrow-shouldered. But his gray eyes watched her while she assessed him, and if her woman's intuition told her anything, she didn't think he was so under the demon's control.

"My mother's not a master at anything. Her abilities are limited at best." Except for when it came to dealing with poltergeists. Alana's lips parted for an instant.

"Think of something?" The doors opened, and Tarn pulled her into a darkened hall. "You had one of those light-bulb-moment looks."

"She sent me to my uncle's place for training because he's much more powerful. Why would she do that if she could train me instead?"

Yet, her mother had—to deal with spirits. But what difference would that make? Alana's father couldn't have thought that was important. Cold air whirled around her, making her shiver. She squeezed rainwater from her hair and tried to do the same with her shirt.

"The demon world is too organized, too boring. We need chaos to liven things up. But we can't in the demon world. Lesser demons outnumber us. On several occasions, Earth world has been our stomping grounds. Who do you think started some of your most violent wars?" He ran his hand over the door, and it slid open. He yanked her into a spacious room filled with black leather couches and chairs, but at once she sensed pure evil.

The electrical charges crept over her skin, making chill bumps erupt. Poltergeists. Spirits of those who were evil through and through.

Tarn made her sit on one of the couches, and she hoped she ruined the leather with her wet clothes. But the leather was icy cold and made her shudder.

"You'll stay here while I locate Ferengus and Gryndal. My guards will keep you here, so don't think of leaving. I would bring my partners in crime here, but I'm afraid I would have a fight on my hands." He gave her a contrary smirk. "If you're hungry, the fridge is full of human-type food and a few things you've probably never heard of." He looked at the warlock, who was still focused on Alana. "Stay here until I need you to open the portal."

Tarn slid the door closed on his exodus.

Before she could say a word to the warlock, five poltergeists—three men and two women floated into the room. To the normal viewer, they wouldn't have been visible. With her special gift to deal with poltergeists, she could see most of them as not quite in solid form, but close to it.

As her mother had taught her, she targeted the leader of the group. No matter how sinister they were, someone always took charge. He or she would be the most dangerous. Alana had never attempted to deal with more than two on her own at once though. Seeing as she had no choice, she took charge and hoped the warlock wouldn't interfere.

"Tell me your name and the crimes you committed," Alana said, her voice sure and steady as she directed her command to the balding spirit who looked like an ex-football jock midway past his prime, the muscles having turned to flab. His dark eyes held the most contempt for her and the way he hovered threateningly close assured her that he led the pack. "Tell me why you're here."

The spirit moved even closer, chilling her to the bone. "To kill you."

"If you killed me, Tarn would make you live a million more horrors. If you tell me about yourself, maybe I can save your soul and release you from this world. He'll never be able to use you again." She couldn't save souls, but she could move the spirits from Earth world to another.

"Maybe I like causing horror."

"Ah, you were a bad boy and you want to continue to be one, is that it?"

The other poltergeists laughed in a hauntingly sick way.

"Well, see, I was giving you a choice of living a life of horror—and I didn't mean that you caused—or freedom." She let out her breath and waited. He sent a glass careening off the coffee table, and it shattered on the wooden floor. "My mother always taught me to give you guys one more chance, probably more than *you* deserve. But I'm done being nice."

She began a chant, but his icy hands seized her throat and began to squeeze. Choking for breath, she tried summoning wind, and to her surprise, her wind spell morphed into something she hadn't expected.

The wind sucked at him like a mini-tornado, pressuring him to release her. Losing his grip on her neck, his jagged fingernails gouged at her cheeks, but she barely felt the burning pain as the ice-cold wind whipped her hair into her eyes, and she tried to catch her breath. She continued to chant, the spirit fighting to reach her again. Despite the wind swirling around him, he grabbed her wrist and held on with one hand, the rest of him being pulled into the vortex.

Digging at his fingers, she managed to break his grasp. Once he lost his iron grip, the wind yanked him back. His face contorted and turned slightly green. Like a feather plucked up into a whirlwind, he couldn't break free. Cursing and flailing his arms and legs, he was sucked upwards toward the high ceiling. Then with a blood-curdling scream, he vanished.

The other poltergeists hovered nearby but didn't approach. Expecting trouble with the warlock, Alana cast a look in his direction, but he folded his arms and gave her an appreciative nod.

Exhausted, Alana shut off the wind. As much as dealing with the jock spirit had taken out of her, she wasn't sure she could manage four more ghostly entities. Diplomacy had to prevail with at least a couple of them unless maybe the warlock was willing to help. Though she doubted he could deal with the spirits anyway.

A female slid closer, her hair teased and stiffened with heavy-duty hairspray piled high on her head, and her leather miniskirt and spandex shirt looked like it should be worn by a woman, ten years younger, stretching tight over her curves. "I killed my kids and my husband for the insurance money I and my boyfriend got." Her brow cocked as if to say, 'So what's it to you?'

"Do you feel any remorse?" Alana doubted the woman did. Who could kill for money and have any human feelings? And people thought all demons were bad.

"Yeah, I feel a ton of remorse, girl." She gave a haughty laugh. "We got caught and got fried."

The warlock chuckled.

The poltergeist circled Alana and touched her hair. "What *are* you, anyway? Not exactly human, are you?"

"I give you the same choice as the other entity. Give up easily and leave in peace, or..." Alana shrugged.

"We can't kill you, Tarn told us. Just keep you here. But he said nothing about you being able to destroy us. That changes the rules. All bets are off." The female spirit lunged at Alana.

Still weary from using the first spell on the flabby "Goliath" jock, Alana didn't react quickly enough before the poltergeist raked her nails across Alana's neck and seized her throat.

Alana cast the wind spell, but it didn't have the same power as the first time, and she was afraid she couldn't use it again to any advantage without resting longer. The woman held on tight, though she wasn't as strong as the man, but because the wind spell wasn't as viable, the situation was much the same.

Trying to keep up the chant, Alana struggled to extricate the woman's long, thin fingers from her throat. The oxygen was being cut off from her brain. Her mind faded fast. *Concentrate! Don't let her win!*

The warlock remained silent and unobtrusive. The other spirits hovered around watching with wicked delight as if they were spectators observing a gladiator in the pit, fighting against a lion, except Alana had lost her shield and sword.

"Do you want to know how we killed them?" the spirit asked.

Now the murderer's concentration was focused on her past deeds. The woman's fingers loosened around Alana's throat.

"Tell me," Alana said but didn't hear a word the woman said while she concentrated her efforts on the wind spell.

For several precious seconds, the woman rattled on. "It was the most exhilarating high to see my husband dead on the floor of our bedroom, blood pooling on the—" the woman said, then shrieked when she lost her grip on Alana's throat, the wind whipping her up toward the ceiling and she quickly slipped into oblivion. Or some- where that her kind would end up.

Horribly drained, Alana collapsed on the couch. Three more poltergeists to go and she was afraid now that none of them would go quietly into the afterworld they'd created for themselves.

She realized, too, that the wind had dried her clothes, and at least she was no longer shivering.

Scraggly looking with dirty long hair, a man scratched at his bruised and needle-marked arms and drew closer to Alana. His gaunt face was drawn, and his yellowed eyes barely seemed to focus on her.

"Drugs made me kill my girlfriend and baby. Drugs," he said. "If my dad hadn't gotten me hooked on them—"

"So you feel bad that you killed your girlfriend and baby?"

"Yeah."

"The only thing you feel bad about is you don't have any more coke," the last woman said.

He snickered. "Yeah, my dad was holding out on me. I killed him, too."

Alana narrowed her eyes. "Too bad you didn't have a decent mother to raise you."

"She was too busy hooking."

"We all make choices in this world. You made yours." Alana tried the wind spell, but nothing happened. She swore under her breath and used a standby spell.

The spirit seized her neck with frigid hands and started to choke her.

She surrounded herself with spirits of her own making, just as deadly as the one who tried to choke the life out of her. Her mind blackening, she hoped the spirits she called forth would take care of the ghostly drug addict before she lost control.

His rough hands loosened on her throat. She coughed, trying to catch her breath. Black-robed wraiths dragged him away, and he screamed in terror, kicking and flailing.

"Postpartum depression. I killed my babies. I deserve to live an eternity in hell," the young woman said, dropping to her knees. *Truly remorseful?* "Other women prisoners hated me for drowning my three children. They murdered me, but I'll never find peace. I won't hurt you. The demon can't make me hurt you."

"You can't ever hurt another living soul." Glad Alana could free an agreeable spirit, she chanted the spell to release her.

The last man sank to his knees. "My dad abused me. I'm one of those sicko cases that could never be rehabilitated. I didn't deserve to live, and I was glad I finally died. I don't want to cause any more pain."

She nodded. "Be free from Earth's bonds." She sent him away and instantly, the place felt at peace, and the air smelled of roses.

The warlock clapped his hands, a slight smile tugging at his lips. "I'm Connor, by the way. Very good job. What do you do for an encore?"

"Why didn't you help me?" She touched the painful scratches on her face and felt moisture. Her fingertips were covered with blood.

"I can't do anything with spirits. That's why Tarn left them to guard over you...and me. I take it he didn't know you had that ability. And as for healing you? I don't have that ability either."

She rushed to the door and tried to open it, but it didn't budge.

"It's configured to his touch only."

"So what do you do other than open portals for the sick bastard?"

He shrugged.

She tried to open the portal, but nothing happened.

"He has got some kind of shield in here, so I can't open one and escape back to Earth, either."

"You could have told me." She peered out the window, some forty floors above the ground.

"Can you fly?"

She gave him a barbed look. "Do I look like a bird?"

"What does a Kubiteron do?"

"Heals. Commands the wind. I don't know what else."

The warlock hurtled a couch through the window using his mind. "I can't fly either, but I can make a couch fly."

"Levitation!"

"Can you do it?" he asked, his brows arched.

"On others."

"Same here," he said. "Just don't drop me."

"If I drop you, I'll send your spirit to the good side." She smiled.

"I don't trust that wicked look of yours. I'm sure for helping the Matusa you would rather I fried for all eternity."

He had that right. She could be dead meat, just because Connor helped the demon bring her here. "So why do you help him?"

She leaned out the window and felt a stiff wind at the elevated height. "Have you ever opened a portal above ground?"

"Hmm, no. If we jumped through it, wouldn't we fall forty feet somewhere on Earth world?"

"Could be. Listen, I don't like heights, so get this right, okay?" She climbed onto the windowsill, her legs and arms shaking. "Do it."

"You sure are bossy for being a witch."

"I'm half demon." Her eyes flared red. "And proud of it."

He shook his head. "I don't think I'll ever get used to the fact there's a demon world and some of them are living on Earth. Here goes." He lifted her from the window and started to lower her.

At the same time, she lifted him and pulled him out of the window. She struggled against the force of the wind and kept working him toward the ground, but only at the same height as he moved her. She would not release him until he did her.

Before they reached the ground, she sent a message to Hunter, *"If you're in the demon world, return home. I'm almost free to return and will meet you back at my house."*

When they reached the ground, Connor opened the portal before she could summon the energy. Before she could enter it, he grabbed her wrist and pulled her through. She was several blocks away from home, but immediately sent word to Hunter, *"I'm back."*

"Now what do we do?" Connor asked.

"My uncle is destroying summoning books. If you could hook up with him, he would be pleased to have your help."

"If I had a friend like you—"

Hunter, Samson, and Jared ran toward her.

"I'm afraid my demon friends wouldn't like that." She gave Connor her uncle's number. "Call him. He could put you to good use."

When she saw Hunter's angry expression, Alana quickly shouted, "He's on our side, Hunter!" Turning to Connor, she patted him on the shoulder. "Possessive Matusa."

Connor shook his head and strode off. "I always miss out on the interesting witches."

23

Hunter grabbed Alana's arm and pulled her back to her mother's house. "What happened? You're hurt."

"The demon pretending to be my father was the Matusa who killed his summoners and could change his demon type at will. He was going to meet with Ferengus and Gryndal. I'll be fine."

Jared shook his head. "I've never heard of a demon like that."

"Well, believe me, one minute he was a Kubiteron, the next, Matusa."

"So he didn't know Gryndal was dead." Hunter smiled. "Good. He probably doesn't know Ferengus is running around in a swamp in the demon world either."

Alana punched in her uncle's number on his cell phone.

"Alana? Where are you?" Uncle Stephen asked.

"Home, but mom's not here."

"She's here. You're in some serious trouble, young lady."

She touched her face where the cuts still burned. "Yeah, Uncle Stephen. I sure am. Have you destroyed the summoning books?"

"We've canvassed the States for them and destroyed all the ones we found at the stores you'd given us. We've done sporadic checking of other off-the-wall stores but found nothing."

"Good. Then all we have to worry about is anyone who already has the book."

"Already done. We've checked any purchases made at any of the stores and tracked them down."

"That's great. I'm going to get rid of a couple of poltergeists Mom was scheduled to do, then..." She looked at Hunter. "We have two more Matusa to destroy. I can't return home until then. There's a warlock who helped me escape the last Matusa, so if you have a job for him, maybe he can help, too."

"Tell me more about him."

"Connor wouldn't tell me his powers but helped me escape the demon's apartment through levitation. He'd been helping the demon get to our world by opening a portal for him, but he said it was because he was forced to."

Hunter grunted.

Alana looked at his sour face. "Okay, Uncle Stephen?"

"I'll check him out." He sounded just as untrusting.

Why would the warlock help her, then turn against her?

"I can't convince you to come home, Alana?"

"They'll come for me there before long. Mom's house isn't safe, either. I'll be in touch when I can."

"Your mother wants to talk to you."

Her mother sighed heavily into the phone. "Alana, your father came for you. That's why I sent you to your uncle's place."

Alana's heart sped up. "My dad?" She couldn't believe he would come to see her.

"He wanted to take you to the demon world. I couldn't let him."

Alana's head spun. So, her mother wasn't looking at renewing a relationship with a warlock. Why didn't she tell her? She hated how her mother kept her life so secret from her. Maybe she thought Alana might choose to stay with her father. Her mother should have known better. "The Baltimore Matusa said my dad wasn't summoned. That he selected you."

Silence.

"Mom?"

"I'm thinking."

"You were drunk," Alana said, still disgusted.

"Alana, shhhh. I'm thinking."

"I'm a...gate guardian."

"What?"

"My dad thought your abilities transferred to a child of his would make a good portal guardian. That's why I keep getting pulled to them. Dad was also a gate guardian. So I think you summoned the portal and not a demon. Dad came to the portal."

"But you said he selected me. Besides, he wouldn't have really been there, right?"

"Oh, yeah."

"I summoned the portal...and summoned a demon. I'm sure of it. But things kind of blurred after that."

"But you remember him making love to you."

Silence.

"Don't you?"

"Yeah, your dad was really special. But you're right. Something strange happened. I...don't think the demon I summoned was your dad."

"How—"

"I think...I think the demon I summoned meant to harm me. And your father somehow came to my rescue."

Her Dad saved her mother? She had to know the truth.

Hunter tugged on Alana's arm. "It's not safe here. The Matusa pretending to be your dad will return when he discovers you've escaped."

She took a deep breath. "I've got to go, Mom. Keep yourself safe." She ended the call. "I've got to zap a couple of ghosts, but I need to rest first. I doubt staying at my mother's place would be safe. Do you have any other suggestions? You guys want to watch a witch in action?"

Hunter yanked open the door to the rental car. "Yeah, I want to see you take care of some of these sweet spirits. I thought you said you don't zap ghosts, by the way."

"After the last few..." She let her words trail off.

Jared hopped in the backseat with Samson.

"This I've got to see," Jared said in his cocky way.

When they arrived at the Holloway Mansion, the parking lot was deserted, except for one car sitting near the old colonial-style building. A light flickered on and off in the dining room.

"Now or never." Alana climbed out of the car.

"What do you want us to do?" Jared asked.

"Do you know any protective spells?"

Jared vanished. Alana chuckled. "Cowardly lion."

Alana knocked on the front door and a fidgety, gray-haired woman opened it. "W-we're closed."

"I'm Alana Fainot, and I'm here in my mother's place to exorcise your poltergeist. You're the manager, Mrs. Johnston?"

The woman nodded and glanced at Hunter and Samson.

"They're learning the ropes of the business."

"You seem kind of young, but, well, I'm glad there's so many of you because there are three of them. W-what do you need me to do?"

"If you don't mind...leave."

The woman's violet eyes widened.

"For your own safety. Please."

Though Alana was telling the truth, she also didn't want the manager to witness how she dealt with the poltergeists.

"Yes, yes. Good idea." The woman hurried outside and shut the door.

Alana cast a protection spell over her companions. "Sometimes they work. Sometimes they don't."

"Like against demons," Hunter said.

"Yes. Every spirit is different. Some are extremely sinister; others are goaded on by a leader. I always target the strongest first. But I never know what will work against them."

She walked across the wood-paneled floor and entered the dining room when the light suddenly flickered off.

The sun still washed the room in a warm light through wide-paned windows. Ten tables covered with white cloths waited for patrons, each decorated with a vase of fresh red roses cut from the gardens in full bloom out back.

"I'm here to help you," Alana said.

Hunter and Samson's backs were stiff, and their gazes shifted around the room.

The light fluttered twice, then stayed on in the crystal chandelier hanging from the ten-foot-high ceiling.

Alana folded her arms. "Did a demon force you here?"

A low growl filled the room.

All at once, Alana wished her mother was here and they were working as a team.

"I take that as a yes," Hunter said under his breath.

"Matusa," the room seemed to whisper with hatred.

The hair on Alana's arms rose to attention. "The one who sent you here?" Or was the ghost referring to Hunter? She had to know which, though she was sure Tarn was stirring up the poltergeists in the area since he used them to guard her at his place.

Something icy brushed the scratches on her cheek and her heart leaped in her throat. "A Matusa called you forth? Tarn?"

Frigid fingers embraced her neck, then slid away. The actions were seductive, not threatening, but the entity couldn't help but creep her out.

"What's happening?" Hunter moved closer to her. "Your breath is frosty."

"I'm okay. Stay back." She assumed the spirit was no threat to her, but she feared Hunter's interference might provoke it.

Hunter glowered at her but didn't move any closer.

Samson watched with rabid attention, his hands fisted at his sides.

The entity brushed against her lips this time, making them feel as though she'd pressed ice cubes against them. "Are...are you a Matusa?"

Hunter's eyes rounded. "What the..."

"Matusa," the creature repeated.

"Did...did Tarn kill you?"

One of the flower vases hovered above a table, then flew into a wall, broke into bits, and fell to the floor with a crash.

Her mind racing back to what she'd read on the banker's computer, she tried to recall the messages. The Baltimore Matusa had a dispute with another Matusa over territorial rights.

"Indigo? Is that your name?"

"Kubiteron." He said her demon type with longing.

Near the dining room entrance, Jared said, "This is *just* great."

She glanced back at him but saw no sign of him—still cloaked. "Do you want to get back at Tarn?" Alana asked the poltergeist.

Hunter frowned. "I don't think this is such a good idea."

"We'll call him forth, Indigo. We'll destroy him. Will this appease you?" To Hunter Alana telepathically communicated, *"I'm not certain I can exorcise a Matusa poltergeist. I have to try and pacify him instead."*

Hunter let out his breath. "You're the expert, but what if Tarn can control him?"

"Indigo wouldn't allow it, would you?"

The air around her grew cold again and a frosty breath said next to her ear, "Kubiteron."

Chill bumps raced down her spine. "Summon Tarn," Alana said to Hunter. "Samson, you do what you do best."

"What about me?" Jared whispered.

Alana raised her brows. "Same with you."

Hunter opened the portal. "Are you sure about this?"

She stared at the blue-green light as the wind whipped her hair about. "Yeah. Go ahead. Let's get this over."

Hunter attempted to summon forth Tarn and Samson vanished into mist. Alana hoped Tarn hadn't gone to Florida looking for Ferengus and Gryndal.

When he didn't show, she expressed her concern out loud.

"Well, he won't find Gryndal anytime soon," Hunter said.

She frowned at him. If the spirit knew Hunter had killed the Matusa when Indigo and Ferengus had been partners...

"Ferengus killed him," Hunter said, seeing the expression on her face.

"Ferengussss," the poltergeist repeated.

"Yeah, he struck both of us with a lightning bolt, but Gryndal had been weakened after some kind of swamp creature attacked him. Ferengus planned to kill us both." Hunter shrugged. "Seems he's as devious as Tarn. It would serve him right if Tarn plans to kill him next or vice versa."

"Ssssummon Ferengussss," the poltergeist whispered.

Hunter winked at Alana and gave her a dark smile. Arrogant Matusa. He was only lucky his ploy worked.

Hunter summoned Ferengus this time and the demon appeared.

"Oh, not again," Jared groaned.

Ferengus glanced in Jared's direction, but Hunter attacked the demon with a swift kick to his chest.

Ferengus fell back. The poltergeist whipped around him, turning Ferengus's black brows and his long hair frosty.

The mist surrounded Ferengus, and Hunter swore under his breath. "Samson, I can't see to strike him. Get away from him!"

Ferengus made a lunge for Alana but suddenly fell on his face. She couldn't see Samson in the mist, but she assumed he'd become more solid to trip the demon.

Hunter kicked Ferengus in the stomach and the demon howled, but the mist swallowed him up again. "Samson, I swear I'll kick your butt next if you don't get out of my way."

"We work together," Alana said, "and let Indigo have his chance, too." She only said it, meaning to keep the demon poltergeist on their side, but suddenly his cold touch swept over her lips again. She fought stepping away from the iciness and the repulsion she felt for him.

The front door opened and slammed shut. Alana worried Mrs. Johnston was checking on their progress. Before Alana could head out of the dining room and chase the manager back outside, Jared warned, "It's Tarn and that warlock, Connor."

So Connor wasn't done being Tarn's lackey. Tarn's arrival didn't help matters. Alana tried a lightning spell on him as her uncle had taught her, but nothing happened.

Hunter jumped away from Ferengus's outstretched claws as Tarn tsked. "Haven't you killed this guy yet?"

"I'm working on it," Hunter retorted.

Tarn chuckled low, sending a wave of unease washing through her. "Kill them all but the Kubiteron. She's mine."

"You can't be commanding your warlock to do your dirty work," Alana said. "He can't do anything more than a levitation spell." She knew better than that. That he hid his powers from her because he was still in league with the Matusa.

Tarn smiled. "He told me how proficient you were in getting rid of poltergeists." He turned his attention across the room. "If I don't save you, Indigo, she'll also send you to oblivion."

"You already killed him, remember? I don't think he's too happy about it."

"You're creating a ripple in my plans if I have to keep you under my control, Kubiteron."

"The poltergeists? Did you plan to use them to terrorize the human population? Better than having to deal with Matusa who might try to take over your rule, right?"

His face was shadowed as he smiled again, and then he cast blue smoke at Hunter.

Her heart racing, Alana cast her wind spell and blew the smoke back in Tarn's direction. Since it was his spell it wouldn't harm him, but the smoke hit Connor, and he grabbed his throat and began to choke.

Tarn cast a spell at Alana this time, but she didn't have a clue what the effect would be, so she erected a water wall. He laughed. But then Tarn seized his own throat like Connor had done. The warlock was either passed out or dead on the floor.

Taran's face turned whiter and his eyes bulged as he fought the unseen force. The poltergeist? Jared?

Hunter and Ferengus were lost in the mist, though painful-sounding grunts and groans came from there.

A hand touched her shoulder, and she jumped away from it and whipped around.

At once, she felt the connection and saw a slight resemblance to the male Kubiteron standing before her. His hair was as golden blond as hers and his eyes as sea green. He even had the same dimples when he smiled.

He glanced at the room full of demons and nodded. "You have done well, Alana, for not being trained."

She opened her mouth to speak, but he silenced her with a wave of his hand. "You have a Matusa, Elantus, and Samuria working for you to help you guard the portals."

"The hell she has," Hunter said from somewhere in the thick of the mist, then "oofed," as if Ferengus had gotten the better of him when he was distracted.

"You've even managed to garner the help of a Matusa poltergeist. More than I could ever have hoped for. When I was a young gate guardian, I never had that much help. Therefore, in deference to your mother's wishes, you will continue to train with her and hone your witch's skills further."

She couldn't believe her father was here now!

"For two months of the year, I will teach you how to manage gate guardian duties. For one, how to stop from being pulled to a portal when you're driving a car or..." He smiled. "...taking a shower."

Her skin heated with annoyance. He'd been watching her all this time? He was worse than a Matusa. "What about my mother?"

"She's special to me."

"She has been pining away for you all these years."

Her father laughed. "Is that the story she told you?"

Alana glanced at Taran lying on the floor. His face wore a death mask, his hands still clutching his throat. "Jared? Indigo?"

"Taran'ssss dead," Indigo said.

"Yeah," Jared said, reappearing. "Indigo and I helped Taran leave this world together."

Hunter stepped out of the mist, his face flushed, his chest and cheek bloodied.

"Ohmigod, no! Hunter!" Alana rushed to grab his arm.

"This time Ferengus is dead." He clenched his teeth and leaned against her.

"We have to call your father."

Hunter grunted.

Samson reformed, and the mist dissipated. "I'm sorry if I got in your way."

Hunter shrugged and grimaced. "We got him, didn't we?" But he cast Samson an irritated look.

"You want to call Bentos, or should I?" Alana held onto Hunter and felt his body temperature elevating.

"I want you to leave before he arrives in case he still tries to claim you," Hunter said.

"No way. I'm staying right here until he heals you."

Hunter scowled. "Maybe your father can teach you to respect the Matusa."

Her father's eyes sparkled with humor.

Alana and Jared helped Hunter to a chair, and he leaned his arms against the table. He wasn't in any shape to summon anyone. She called to Bentos, summoning him to help his son once again, hoping he would do so and leave her alone.

Almost immediately he appeared, and she wondered then why they hadn't had to return to Dallas first to be close to where he lived.

"I was trying to track you down, Alana," Bentos said, his smile smug. He turned his attention to Hunter and shook his head. "When will you call just to visit me as any good son would?"

Hunter offered a disgruntled snort.

Bentos smiled. "It is good that I admire you, son. It is not often a demon has a half-human child he can be proud of. None of our kind have ever worked with a Kubiteron gate guardian." He cast a glance at Alana's father.

"You can't have Alana," her father said to Bentos.

"Come now, Pappalios. You would not deny my claim to her."

"She has already been claimed, and she has returned the interest."

"Yeah, and she beat on my chest to prove it," Hunter said, sounding proud of the fact.

"I...why you arrogant jerk!" Alana's face flamed and the heat quickly consumed her. "I had to start your heart—twice. I should have let Samson beat on you."

"I'm her match," Samson said to her father, his chest puffed out. "It has to be a Samuria."

Indigo swept around her, chilling her. She'd forgotten all about him. "Tarn's dead now. You have avenged your murder. You can leave this world now."

"Kubiteron."

"Oh, for heaven's sake. You want to find peace."

"With you." Then Indigo slipped away.

Jared pointed at the warlock. "What do we do with him?"

"I can't wipe a warlock's mind, but maybe my uncle or his mentor or someone else they know might." Alana turned to her father. "What did you mean that my mother was telling me a story about you?"

"She couldn't tell you I was her demon lover, not until you began to experience your demonic abilities. Then when I said I would take you away to learn your skills, she panicked and tried to hide you from me. She worried I would take you to the demon world and never return. She'd hoped your uncle could teach you skills to keep you away from me. I knew where you'd gone and watched you."

"Even in the swamp?"

Her father's ears turned a little red. "Some of the times I lost you, I have to admit. You're hard to keep up with."

"So you loved my mother."

He bowed his head.

Her heart shot straight to the ceiling. "Always?"

"Yes, Alana. And watched you grow all these years. You didn't give the boy a nosebleed in class when you were nine. You were too young to use any of your abilities, witch or demon. I did."

Ohmigod, if she'd only known. "I would have made you a Father's Day card."

"It was enough to watch you grow up."

"You can cloak yourself like Jared?"

"Yes."

Hunter groaned. His father dug his extended claws across Hunter's chest. She cringed at the sight and wished she could have healed Hunter instead.

"What about him?" Jared pointed at Connor, still passed out on the floor.

"I'll call Caroline and tell her to get some help for him," her father said.

"So, what do we do now?" Jared ran his hands through his disheveled hair. "We've gotten rid of the Matusa who were causing trouble. Your uncle has destroyed all the summoning books they could get hold of. It's still summer vacation and—"

"We have a week left at the hotel," Hunter said, rubbing his chest.

"I wouldn't mind riding some of the rides." Samson smiled.

Alana nodded. "I'm game." It would be much more fun than returning to her uncle's home and practicing more spells. "Besides, I need to remove a couple of barriers I erected the last time we were there."

"I'll let your mother know where you're going for a week," her father said.

"I've got to help a couple of other ghosts leave here and Trendy Donuts."

"What about Indigo?" Jared asked.

Alana lifted a shoulder. He'd helped them fight the sinister Matusa. If he didn't bother anyone and didn't want to leave Earth world yet, maybe it wouldn't be such a bad thing.

AFTER EXORCISING the ghosts at the mansion and donut shop and saying goodbye to her father, she intended to give a Dad's Day card to him in a couple of weeks, and then they boarded a flight to Orlando.

Exhausted, everyone slept for part of the flight, until Alana felt too chilled. She reached up and turned off the overhead air vents, then felt the cold brush against her cheek.

Slumping against the seat, she pulled the thin airline blanket higher. Maybe she wouldn't have to tell anyone about her secret admirer. She hoped she wouldn't have to try and exorcise him anytime soon, figuring he might be more than she could handle.

She glanced at Hunter who frowned at her. "What?" she asked, totally annoyed.

"You brought him with us, didn't you?"

"Who?"

Hunter wrapped his arms around her and pulled her close. "Frosty the ghost. Don't worry. I'll keep your fires burning."

"You are so—"

"Yeah, and you love me for it. Admit it, Alana. You beat my heart right into submission just like any good demon mate would."

Indigo came back for another pass, and Hunter tightened his hold on Alana. She smiled. Never in a million years did she think being half-demon could feel so right.

Her world would never be perfect, but she figured right this very minute, it wasn't half bad.

The End

FOLLOW the demon guardians in the next installment—Demon Trouble, Too—where the guardians continue to get themselves into serious danger.